Je [...]
Enjoy [...]
snippets in the [...]
Jack Randall

the synthetic race

Jack Randall

PublishAmerica

Baltimore

First printing

ISBN: 1-4137-1427-7
PUBLISHED BY PUBLISHAMERICA, LLLP
www.publishamerica.com
Baltimore

Printed in the United States of America

This book is dedicated to my wife, Patricia, who has many times endured my writing long past midnight in the loft in our bedroom where my desktop computer is located.

It is also partially dedicated to my blue-point Siamese cat, Vincent, who always accompanies me up into the loft when I am writing.

I feel greatly obligated to Dr. Isaac Asimov for starting my interest in science fiction. As he always said in my biochemistry class at BU Medical School—"good science fiction is just one or two steps away from reality; and can sometimes help to discover those steps". I started this novel back in the '50s, before the *Six Million Dollar Man or Woman* and television series like *Star Trek* and *Babylon Five* were presented; but a busy life in vascular surgery caused me to put off finishing the last few chapters until now. All the subsequent great science fiction television and movie series have served to make my novel easier to comprehend now than it would have been had I finished it back in the '50s. I appreciate the help these fine shows have given to better enjoy my novel.

Zandor glanced nervously at his timepiece and walked once more across the floor between the telescreen and the Portal, his pacing making a staccato echo in the empty laboratory. Suddenly the warning buzzer sounded and the dull black color of the Portal slowly became a shimmering dark green as his friend Dort quickly stepped through. Relief slowly flooded across Zandor's face as he viewed the obviously quite pleased expression on his older colleague's face.

"Then the Council has voted in favor of our expedition?" he asked, trying to suppress his rising enthusiasm.

"Yes, in a manner of speaking," answered Dort, "and even the Prime Mover was impressed by our theories. The Councilmen did find it difficult to believe, however, that any creature made of such perishable material as seen in the lower animals here on Mekan, could possibly survive without a protective synthetic body in even a relatively non-hostile environment. They didn't see how such creatures could tolerate the constantly erupting energy shifts from within and without on this emerging planet that I told them we had observed. Several of the other Councilmen who were not in favor of our expedition have suggested openly that our instruments are perhaps not able to record accurately any such life forms from a galaxy so far distant from our own system. When I tried to explain your new application of the recent time warp mechanism with wave optics I'm afraid I lost most of the Council after my opening remarks, except for the Prime Mover and another elder Councilman named Zar."

"How many of the Council were against us?" asked Zandor.

"Almost all of them except for the Prime Mover and Zar as far as I could judge," remarked Dort dryly.

"Almost all!" burst out Zandor. "Then how on Mekan did you convince the Prime Mover to let us proceed with the expedition? You know it will necessitate our using his new Starship, since the expedition will never be able to travel that distance and back in a time practical for the exploration and hopefully, experiment. How did you do it with so many against us?"

The older Gnorman's eyes twinkled slightly as he deliberately allowed his younger friend's impatience to build up to near fever pitch.

"Now, slow down, Zandor. It's as much a mystery to me as it is to you. Suffice it to say that apparently he and another Councilman, Zar, were able to convince the rest of the council that our experiments were impressive enough to warrant recognition. It is possible, of course, that he may believe we will be out from underfoot if we set out on this expedition. After all, the Starship is an experimental one, and there are no guarantees that we will make it to this planet and back again. At any rate, he has decided to let us use the new Starship; and has given us full outfitting privileges for our expedition! With our ability to go backwards and forwards in time with the time warp mechanism, and the time wrap drive on the Starship, we ought to be able to get to the distant planet we have discovered and see if our theories of spontaneous evolution of the governing substance within a naturally-evolved body are possible."

"Do you realize," asked Zandor, "what this will do to the accepted doctrine of the development of the Gnorman if we are proved correct by this distant planet experiment?"

"Yes," replied Dort, "it will shatter that doctrine completely. And it will bolster tremendously the old myth that Gnormen were once different from the synthetic metal, plastic, and chemical beings they are now and were more like today's living lower animals abundant here on Mekan. The myth states that they were, at one time, composite creatures of metal, plastic and something living placed into this body to govern its actions. Some of the oldest Gnormen today say they remember stories in their earliest years of these composite beings that had a living governing substance placed into their heads to control the rest of the body. Eventually, however, the Council's Life Factories were able to synthesize this governing substance so that a more durable chemical, metal, and plastic duplicate was able to be substituted for the former living substance. The myths went further back and suggested that in the dim recesses of time on our planet there were actually bodies that spontaneously grew to house the governing substance, which also spontaneously developed in harmony with the rest of the developing body. These bodies also were able to reproduce new bodies from parts of their own unit, including a new governing substance; somewhat similar to how the lower animals do it here today on Mekan. This, of course, makes sense; for where else would they have obtained a living governing substance for use in the composite body?

" This, as you know, has led to our theory that perhaps if these creatures existed, they may have begun to realize the danger of the vulnerability of their bodies. Perhaps it would have led them to develop more durable metal, plastic, and chemical ones to house their governing substance which they may have at first found too complicated to fabricate."

"Yes," added Zandor, "eventually, however, they learned to manufacture even the governing substance and all Gnormen have been fabricated totally by us in the Council's Life Factories ever since."

Dort's face became clouded. "If true, our theory could certainly lead to much discontent on Mekan. The Council and our Life Factories would lose much of their power and prestige; especially if there were enough Gnormen who would like to go back and claim our lost heritage of spontaneous development instead of the durability and longevity of our present synthetic bodies. Even though our synthetic body and governing substance does develop somewhat spontaneously during the time in the Life Factories, a total initial spontaneous life form would have to predicate a very different Creator than our Life Factories. This, of course, would lead to considerable loss of prestige and power to the Council, compared with what it now possesses. I presume this is why they do not support our theories and our expedition. If we were to prove that on a distant planet there were life forms that could spontaneously evolve into a creature capable of activity equivalent to our own, then we will have lent credence to the possible fact that Gnormen may have been developed originally from such an ancestor because of a need to protect a fragile and dying race. The Council and our Life Factories could be the result of the evolution of this need."

A sudden cloud crossed the intensely absorbed facial expression of Zandor as another problem came up in his mind.

"What about this new Starship?" he queried. "Has it been tested? Remember, this will be the first time anyone has attempted time-adjusted travel beyond our own galaxy."

"Actually, Zandor, that is no longer true," said Dort. "The Prime Mover himself has been out to our nearest neighbor, Centus IX, and he says that the ship operates flawlessly. Unfortunately, what he was doing out there he didn't reveal to me. He did tell me, however, that with its new time warp drive that you are familiar with, he has calculated that our journey to our targeted planet will take us about six months to complete each way, leaving us enough fuel for about four months of scouting time to set up our experiment. This, of course, is if there are spontaneously developing appropriate creatures present on the planet. By using the time warp mechanism after traveling this tremendous distance, each successive flight can be made to be millions of the target planet's years apart. I figure that we should be able to configure time to be able to view the results of our speeding up of evolution on this planet in about the time it takes us to get there, come home, and return there again. This will mean that we will hardly have returned to Mekan when we will have to make the return flight for evaluation of our project.

All this activity concerning inter-galactic flight, including the first really long distance test run with the new Starship, seems exceedingly strange for the Prime Mover to be concerning himself personally with. Even more unusual, he has taken it upon himself to personally set up our expedition; and from my initial perusal of the checklist for equipment, it has been arranged far more satisfactorily than I could have hoped for. Another unusual occurrence; he wants you and I to be his guests this evening; and he arranged this meeting deliberately quite secretly so that the rest of the Council is not aware of it."

"Well," said Zandor, "if we're to visit so mysteriously with the Prime Mover tonight, let's hurry and finish this last acceleration experiment so we won't be late."

As one of Mekan's three satellites slowly began to rise over the horizon, Dort and Zandor stood in its rosy glow before the Portal in the laboratory and set the coordinates for the destination given to Dort at the Council Hall by the Prime Mover. They stepped through the Portal and found themselves in a small, windowless room lighted only by an incandescence that seemed to emanate from the walls themselves. As they glanced around the semi-lighted room a voice suddenly directed them to stand under a large circular rod that hung from the ceiling at one end of the room. A faint hum started and a beam of light began to emanate from the rod on the ceiling, enveloping the two Gnormen. In another instant they found themselves in a well-lighted large room bathed in the same type of light and standing directly underneath a rod on the ceiling similar to the one in the small room they had just passed through. A door opened and Zandor saw the Prime Mover striding toward them with an easy smile on his face.

"Well, gentlemen, how did you two like our new personal Portal?" he asked. "This method is similar to the standard wall Portal but its coordinates are not obtainable by standard means; it serves as an efficient deterrent to unwelcome visitors. How do you do, Zandor; Dort has told me much about you and your evolutionary theories—or perhaps I should say revolutionary."

A faint twinkle appeared in the eyes of the Prime Mover. He was a tall Gnorman, with the easy grace and movement of one well skilled in physical activities; a fact that surprised and impressed Zandor considerably. "Welcome gentlemen, to my sanctuary."

Zandor was puzzled. "Does the Prime Mover have need of protection in Mekan? Unrest seems an exceedingly unlikely occurrence in our calculated, well-balanced Gnor society."

"It is not for protection from Gnor society at large, Zandor," answered the Prime Mover, "but from certain of the Councilmen, that I avoid an unannounced visit; but come, let us relax in sensorchairs while we chat."

As they began to relax in the soothing sensation afforded by the sensorchairs stimuli to their multiple peripheral circuits, the Prime Mover looked up and began to speak.

"You know, Dort, if there are such creatures as you have theorized they probably would be able to affect the same results that these sensorchairs create by taking in a chemical and having it travel through their bodies and envelop their neuronal circuits. I think that might be an interesting ability to have, don't you?"

"You must forgive my impatience, sir," replied Dort. "My curiosity as to why the Prime Mover has become so interested in us and our experiment is so great that it has caused me to forget my manners; but just why is our expedition so important that you would override most of the Councilmen's displeasure with our venture? Why, even some of our co-workers in the Life Factories don't accept our ideas."

"All in good time, Dort," said the Prime Mover. "But first, you must pardon me while we ascertain the status of your friend here; although his theoretical abilities probably preclude us even having to do it." He turned toward a far door and said, "Zar, would you please come in now?"

With this the same door the Prime Mover had entered through in the far end of the room slid noiselessly open again, and the elder Councilman that Dort had seen with the Prime Mover at the Council Hall rapidly came over to the trio. The Prime Mover introduced Councilman Zar to Zandor; the Councilman then produced a small black instrument he was carrying with him.

"If you would permit me, Zandor," the Prime Mover said, "I should like to monitor the rear of your head for a moment."

As Zandor visibly became somewhat apprehensive the Prime

Mover hastily explained, "Please do not be concerned Zandor; Dort, I must apologize, has already been monitored without his knowing it. This process is not painful or harmful in any way; it just gives us some vital information we must know about you that we already know about Dort."

The Councilman rapidly passed the glowing instrument back and forth behind Zandor's head several times. With obvious relief he noted the readings obtained and nodded significantly to the Prime Mover. "There is no question about it; he too, is one," said Zar.

Zandor looked alarmed. "What do you mean? What on Mekan are you talking about?" He looked at his older colleague for explanation.

Dort looked as puzzled as his younger friend. "I'm sure I don't know, Zandor, but hopefully the Prime Mover will enlighten us."

"Of course," said the Prime Mover, "and please forgive this rather bad transgression on our parts. You are obviously quite familiar with the old myth of the supposed earlier beginnings of Gnormen here on Mekan; indeed, your theory and expedition, if successful, would just about prove this myth to be factual—is that not true?"

"Well, we have believed so," said Zandor. "This, of course, would presumably lessen considerably the power and prestige of the Council and our Life Factories; which we thought accounted for their distaste for our theories and proposed expedition."

"Exactly," said the Prime Mover, "and you are probably wondering why Zar and myself, supposed leaders of the Council, are backing this expedition which is so frowned upon by the rest of the Council?"

"Well, it certainly has been in our minds," answered Dort.

"First let me tell you that your theories are not theories, they are fact! I realize this may sound incredulous to you, but if that is hard to believe wait until you have heard what I am about to say. Not only were so-called composite living beings present in the past on Mekan; they are present today—in fact, all four here in this room are just such beings!"

Dort and Zandor were stunned. "You mean we... are... composites?" Dort stared in disbelief at Zandor, who was in a similar state of shock at the statement as his older friend.

"We didn't know about Zandor until just now," stated the Prime Mover, "although we assumed he was one because of his advanced theoretical ability exhibited by his and your present work."

Zandor, incomprehension still in his eyes, questioned the Councilmen, "You mean that Dort and I are not just plastic, metal, chemical and synthetic governing substance, manufactured in our Life Factories here on Mekan? What are we then?"

The Prime Mover looked earnestly at his two guests. "The theory is true that there once were two types of creatures on this planet and in this galaxy that took in raw material and oxygen and converted it to energy for growth and maintenance and reproduced themselves from within their own bodies. Their life form started as a single cell which took in raw material and in time grew into a mechanism much more complicated than the present day Gnorman; at least as far as its governing substance was concerned. Our present Gnor body itself, however, is much more advanced than what these creatures possessed. But the governing substance within their head was far superior to ours at the height of its development. It came from spontaneous growth and development from this same original single cell which was carried within the body of one of two types of these creatures. When a specific cell from one of the two types was introduced into a cell from the body of the other type, then this single enhanced cell would begin to grow and develop into a new creature. When it had reached a certain stage of growth and development, the new creature was shed from the first creature's body, where it then began to grow and develop into a mature being on its own. This development was not unlike what we see in the lower animals present today on Mekan. Even our Gnorman, when he is first produced in the Life Factory, is without any useable knowledge; but gradually his synthetic governing substance learns and he begins to function effectively at his chosen work. The only difference from the ancient natural living creature was that in its early life, it was small in stature and coordination; not at all like the fully developed and coordinated Gnor body from the Life Factories. The new living creature, as time went on, grew larger and better coordinated until it reached mature proportions; similarly as the lower animals do now."

"But what happened to these creatures?" asked Dort. "If they were that successful, and with a more complicated governing substance than the present day Gnorman, why did they disappear?"

"What happened to them has a long, complicated history," replied the Prime Mover. "I will try to relate this history as clearly as I can, and I even can show you what they look like later on. Suffice it to say that these marvelous, self-sustaining and self-duplicating bodies were, however, extremely fragile and vulnerable. Instead of a several hundred year life span as our current Gnor bodies have, these creatures were lucky to live to be 100 years old. They were therefore exceedingly dependant on their ability to reproduce in their younger years to keep them from becoming extinct; as some of the lower animals have already become here on Mekan. This factor became an overpoweringly predominant instinctual feature in their evolutionary pattern. It caused them to seriously overpopulate the planet as they gradually came to conquer some of the natural forces which in the past had decimated their ranks at an early age. This overpopulation led to the unrest of the consequent competition it engendered and multiple encounters between one another broke out which they called 'wars'. This caused further depletion of many of the youngest and best in their population. They became very aggressive and violent creatures because of the overpopulation-engendered competition, which added to the many physical conflicts that arose sometimes over very trivial misunderstandings. They eventually were able to stop the larger physical encounters or wars when they fully realized their devastating effect, but this unfortunately led to further overpopulation. In turn, this began to cause another serious problem— that of pollution of their surrounding environment. Large numbers of these creatures began to die off because of this increasing pollution of the raw materials and the atmosphere, and the growing difficulty of providing enough non-polluted raw materials to keep all these billions of creatures alive. In addition, tiny microscopic organisms and killing rouge molecules came into being that they were unable to eradicate with their science, so even more of the population was destroyed. Unfortunately, through all this the one thing they never seemed to be able to change or modify was the overpowering innate urge that drove them to reproduce; and they apparently never developed any measures to stop or control it. Finally, in the midst of a growing sea of calamity, a few brilliant creatures devised the idea of building a synthetic body to house their governing substance. This body would tolerate the pollution around them for indefinite periods. They developed a battery pack for power with an internal apparatus that used the magnetosphere of the planet to create an electric current to recharge the batteries and supply the power needed for them to function as they moved through its magnetic field. That, as you know, is why every Gnorman is instructed to walk every day. The only raw material intake would be a daily small amount necessary to oxygenate and nourish their living governing substance. They developed a nutrient fluid that would penetrate their governing substance making a vessel supply to the organ unnecessary. What they eventually developed were the composite bodies that are actually almost indistinguishable from our current ones that also, as you and I, have to have a capsule of concentrated raw materials and oxygen daily to maintain our governing substance.

"After many years of partial successes but mostly failures, they gradually began to accrue a sizeable number of functioning composite creatures. The living governing substance was floated within a fashioned protective head in a nutrient bath that contained all the oxygen and raw material necessary to sustain it with the aid of the daily capsule supplements. The mouth, vocal cords, tongue, and teeth of the living creature were retained to take in the capsular nourishment and to enable the composite to speak. A bellows mechanism within the composite's chest took in and expelled the gas from the environmental atmosphere enabling him to speak; so he no longer needed the lungs the living creatures had to breathe and speak with. The natural governing substance had had circulatory vessels that delivered and removed substances to and from it in the living creatures. Gradually these now unneeded vessels were slowly absorbed for nutrients and eventually disappeared. The nutrient fluid developed had chemicals within it that allowed these nutrients to pass throughout all of the governing substance with ease. Another remarkable thing that happened was that the lower end of the living governing substance actually learned on its own to connect to the Gnorman's lower electrical body circuits; somewhat similarly to the way it happened naturally in the living creatures. This end plate connection area has been worked on for centuries and has been dramatically improved to its current almost perfect state.

"However, there soon grew up a tremendous hostility between the composite creatures and the natural creatures which eventually led to open warfare with almost an extinction of the natural creatures. But because of the need for living governing substance to power the composite beings, colonies of the creatures were kept alive and strictly regulated as sources of this organ for the composites. When a governing substance within a natural creature had sufficiently matured, and a need arose to replace a traumatically destroyed composite creature's governing substance or create a new composite, the governing substance was removed from the head of the natural creature and placed into the head of the composite Gnorman. The connections from the living governing substance to the circuits of the rest of the Gnor body gradually fused spontaneously in the Life Factory, thanks to the developments mentioned before which encouraged this to happen; and the new governing substance began to control the Gnorman's body. The living body of the natural creature was thus destroyed, but its governing substance (and essentially it) continued functioning as before but with a new almost indestructible synthetic body with a several hundred year life span. This was not a very moral time for our ancestors because of the enslavement of the natural living creatures essentially against their will.

"But an interesting phenomenon occurred with the newly created Gnormen concerning the innate urge to reproduce that was present in the natural creatures. It had been agreed at the start that only one of the two creature types would be fabricated as a Gnorman, and the larger of the two was chosen. After a while, with none of the second type of creature around, only a few of the composites retained that reproductive urge and eventually it died out completely. Instead it seemed to be replaced by increased creativity and intelligence in almost all of the composites. And in addition, almost all of the natural creature's memories eventually disappeared and would only occur as unusual dreams that the Gnormen couldn't explain. You have probably had such unusual dreams yourselves from time to time."

Zandor seemed puzzled and interrupted the narrative of the Prime Mover. "Yes, sir, some of the dreams I have had contained very different looking people in them and doing some very unusual things together that had no meaning to me. But, sir, if we are all composites, where is the farm that houses the natural creatures? And why create the story that the Gnorman's complete body and governing substance is synthetically manufactured within the Council's Life Factories?"

"Because," the Prime Mover responded, "in most cases the Gnormen are just that. But let me go on and it will become clear."

He continued his narrative. "As the years passed, from time to time there was unrest at the natural creature farm. You see, not all their governing substances were able to be utilized since their life span was so short compared to the hundreds of years for the Gnormen composites. This protracted Gnorman life span was achieved by the development of the revolutionary new raw material delivery system to the governing substance mentioned before. This delivery system has been steadily improved over the centuries and we are benefitting from it today.

"Life on the farm was certainly not very desirable for a life form that was actually equal or even superior to its controllers in every aspect except for longevity, durability, and strength. Consequently, riots broke out, and some of the creatures escaped and had to be hunted down. Finally, all the natural creatures were moved to a maximum security area within a hollowed-out area on one of our satellites, where escape was impossible. That is why, Zandor, you didn't know where the farm was located. Very few people know about this farm. In these close confines on the satellite, with only a small hope of ever escaping the situation they were in, these creatures became depressed and began to die out early in their life. It became harder and harder to maintain the usual number deemed necessary to have on hand in case of destruction of some of the Gnormen in some unforeseen calamity. Eventually, the remaining small number of natural creatures accepted their lot in life and even began to be proud of their contribution to Gnor society. They developed a strong camaraderie with their Gnor controllers who eventually grew to admire and respect their superior intellect. The controllers began to allow them as much freedom as possible on the satellite. In response the creatures helped their controllers develop most of the improvements to the construction of the Gnormen that we see today. They truly understood the cataclysmic problems that had caused their ancestors to disappear and began to identify themselves quite correctly as saviors of the Gnor race by their efforts at advancing its evolution. They no longer minded dying, since in reality they would still be living, and for a much longer time than they ever could in their own fragile living bodies.

"Unfortunately, the diseases from the past, along with an unforeseen radiation problem from the digging on the satellite, had affected their reproductive ability; and the number of natural creature's governing substances now available for transplant became dangerously low.

"At this time, in a very primitive fashion, one of the more brilliant natural creatures first became able to duplicate with a chemical substance enmeshed within a plastic and metal matrix some of the essential lower activities of the naturally-occurring governing substance. Stepped-up research on this finally led to the ability to totally replace the living governing substance with a synthetic one. At first all looked very well indeed regarding the possibility of not needing any future new composites. If this could be accomplished, the natural creatures would be able to be liberated and continue on their own on their satellite or anywhere else they desired to go. They would still be able to contribute with their intellect and creativity to the forward progress of Gnor society. This fabricated governing substance was placed into a mature Gnor body and like the living governing substance, required a certain amount of time and programming before it could function effectively. The Gnormen, as is true today, went through an intensive training period within the Life Factories until their synthetic governing substance was programmed well enough to allow them to assume a role in the outside Gnor society.

"It soon became apparent, however, that the synthetic governing substance did not work as well as the natural one, and that there was a limit as to how much learning could be assimilated by these completely artificial Gnormen. As you know, there are far more menial activities in our Gnor society than there are theoretical creative ones; and the bulk of these menial jobs are now held down by these synthetic Gnormen. All of the creative, theoretical positions, however, are still held down by composites like us. Research has gone on feverishly but to this day nothing has been able to improve the synthetic governing substance. Our brilliant chief designer, Jol, is sure that he will eventually create what we need, but more time is needed for research to accomplish this.

"It was decided long ago that it would not auger well for Gnor society to know that it was composed of different kinds of Gnormen; especially since one type was so superior to the other. That is why all Gnormen take the same raw materials capsule daily for their governing substance, even though the synthetic ones really don't need to do so. Consequently then, the truth became myth; and was buried by the relentless efforts of the rest of the current Councilmen; whom, as I am sure you now realize, are all completely synthetic Gnormen. Zar and I are the only remaining composites at this level of Gnor society."

Now Dort seemed puzzled. "But how did the synthetic Gnor Councilmen gain such control if they are so far inferior to the composites?"

"They are only inferior as to higher abstract thinking; this is in the frontal section of the natural governing substance and so far has been unable to be duplicated by the Life Factories. Political activity, cunning, and practical lower level organization is actually better handled without the interference of abstract creative thinking. In fact, even in the long past time of the natural creature's ascendancy there was a preponderance of this type of person in control of society. It was a leading factor in many of the physical encounters or wars that were present in those days. Thus, the Council has come to be made up in large number of the best of these synthetic practical organizers; and it is they who have the power to direct the composites in their research as you already know."

Zandor looked at Dort with a significant nod. "I always felt that way about our project director. This certainly backs up my suspicions." Then, to the Prime Mover, "But why then is our expedition so important to you, since it is now obviously unnecessary to prove our theories?"

"Unfortunately, a recent space plague brought in to the satellite farm has completely wiped out all remaining natural creatures save for one 35-year-old young doctor who was in my fortress studying to eventually replace the aging doctor at the farm. You will meet him eventually; his name is Dr. Dik Ran, and he is the only living natural being left on Mekan. The composite controllers did everything they could think of to try to save the rest of them, but they eventually all perished. This caused great grief to Dr. Ran and the controllers at the farm who had by now become deeply attached to them as friends and colleagues. As far as is known, other than Dr. Ran, there are no remaining live natural creatures anywhere within this or neighboring galaxies. That is what I was looking for in our new Starship out at Cygnus IX. Your proposed experiment to cause a specific type of life form to evolve rapidly on that distant planet you discovered has given us hope that with our new Starship and the ability to move forward and backward in time with our time warp mechanism you might be able to get us a new supply of living governing substance. Without composites we will never be able to develop synthetic duplication of the higher centers in the living governing substance. The life of a composite may range into several centuries, but it is much shorter than the thousands of years a totally synthetic Gnorman enjoys. The governing substance, even though freed up from dependence upon lifetime-limiting vessels for nourishment, eventually breaks down and stops functioning at about 900 years. Thus, unless a supply of natural governing substance is located soon enough, the remaining composites will die off never to be replaced; and our race will become permanently stagnated at its present level. At the least, this is a terrible legacy for our living ancestors that gave so much to try to improve the Gnor race and its future generations."

Dort exchanged a significant glance with Zandor and a hint of apprehension crossed his face.

"You know, our instruments have detected life forms that are evolving on this distant planet; but they are very early forms. Even with the time warp mechanism advancing and retreating time over very long periods, when we arrive on the planet there still may not be enough time for a high enough type of living creature with suitable governing substance to evolve."

"This we understand," said the Prime Mover, "but we also understand that you have some theories about possibly speeding up this evolutionary rate; especially as regards the governing substance."

"Well, yes, we do," replied Dort. "Zandor and I believe that certain chemical and electrical manipulations, including some introduced genetic makeup from lower animals that we may have evolved from here on Mekan, may enable the governing substance to be selectively accelerated. We are hopeful that the creature that evolves with our enhancements will have a governing substance similar to ours and capable of much more activity than its concomitantly developing body can utilize. Now that I think of it, if this excess governing substance organ were placed into a Gnorman, there is a good chance that much more of it would be able to be utilized. The Gnorman body is much more complex and actually could be made even more so, enabling more of the governing substance to function!" With the last realization of what he was saying, both Dort and Zandor became visibly excited.

The Prime Mover interrupted Dort with great excitement as well. "You see! You see! That's exactly what we had in mind. In other words, we are hoping that you will be able to accelerate evolution enough on this emerging planet's creature to come up with a suitable governing substance that will be in time to continue composite Gnormen lines. This will enable research by them to continue to try to design a synthetic governing substance that can replace the living one."

Dort looked thoughtful. "Yes, I see. Perhaps it can be done. But tell me, why don't the other Councilmen sanction this? It would seem it might be just as beneficial to them."

"It is the old story that was prevalent even with the natural living creatures in the past before us," said the Prime Mover. "The Councilmen do not have the intellectual capacity, ethics, or morals of the current composites that took centuries to develop; nor will they have the intellectual capacity of the proposed new artificial Gnormen if the higher centers of the natural governing substance can be synthesized. They fear that they will be replaced and lose their power if these new beings are able to be created. Zar and I have reason to believe that the recent space plague at the satellite farm was deliberately induced. In addition, several composites have met with rather strange accidents lately, and have fallen sick after their raw material capsules were replenished. It has become increasingly evident that there may be a plot present to destroy all composites before any progress being made by them on the synthetic higher centers of the governing substance can be completed. As you can see, since the Councilmen control our Life Factories where you and the rest of the composites are working, the situation is very serious. That is the reason for our protective Portal. Without you knowing it, we have also clamped a tight lid of security around you and your project. Your raw material replenishment capsules have been carefully checked and stockpiled for later use. Do you see, gentlemen, how much we and our future society may be depending on your project?"

Dort again looked thoughtful. "I do see, Mr. Prime Mover, and if we are to leave on schedule next week we must make many preparations now. We had better get back to the lab and get started on them." He rose and looked at Zandor who nodded and also rose from his sensorchair.

"Before you go," the Prime Mover said, "I know you would be interested in seeing pictures of the natural creatures that you have never seen and from whom your own governing substance was obtained. I would have introduced you to Dr. Ran but he is on the satellite farm at this time."

He rose from his sensorchair, approached a projector on the edge of a nearby table, and snapped it on. Two holographic figures instantly appeared in the center of the table; one larger than the other and shaped differently. The smaller figure was more rounded and had two mounds on the upper front part of its torso. The larger figure was more representative of the current Gnormen but smaller, with a strange organ dangling down from the middle of its two legs. The smaller figure didn't have such an organ but instead had an opening where the larger figure's organ was situated. There was also an opening in the rear of each creature just back of the organs opening in front. There was hair on each figure's head similar to their own hair, and both had hair where their legs divided off their abdomen.

Zandor looked incredulously at the two holographic figures on the table before him and spoke to the Prime Mover excitedly.

"Sir," he said, "I have seen creatures like this before in my dreams! The larger figure often would be handling those strange mounds on the upper torso of the smaller figure, and then they would clasp together tightly and roll back and forth. I always felt a sort of exhilaration when this was going on; I don't know why. And what is that organ and aperture between their two legs?"

"A very astute observation," said the Prime Mover. "Your dreams are probably the fading memories of the creature whose governing substance you have. That organ on the larger figure and the opening on the smaller figure is what could have led to their extinction for that is how they reproduced their new creatures and how serious infections were introduced to cause large numbers of them to perish. This reproductive urge was instrumental in causing the overpopulation of the planet, spread of very serious infections, and consequent decimation of great numbers of these creatures over the years."

"How did they accomplish this reproduction," asked Dort.

"That organ on the larger figure", explained the Prime Mover, "was introduced into that aperture on the smaller figure. Apparently the pleasure this maneuver created was extremely enjoyable to both creatures. I believe, Zandor, that the feelings you had in your dreams was some part of that stimulus. Later, the material deposited into the aperture by the larger figure combined with a similar substance within the smaller figure and this gradually grew into another creature within an organ in the smaller figure's body. In time, after it had grown a certain amount, this new creature would leave the smaller figure's body through the same aperture and begin to mature on its own as a totally new creature. Those two mounds on the front of the smaller creature were what it used to feed the developing new creature it had just shed from its body. In essence, then, these two creatures had their own 'Life Factories' within each other. And with credit to the utility of these openings and organs, they were also used as ways to get rid of the waste products from their ingested raw material as well. You can see how these creatures were very similar to the present day lower animals still on our planet, but with considerably higher development of their governing substance."

Zandor looked at Dort and said, "You know, the larger figure does look a lot like we do; sans the organ, of course. I guess that would be true since the original Life Factory specimens must have been modeled on his figure."

"That's correct," said the Prime Mover, "but the Gnorman body was made bigger and stronger with many more physical abilities than his smaller natural cousin. I believe the reproductive organs were probably not developed for a Gnor body since that urge had often been the source of the creatures' overpopulation, jealousies, and wars, and the original designers didn't want that to happen again. I did find out, however, that the two types of Gnormen, designed similarly as the two types of natural creatures, and possessing such organs, were developed in a few cases for the local pleasure stimulus effect, but they were largely discontinued for the fears expressed above."

"You mean," asked Zandor, "that there were two types of Gnormen developed and they had those same organs that caused such pleasure? Why didn't they continue these Gnormen?"

"As I said before," replied the Prime Mover. "They were afraid the Gnormen might be influenced adversely as the natural creatures had been in the past because of what this pleasure-filled urge might create."

The Prime Mover and Zar escorted Dort and Zandor to their special overhead Portal. "I'm sorry to have to inflict all of this on you at once, gentlemen, but time is of the essence. Only one thing; to protect yourselves, please stay within the confines of your laboratory as it may not be safe for you to return to your apartment. When you have completed your preparations and are ready to leave, notify me, and we will escort you to the Starship for takeoff. We'd love to go with you, but we are needed here to keep things stable and protect the remaining composites. Thank you gentlemen, and may your expedition be successful for the sake of the future of our Gnor society."

With that there was a crescendo hum, and an increasing intensity of light enveloped Dort and Zandor, transporting them back to the windowless room. They set up the coordinates on the conventional Portal and stepped through into their laboratory.

Zandor looked at Dort. "Composites! Not only were and are there such creatures but we're each one of them! I'll never look at my raw material capsules ever again in the same way! And now we're off on a mission to keep composites alive to continue the evolution of the whole Gnor race; in a Starship whose drive is still theoretical in many aspects! It's a lot to assimilate in one night, Dort, don't you think? I remember the Prime Mover telling us that the living creatures used to take in some liquid material to help them relax. I wish we had that ability now. I think I'll just sit in the sensorchair for awhile to see if it will help unwind my circuits. Will you join me?"

"I had thought," said Dort, "to start out with the problem of atmospheric control on the new planet. But perhaps you're right; a little meditation and relaxation would certainly be helpful at present."

They were two and a half months out into deep space when they encountered their first significant problem. The bridge crew was made up of eight Gnormen; Dort and Zandor; the captain, Zeltor, a long-time space enthusiast and a composite; Rol, the space navigator and another composite; and three crewmen and a laboratory technician, all synthetic Gnormen. It seemed that during the extreme length of time that had passed due to the time warp mechanism's effect, the atmosphere of the approaching planet had expanded tremendously, so that there might be a heat problem to the Starship's hull in entry through it to the surface of the planet.

"We will have to slow the ship significantly to ooze through this thick atmosphere," said Zeltor. "Fortunately this great ship will be able to slow down and hover to get us through safely. At the speed we've been traveling even this Gnor metal ship might burn up trying to bust through this thick atmosphere."

"It is interesting to realize that this blanket of atmosphere could be an advantage to a vulnerable chemical life form," remarked Dort. "It could certainly serve to protect them from their star's radiation if it has the same situation with an ozone layer like that present on Mekan. Still, it could pose a problem here for us to get through to land."

"I don't think we will have too much trouble with it save for the expenditure of some more fuel," said Zandor. "We can double the force field around the ship and slow down dramatically. This should take care of most of the heat problem during our descent to the planet's surface. We can check this out more carefully when we get to the planet. Say, Dort, we are close enough to the planet now to use that modification of the time warp optics device we used back on Mekan to view this planet originally and that I had installed on the ship just prior to our leaving Mekan. Shall we try contacting the planet now?"

"Fine," said Dort. "I'm anxious to see what type of evolution has occurred on the planet since the last time we viewed it back on Mekan; especially since our time warp mechanism has caused a lot of time to have gone by since we last viewed it. He glanced over at Captain Zeltor who was busy at the instrument console. "What say, Captain, can you and Rol tear yourselves away from that control panel long enough to join us up front on the observation platform for a view of the new planet ahead and what's waiting for us there?"

"A pleasure," flashed back the captain. "Let me adjust this fuel monitoring computer and Rol and I will join you shortly."

On the observation platform the four Gnormen glanced with nervous anticipation at the information beginning to arrive through the computer banks from the time warp optics device installed by Zandor. The planet ahead was about the same size as their planet, but its atmosphere was definitely more dense than that of Mekan.

"We were certainly right about that atmosphere," said Zandor. "It's at least twice as dense as that on Mekan, but has a roughly similar mixture of gases with a little more oxygen than we have on our planet. There seems to be a much wider expanse of the oceans now present than what we saw on our original time warp wave optics device scan from Mekan. They also seem to be much shallower than before as well."

"About how many years of this planet's time have you caused to pass since you last viewed it at home, Dort?" asked Zeltor.

"As near as I can judge from the time warp mechanism we set I'd say about 150 million years of this planet's time has passed. When we originally scanned this planet back on Mekan, we figured it was already about 300 million years old and had life just beginning in the warmer edges around the oceans. That, of course, was why we were excited about using this planet for our evolution experiment. It seems that these oceans are much more shallow and warmer now than on our previous scan; I suppose it's the effect of the planet's star heating up the more shallow seas. Let's see if we can pick up any life forms on the surface. The last scan showed a predominance of small creatures, mostly living in the seas; but there were a few that could be found both on land and in the seas.

Zandor! Look at this! The scan has picked up a creature of unbelievable size! And now there's more... and more! Why, this planet is teeming with creatures from tiny to unbelievably large size! With obviously such prolific physical evolution, I wonder if there are any creatures already evolved with governing substance that we could use."

"Well," spoke up the navigator, Rol, "we'll know soon enough when we land—as far as I can calculate about ten more hours of this planet's time. I noted that this planet rotates on its tilted axis about twenty-four hours from when one spot on its surface faces its star again. It also has one satellite that strangely enough only has one side of it that faces the planet at all times because of its and the planet's rotation. This might be helpful to us when we return again after your experiment to speed up evolution. We could set up a base on the far side of that satellite and not be seen by anything on the planet itself. I suggest we start the preliminaries for the descent through this thick atmosphere and our landing if we do so. We can orbit for awhile and check out what is going on below through the telescreen."

As the Starship advanced through the planet's outer atmosphere Zeltor placed it into a low orbit so that they could survey the planet's surface and its life forms visibly over the telescreen. The four composite and three of the four synthetic Gnormen all stood in the upper observation bridge of the Starship before the telescreen where Rol and Zandor were making the final adjustments to the device.

"Well," said Dort, "now we'll know what spontaneously evolved life forms can look like. From the various sizes and shapes noted on our long range scans the actual viewing of these creatures should be nothing short of phenomenal!"

Suddenly the telescreen before them sprang into life and the seven Gnormen stared in open wonder at the panorama unfolding before them. They were looking down upon a large meadow at the edge of a deep swamp. Trees somewhat similar to those seen on Mekan but infinitely larger and more densely leafed surrounded the outer edges of the meadow. Wispy, blue-grey patches of fog floated across the meadow from the swamp. On the edge of the meadow, knee-deep in the adjacent swamp ooze, stood an enormous beast with a relatively small head. It was stolidly tearing off large chunks of grass and bushes with its mouth and swallowing them down its long neck in one convulsive effort after another.

"Unbelievable! Look at the size of that creature!" exclaimed Zandor. "And yet, its head is so relatively small it is not possible that its governing substance has evolved to the state necessary for our use."

29

"No," said Dort, "the scanners show that the governing substance in that creature is tiny and underdeveloped, and those other beasts over on the right edge of the meadow are similar creatures, although not as large. And see! One just flew by in the air! Imagine! These creatures have evolved the ability to fly! Still, the scanners show that even their governing substance is not developed enough for our use. No, Zandor, if we cannot find any creature here with a governing substance already sufficiently developed enough now to be utilized in a composite, then our experiment will definitely be necessary to allow the evolution of a governing substance suitable for our use. We will have to find a creature on this planet with the potential to develop the governing substance we need, and then set up our experiment to help it evolve appropriately. We also may need to find some way to protect it from some of these fierce, massive creatures, many of whom seem to enjoy devouring the smaller creatures around them."

As the Starship orbited the planet just beyond its outermost atmosphere, the Gnormen searched through the myriad of creatures that appeared before them on the telescreen for a suitable subject for their quest. Although there were countless thousands of creatures of all sizes, descriptions, and habits in the sea, on land, and in the air; they were unable to locate one they felt already had a suitable governing substance to use now or even for their evolution experiment later. They determined that all these creatures had developed spontaneously from one another, almost exactly as the Prime Mover had described the early life forms on their own planet. This planet's creatures all maintained their living state as the lower animals did on Mekan; by taking in raw material through their mouths and apparently converting this material by internal means into the energy necessary for their functioning. It was not at all similar to the battery power energy supply in the thorax of Gnormen, recharged constantly by motion through the magnetosphere of the planet; although Gnormen did ingest raw material capsules through their mouths daily for their governing substance. Fortunately, this planet had well developed magnetic lines of force like their home planet Mekan which enabled them to recharge here just as easily.

Dort stated, "I guess maybe we're not that different in some ways; we do have to take raw material in for our governing substance. I guess that shows our ancestral roots were probably quite similar. Indeed, the Prime Mover told me that on the satellite farm the living creatures did this regularly as well. I believe these facts auger well for us finding a creature here that we will be able to induce a successful enhanced evolution of a governing substance that we will be able to use."

The creatures below seemed to be divided into three types as regards the kind of raw material they utilized. Some took in only plants; others only small six- and eight-legged creatures that had almost no governing substance; while a third group attacked other smaller creatures of the same or similar groups, destroyed and devoured them! It was this last group that was particularly repulsive to the seven Gnormen; it was alien for them to accept this wanton destruction of another, often identical being.

On the third week of orbiting the planet, the Gnormen still had not found a suitable candidate for their experiment, and were about to give up the project and return to Mekan. Zandor suddenly stopped the sweep of the telescreen along a fertile meadow at the edge of a forest of trees. He adjusted the controls to return the scan to the branches of the bordering trees.

"There! Look!" he cried excitedly. "Dort, see that small creature there? It's the one with those wide, beautiful green eyes. Could it be we've found our subject? Its eyes, skull, and teeth are different from the land, sea, and air creatures we've been looking at for three weeks. Unless the scanners are mistaken, this animal, with a little enhancement from us, may be able to develop a fairly respectable governing substance in time."

Dort peered intensely at the screen and excitement began to mount in him as well. "I believe you're right, Zandor! Here we've been looking in the sea, on the ground, and in the air, but have neglected the trees—perhaps the safest spot in such a teeming, hostile world such as this. A creature with some reasoning ability would naturally go to the area of least possible danger; and in this world, I'd say it's the trees. That creature is obviously our subject if it has the governing substance the scanners are showing us. We must capture one and determine if this is true or not. Zeltor, Rol, gentlemen, let's prepare to get through this atmosphere and land—we've much to do!"

"We must recheck all of our calculations," said Zeltor. "I don't want to be left on this ferocious planet. We must not waste any more fuel than we have to. "We do have to get back to Mekan, you know."

They all exchanged smiling glances and set to work to prepare for the landing.

As they descended through the atmosphere Zandor utilized extra fuel to build up the strength of the force field around the Starship. The area immediately adjacent to the field began to go from a dull red glow to a white hot area ringing the entering portion of the force field around the front of the Starship and tapering to a red glow on the last portion of the field at the rear of the vessel.

Zeltor suddenly noted an alarming rise on one of the temperature gauges on the control panel in front of him. A hasty survey of the computer data showed that power had been directed away from the left front force field which, if continued, would shortly result in failure of the field and probable eventual burning up of the Starship!

"Zandor!" shouted Zeltor. "Check the power to the left front force field; quickly! A few more minutes and the field will fail and we might not be able to build it back fast enough to prevent irreversible heat damage to the ship!"

Zandor hastily checked the control panel in front of him and manipulated several controls in quick succession. "The controls don't seem to be responding from here; and yet there are changes continuing that could only happen with some direction from somewhere else. Rol! Quickly! You and Dort check the compartment below where the manual override panel is located. And Dort, you'd better take hand lasers with you!"

The two Gnormen swiftly descended the companionway to the compartment below with Dort leading the way with his hand laser drawn. As they dropped to the floor of the compartment one of the synthetic Gnor crewmen, who had been working feverishly behind one of the manual control panels, made a lunge for his laser which was on a work bench close by. Dort fired a blast that caught the Gnorman in his mid section and he crumpled in a heap, his chest a mass of molten metal and burnt plastic. Dort quickly examined the damage behind the control panel and noted where several circuits had been crossed and shorted.

"Rol," snapped Dort, "tell Zandor the trouble is in the manual override and that I can have it properly adjusted in a couple of minutes. Tell him not to open the left force field tie-in until I give the word. And don't tell him what transpired here yet; remember, there are three other synthetic Gnormen on board."

Rol relayed this message to Zandor over his communicator. Dort hastily made a final adjustment and gave Rol the signal for Zandor to tie in the left front force field once more. A slight throbbing was initially felt by the two Gnormen, but this gradually disappeared as an ear-shattering whoop came over Rol's communicator.

"It's working!" shouted Zandor. "The field's building back! I guess we made it, Zeltor! That was sure a close one!"

Dort and Rol approached the weapons locker in the lower compartment and locked it; taking the key with them. Then they returned to the bridge of the Starship with their lasers sheathed, and noted that the other three synthetic Gnormen were completely occupied in the landing procedure of the Starship. They resumed their positions as the Starship began to settle toward the rapidly appearing planet's surface below. Shortly they were flashing over one of the oceans and approaching a large island continent in the southern hemisphere.

"Let's deliberately not do anything on this continent, Dort," said Zandor. "It is quite isolated and we can see the difference in the governing substance that evolves naturally here on this continent as compared to that which we will influence on the other continents."

"Good idea," said Dort.

The Starship quickly passed over the large island continent, traversed the ocean going north and passed over a much larger mainland continent, from its eastern edge to its western edge. Zeltor skillfully brought the craft to rest on a high mountain top above the tree line at this side of the continent so they would be able to reconnoiter from this area without the Starship being in any danger from the large beasts in the swamps far below. The other three synthetic Gnor crewmen had finished their tasks and left for the crew quarters below.

"Now," said Zandor, after complete landing procedures had been secured, "Just what happened down there, Dort?"

"Apparently the Prime Mover was right about a conspiracy," said Dort. "One of the synthetic Gnor crewmen was tampering with the manual override on the force fields in such a way that it would have meant certain destruction of the Starship if he had been successful. He tried to shoot us with his laser, but I managed to eliminate him with my own laser before he was able to get to his. We must get to the crew's quarters immediately and be sure there are no more traitors in our midst. I'm surprised and dismayed at this because the Prime Mover assured me that this crew had been thoroughly checked out from a security viewpoint. He also said that he had interviewed them personally and discussed the mission and what it meant to the evolution of the Gnor race. He felt that all were 'in the fold' so to speak concerning the goal of the mission. They all had stated that they would be proud to be part of improving their race and felt privileged to be chosen to go on this mission. Well, let's go check them out; better have your lasers handy."

The four composites descended to the rear compartment crew's quarters where the three remaining synthetic Gnormen were discussing the marvels of the planet they had just landed on.

"Neat landing, skipper," one of the crew greeted Zeltor as he entered the room.

Zeltor questioned the three as to where their fourth crew member was.

34

One of the Gnormen called Cron spoke up, "I don't know what's happened to that sluggard, skipper; but I'm mighty upset about him. I had to do his job as well as my own when we landed and it wasn't too easy handling it alone, believe me!"

When the three synthetic Gnormen were told of the fourth Gnorman's treachery they expressed what appeared to the four composites to be quite genuine evidence of shock, surprise, and dismay at the potential dangerous turn of events that Dort and Rol had thwarted.

Cron spoke up, "You know, sir, there was something odd about him from the very beginning of this voyage. He kept pretty much to himself and never took part in the usual griping about conditions that the rest of us always do just to pass the time. We are certainly grateful that Dort and Rol got to him in time to stop him. Skipper, the Prime Mover talked with us prior to this mission and explained everything to us about why we were going on this expedition and you can rest assured that we all are 100% for it to be completed successfully!" This seemingly quite genuine declaration by the crewmen was good news to the four composite Gnormen and they left the crew's quarters reassured that these three were loyal to the mission.

On the next day the seven remaining Gnormen went about their respective jobs to prepare for disembarking in the scout vehicle on board. When the four composites were alone, Dort said to the others, "I think the other two Gnor-crewmen are sincere; and as for laboratory tech Bar, he has been with Zandor and me for years and I'm sure he's all right." The other three composites nodded their heads in agreement and continued their preparations for the exploration on the following day for the tree creature they had seen on the telescreen.

Zeltor and Dort set out in the scout vehicle early the next morning to attempt to locate and capture one of the arboreal creatures with the large eyes and skull case. Zandor remained with Rol to map out other sites where they could set up additional evolutionary acceleration experiments using the small tree creatures. Rol had made many detailed maps of the continents during their continuous orbital flight outside the planet's atmosphere, and he suggested several sites to Zandor where the experiments might be originated so that they would have a favorable chance at spreading over the entire planet.

"I think that these three sites would be most suitable," he said to Zandor. "Our present site on the western edge of this large northern hemisphere continent, on the east side of the large continent in the southern hemisphere below this continent, and on the exact opposite or eastern side of the continent we are now on. The climate, geology, and their star's radiation will be different enough in these three locations to have some environmental influence on the creatures' evolution. Perhaps it will create different-appearing creatures; although their governing substances should all be exactly the same if our experiment is successful."

"I believe you have picked exactly the right areas, Rol," said Zandor. "Of course, it will all depend on our finding creatures suitable for our evolutionary acceleration experiments at these areas, or able to survive there if we transport them to these spots. Not to change the subject, but I am certainly anxious to see if Dort and his companions in the scout vehicle below have been able to find a proper creature at this present site."

"I feel as you do," said Rol. "By the way, Zandor, it might be wise for us to use the scout vehicle for all of our expeditions on the planet. It contains everything in it we will need for your experiments and can cover this planet almost as well as the Starship with considerably less expenditure of the fuel we may need to get home to Mekan. It has all the safety devices we will need to protect ourselves from the creatures here; and if we have to lift the Starship off and land it again several more times we will be close to the critical point on our fuel reserves."

"That's a point well taken, Rol," said Zandor. "I certainly think we ought to be able to manage quite nicely with the scout vehicle. It is slower; but this might actually be a help if we have to have an extended search for an elusive creature. Let's pinpoint the navigation data for the scout vehicle computers so that we'll be ready to start to any of the sites you have mapped without any further delay."

The scout vehicle skimmed along the treetops at a more leisurely pace now as Dort peered intensely at the scanners in front of him.

"Why, there are multitudes of these huge beasts all through the land below, Zeltor; the scanner's views are almost unbelievable! I guess there's not much question about evolution progressing well on this planet. I believe one of the main reasons for this success is the dense atmosphere here protecting these creatures from their star's radiation. There is a layer of ozone in the stratosphere constantly being serendipitously produced by the long wave ultraviolet radiation from its star that is very effectively blocking out most of this deleterious radiation similarly to what happens on Mekan. There is also some radiation coming from that unstable planet in the fifth orbit that we came by when approaching this third planet. It would seem that the lack of life on that fourth planet might be because its scant atmosphere has not given enough protection to the surface from the radiation from these two sources. That planet in the fifth orbit has already had several pieces pulled off its surface by the massive gaseous planet in the sixth orbit beyond it; the one with the huge red spot in its midst. This giant planet could have easily become a star itself, making this star system a binary star system. What it has done, instead, is to remain as a giant gaseous planet. Because of its tremendous gravitational force, it has caused a stream of hundreds of small asteroid bodies to be pulled off the fifth planet's surface and trail behind it in its orbit, with more asteroids forming all the time. I believe the disruption of this unstable planet is what is producing the radiation from it. If the process continues, the planet will disintegrate entirely and become an orbit of smaller bodies; essentially a belt of many different-sized asteroids. Added to their star's radiation, the radiation this would produce would be disastrous for any vulnerable life form on the fourth planet and would even stress the ozone layer's protection of the third planet as well. Since the plethora of fierce beasts on this planet may end up being a major deterrent to our being able to get an appropriate creature to evolve, we may have to devise something to protect our own creatures from them or even get rid of them in some fashion. Rol told Zandor that he thought this unstable fifth orbit planet may be the key! But he can discuss that with us later; right now we must concentrate on finding those tree creatures with the large head and eyes."

"I have been looking at a myriad of beasts on the view plate in front of me," said Zeltor. "Have none of them been suitable for your experiment?"

"No, unfortunately not," replied Dort. "Although these creatures most assuredly rule the planet at this time, it is obvious that their governing substance and physical structure is markedly inferior. Their functioning is too modified by their surroundings. If the temperature drops, they slow down and cease to function. If the temperature rises, they become more active and need much more raw material to continue to function. Already some climate changes that are beginning to occur have started to take their toll on certain types of these creatures. For instance, in that dried-up lake bed we just passed, there were a number of rotting carcasses of creatures that had become so adapted to life in the water that when it disappeared, they perished. No, our hope lies with this small arboreal creature. The sensors show it has a larger skull case, better set eyes, far superior governing substance, and a physical setup that maintains a constant homeostatic internal chemical environment that enables it to function at top efficiency at all times and in all temperatures. I noticed that our sensor scan of the creature's internal chemical contents was almost identical to the chemical content that we saw in the earlier oceans on our first scan from Mekan. This means that this creature very cleverly has taken the earlier ocean's contents internally into its body, enabling it to live as easily on land as it did in the oceans."

"You know, Dort," said Zeltor with a twinkle in his eye, "a Gnorman is very similarly set up in an analogous way of speaking."

"Exactly, and if our experiments are successful, this little creature's evolution may be enhanced enough to cause his governing substance to arrive at the standard necessary for a Gnorman composite— hopefully in time to save our race from stagnating at its present synthetic level. Wait a minute! Slow down the vehicle, Zeltor. There! In that clump of low trees ahead...I think...Yes! There are four of the little creatures in the top branches of that nearest tree. When we get closer I'll stun them and gather them up so we can return to the Starship with them. Steady now...there! They are almost in position...now!"

Dort pressed a small button on the control panel before him and a tongue of white energy leapt out and enveloped the topmost branches of the closest tree. Previously hidden by the leaves on the tree, four little creatures fell softly to the plush vegetation below and lay very still. Dort quickly punched the scanner consol and expressed relief at once, "They're still alive! And apparently they are none the worse for their stunning and fall. That's a good sign for their toughness and resilience. Zeltor, you stay here and watch the perimeter while I go pick them up. I wouldn't want to be interrupted by one of these tremendous beasts that delight in devouring any and all creatures they can catch. I'll use my gravity pack and the portable Portal to drop down from the scout vehicle and pick up our prizes."

"Good," said Zeltor. "Be careful! Have your laser ready! Are you sure the atmosphere won't hurt your governing substance? Will you need a protective suit?"

"No," replied Dort. "This planet's atmosphere is quite similar to that on Mekan except it has a little higher concentration of oxygen— twenty percent—and is denser. I don't believe I'll need the suit; it would slow me down considerably, and I'd like to gather the creatures quickly and return to the scout vehicle before one of those seemingly ever hungry beasts decides we are all his supper! They probably would find me rather unpalatable though, as most of the metal and plastic that I am constructed of they consume only in trace amounts. Well, I'm away! Remember, watch the perimeter! I'm taking the portable Portal with me to be able to make a quick exit. When I have gathered up the creatures I'll signal and you can bring us all back on board."

Dort slipped through the lower hatch and felt himself dropping into the thick, rather moist atmosphere. He snapped on his gravity pack and adjusted its controls, now floating gracefully toward the carpet of vegetation onto which the four creatures had dropped when they fell from the trees. As he landed a slithering creature that had been hidden by the foliage crashed madly away through the low vegetation, obviously startled by Dort's sudden appearance from the sky. The suddenness of the situation and the great size of the creature made Dort involuntarily draw his laser sidearm; but he quickly replaced it with a wry smile. He then hurried over to the spot where the four furry little creatures lay and stooped to examine them.

"You know, Zeltor," Dort announced through his communicator, "I don't know why, but these little creatures are quite acceptable to my senses; not like the repulsion I feel for those huge, slithering beasts. They're quite warm to touch, and the upper part of their body moves rhythmically with their intake of the atmosphere, just as the lower animals do on Mekan. It seems to be associated exactly with motion of two small openings on their pointed noses. It would seem from the location of these openings that these creatures can test the atmosphere much as we do; but why they do it constantly instead of at intervals as we do is a question to me. Perhaps they can pick up something these beasts give off and thus escape by being aware of the beasts' presence in time to avoid them."

Dort carefully placed the four warm creatures in the container on his back. He then set the Portal extender on the ground in front of him and turned on the controls. Immediately, a large, shimmering grayish square appeared directly over the Portal. Dort signaled Zeltor through his communicator, picked up the Portal extender apparatus and stepped through the gray square. Instead of appearing within the scout vehicle, however, he found himself prostrate in a hole on the other side of the gray square, and the pack containing the creatures had fallen from his back. He quickly jumped up, picked up the container, and called to Zeltor on his communicator. "What happened, Zeltor. Is there something wrong with the Portal? I stepped through and fell into a hole down here."

"Something seems to be wrong with the receiver here in the ship," said Zeltor. "I'm sure I can fix it shortly. Dort! Look there! One of those huge beasts is coming towards you!"

Dort looked behind him towards the edge of the trees on the other side of the meadow. Lumbering across the clearing from the swamp beyond was a monstrous creature, running on massive back legs and with tiny front legs dangling off its upper body. The most frightening thing, however, was its huge jaw containing two rows of fearsome, jagged teeth! The creature was obviously hungry and looking for a meal; and was apparently attracted by the shimmering gray area created by the malfunctioning Portal. Dort quickly drew his laser sidearm as the beast crashed towards him through the short meadow underbrush. Two full power blasts succeeded in slowing the beast down; several more caused it to topple in a heap, spouting a reddish liquid through the multiple charred openings on its body caused by the laser.

Dort heard Zeltor's voice coming from his communicator telling him to try the Portal again. "And hurry, Dort! There are three other huge beasts advancing towards this area, apparently attracted by the smell of the beast you just killed. I'm not sure that one laser will be enough against three of those beasts."

Dort quickly gathered up his equipment and the box containing the furry little creatures and stepped rapidly through the shimmering gray area, arriving immediately back on the small receiving platform within the scout vehicle. He looked down at the scene below where the three huge beasts were fighting over the body of the creature he had just killed with his laser.

"That was a close one, Zeltor," exclaimed Dort. And then with a wry smile, "the daily necessity for raw material intake these beasts have certainly isn't too conducive for peaceful coexistence, is it? Look at that debacle down below! Well, let's get back to the Starship so we can study these interesting little creatures in detail to find out if our long journey will be rewarded or not."

Zeltor maneuvered the scout vehicle around and headed back to the Starship.

Zandor was the first to notice the return of the scout vehicle on the telescreen scanner. "Here they come, Rol; let's get the receiving dock ready. I wonder what they've found. I guess we'll find out soon enough!"

Rol manipulated several levers and switches on the control panel in front of him and the huge outer door on the receiving port slid noiselessly open. The scout vehicle dropped deftly down onto the landing pod under Zeltor's skilled control and the outer door slid shut behind it. Zandor and Rol were already at the head of the stairway leading to the landing pod when Dort and Zeltor started ascending the stairs.

"Did you find anything suitable?" asked Zandor, trying to conceal his obvious intense curiosity about the container Dort was carrying.

"Yes," Dort answered. "We were able to capture four of the creatures we had decided might be suitable for our enhanced evolution experiment. But I had a narrow escape from a huge beast picking up these beauties, didn't I, Zeltor." He said this with a twinkle in his eyes glancing towards the grinning pilot. As the four composites hurried toward the lab in the front of the ship, Zeltor described the encounter Dort had with the huge beast.

"I knew I'd miss some excitement," exclaimed Zandor.

"Well, I guess that's one kind of excitement I'd just as soon not meet up with again," laughed Dort.

In the laboratory Dort placed the container on a table and opened it. As he looked inside he seemed puzzled, and took out one of the limp little creatures in some disappointment.

"Why, they have become lifeless; perhaps our stunning ray was too much for them. Still, they seemed perfectly intact to the scanner when I picked them up." Dort laid the creature down on the table's surface.

"Look!" exclaimed Rol. "The creature is making a convulsive movement of his upper body. See how rapidly he is moving it now— and his eyes are opening—look out!"

And with that the little creature had leapt off the table and was dashing madly about the confines of the laboratory floor. Zandor finally was able to catch it and placed it gently within a small cage where it crouched in one corner, moving its upper body in a rapid rhythmical fashion and staring wide-eyed at its captors.

"Of course!" exclaimed Dort. "Why didn't I think of it before? Breathing!"

"Breathing, you mean like our lower animals do on Mekan?" queried Zandor.

"Well," answered Dort, "the Prime Mover told me that the living creatures on Mekan's satellite farm subsisted on raw food material they ingested and oxygen, which they would inspire into two spongy organs in their chest cavity from the surrounding outside atmosphere. The oxygen was delivered to the rest of their body from these two chest organs by a myriad of vessels of all sizes that traveled everywhere in the body. These vessels contained a viscous fluid that absorbed the oxygen and then was pumped through these vessels by another muscular organ in their chest cavity connected to the vessels. This gas was absolutely essential to their life functions; including especially their governing substance, just as it still is to the lower animals on Mekan today. We don't have to breathe to get the oxygen for our governing substance since it is in our raw material capsules and is stored in the nutrient fluid bathing it. However, we do inspire atmospheric gases to utilize for speaking, as our living ancestors probably did with the oxygen and other atmospheric gases as well. Unlike their spongy chest organs, we have a bellows mechanism within our chest. This performs the task of forcing the gases in and out by our finely developed vocal cords and tongue to produce the sounds we make to speak. But in living creatures, being without this gas for only a few minutes would cause them to expire. That's what happened to these other three dead creatures! They were closed up pretty tightly within the container and used up all the available oxygen. This last fellow must have been the hardiest of the group and we opened the container just in time to save him. We have allowed the planet's atmosphere to come into the Starship and mingle with our very similar Mekan atmosphere we have carried on board with us, so there should be enough oxygen for our little friend. He seems to be all right; just a little scared."

"That rhythmic motion must be the creature's breathing in oxygen," said Zandor. "When he is frightened he must require more oxygen and so breathes more rapidly. Since we don't breathe for oxygen, we don't think about its functioning as we take in gases only to speak."

"Yes," said Dort, "and like the lower animals on Mekan, these creatures have that 'circulatory system' of fluid-filled pipes that carry oxygen and food materials throughout their bodies. That must have been what spurted out of that huge beast I killed with my laser. Well, we should be able to figure out their organ systems fairly well by dissecting the three dead creatures and observing the live one. I can hardly wait to see what their governing substance looks like! The Prime Mover said that the 'tissue' was very perishable. He recommended that it be excised and placed in the special nourishment fluid he gave us if we were to be able to experiment on it at all. I guess we should start the dissection of the three dead creatures at once!"

Over the next several days the Gnormen were able to divine most of the gross functioning of the little creatures' bodies; and they marveled again and again at their similarity to the Mekan lower animals. They found out that the one living creature needed a specific type of raw material, a certain amount of water, and other trace elements to function properly. This was similar to the lower animals on Mekan, but this creature had infinitely more potential for evolutionary development toward a more complex animal. More importantly, their governing substance was a marvelously intricate substance; and much of it was not utilized in the creature's day-to-day activities. Here then, was the perfect creature for their experiments; and an excellent candidate to supply them with the governing substance needed if they could induce the proper accelerated evolution they had come to do.

In the next few weeks Zandor and Dort made several more trips to the three different areas he and Rol had thought would best propagate these evolutionarily enhanced creatures across the planet. They found suitable tree creatures at every site and their experiments on the governing substance of these creatures were completely successful. They eventually managed to accumulate enough of these enhanced creatures to begin releasing them in the three areas they had chosen where they would spread across the planet successfully. By changing the structure of the creatures' governing substance genetic code, and adding other genetic factors of the lower animals on Mekan from which the Gnormen probably had evolved, they hoped to be able to induce the changes necessary to enhance the evolution of a creature very similar to their ancient ancestors on Mekan. And, of course, this creature would have a governing substance they could use!

As the number of these enhanced creatures approached what Dort and Zandor thought was sufficient to set the evolutionary experiment in motion, they began to realize that the huge, prolific beasts that now ruled the planet might wipe out their creatures. This troubled them greatly and there seemed no way they could be sure that this calamity wouldn't happen during the interlude when time had its role in the experiment. It was at this point that Rol suggested a plan that might facilitate just the protection the creatures needed to survive.

"If we could in some way get rid of these huge slithering beasts that are not related physiologically at all to our creatures, I'm sure they would survive and have a much better chance to evolve without any trouble as they have been so enhanced by your experiments."

"Of course that could be true, Rol," said Dort; "but how do we get rid of the thousands and thousands of these obviously dominant beasts now present on this planet?"

"On our flight to get to this third planet we passed by a very unstable planet in the fifth orbit from this system's star," said Rol. "It was being pulled apart by the gigantic gaseous planet with the huge red spot in its midst in the sixth orbit. There are already hundreds of small asteroid bodies streaming after this planet in the fifth orbit and its disruption is already causing significant radiation to the neighboring planets. In time, I suspect this fifth orbit planet will be pulled apart by its giant neighbor in the next orbit. Perhaps, with a few well-placed fusion torpedoes, we could hurry up the disintegration of the planet and thus increase the radiation effect to all the surrounding planets. It would leave a belt of asteroid bodies in the fifth orbit that would quickly lose any radiation effect to the surrounding planets. This would enable our creatures to do well if they could survive the effect of the initial blast of radiation.

Zandor tells me that some of the processes and substances you have given to the creatures to prevent deleterious mutations have their effect by protecting them from radiation. Actually, the biggest protection from radiation on this planet and what has probably been the main reason why such abundant life is present here, is the millimeter-thin ozone layer in the atmosphere. This layer reflects the long UV radiation from its star and what is coming from this unstable planet next door back into space, similarly to what happens on Mekan. The ozone layer there, as here, is formed by this same long-wave UV radiation which is very deleterious to the plants and animals if it gets through to the planet's surface. Quite serendipitously the radiation actually splits the oxygen molecules in the upper stratosphere into unstable oxygen which combines to form the very thin ozone layer. This then causes most of the UV radiation to be reflected from the stratosphere back into space so that very little of it reaches the planet's surface. Thus, all of the plants and animals on the planet are protected just as they are on Mekan. I'm pretty sure we can destroy enough of this ozone layer for a few months to create large holes over most of the areas inhabited by the huge beasts and allow some serious radiation to bathe this planet. The ozone layer should naturally be replenished again quickly as the radiation from the planet's star will continue the process I just described. This will close the holes we created and resume protecting the planet from radiation again as it has been doing. In the meantime, those big beasts will not have had the benefit of radiation protection as your creatures have, and they should quickly begin to die off from its effect. I'm sure some of the plants they need to survive may not do well with the increased radiation either, and will add to their survival woes. We should be able to monitor this from afar on our way home as we did coming here, to see if that is what is happening."

Dort was listening intently as Rol had continued his narrative. "I see!" he exclaimed. "The radiant energy, mainly long UV radiation, will stream by the planet from our disruption of the fifth planet and the natural amount coming from their star. And since we will have temporarily destroyed the ozone layer protecting this planet for five or six months or so, this radiation will kill off most of the dominant creatures now present on the planet and spare our radiation-protected creatures. This should allow our creatures to evolve virtually unhindered. But Rol, how will you destroy the ozone layer since it is constantly reforming from their star's radiation?"

"It turns out that certain chemicals that we have in abundance on board, or can get from substances on the planet below, will easily create large holes in the ozone layer for a while; perhaps three months or more," said Rol. "Simple chlorine and other halogen gases which we have or can get will quickly combine with the unstable ozone and destroy it. If everyone agrees with this plan we can start at once."

"You know, I believe it'll work!" enthused Zandor. "Rol, you and I talked about this on the way in to this planet. You said we might need that unstable fifth planet. Looks like you were right! Let's get together and figure out an effective plan to torpedo it. The disruption of this third planet's ozone layer for a few months should be relatively easy to accomplish with appropriate halogen gas seeding. You know, even if we can't get the fifth planet to disrupt entirely there will be enough radiation effect just from the planet's own star to kill the beasts. And this fifth orbit planet obviously will continue to be destroyed by the giant planet next to it. I'm sure we'll find only an asteroid belt in the fifth orbit when we return here. Zeltor, you and Dort can start preparations for our journey home while Rol and I put together the plans to torpedo the fifth planet and the seeding of the ozone layer."

The Starship hung in space several thousand miles from the fifth planet, while Rol and Zandor completed the final programming of their newly fashioned fusion torpedoes. In this way they would be able to strike the planet at several pre-arranged sites with the torpedoes. If their calculations were correct, the explosions would start a cataclysmic upheaval within the planet's core that they hoped might cause it to break apart within three to five days. The continuing pull of the giant gaseous planet in the next orbit to this planet would help enormously with this effort.

"Well, this is it!" said Zandor. "Rol, I think you should fire the torpedoes since it was your idea."

Rol looked solemnly at the other Gnormen and then pressed a red button on the front instrument panel. Multiple short shudders were felt for the next five minutes as the torpedoes left the Starship on their way to the fifth planet. "As I said before," said Rol, "when we return, if I'm right, the fifth orbit in this star system will be a huge band of mineable asteroids with a planet no longer present. Incidentally, I pulled one of the smaller asteroids into one of the large cargo bays on our way here that was almost pure gold! I thought we could use it at home in the Life Factories as most of our circuitry utilizes gold connections and it's a scarce commodity on Mekan."

"Enough talk!" exclaimed Zeltor. "Let's get out of here right now. I don't want to test our force fields against whatever might hit us from the planet if it blows!" With that, he pushed the Starship into drive and directed it toward the outer limits of the star's planetary system; beyond its last small icebound planet, now in the ninth orbital position.

The Gnormen were not prepared for the celestial fireworks that began as soon as the first few fusion torpedoes landed. By the third day the planet had erupted and exploded two thirds of its mass off into space in the form of smaller planetoids, asteroids, and radiant energy. Many of these small bodies struck the neighboring two planets with concomitant tremendous upheavals there as well. Several smaller bodies were captured by the giant gaseous planet which gained 12 satellites in all, about four of them as large as the third planet's single satellite. The fourth planet captured two satellites and was bombarded mercilessly because of its thin atmosphere. By the fifth day the fifth planet had completely disintegrated and left a mass of trailing asteroids in orbit around this system's star between the fourth and sixth planets; the sixth planet's orbit now becoming the fifth orbit.

"Well," said Rol, "this star system now has only nine planets and a belt of asteroids; just as I predicted; although I didn't think we'd see it this quickly. I'll bet the large beasts got hit pretty hard by the tremendous bombardment of debris and radiation that just came their way. There was very little ozone to protect them thanks to the holes we left in the ozone layer; so they will soon begin to die off from the radiation effects on them and the plants they have to eat to sustain them."

"You were absolutely correct in your predictions, Rol," said Dort. "We should now have the best chance for our evolutionary experiment to succeed! Let us now return to the third planet to make sure our enhanced creatures are all right and are situated well enough to continue their survival and evolution." With that the Gnormen retraced their flight back towards the third planet.

The Starship orbited the third planet while Dort and Zandor completed the final stages in their experiment. Their enhanced creatures had survived the debris shower from the former fifth planet without any casualties they could find; and they seemed to be tolerating the increased radiation as well. The creatures seemed well entrenched in the three areas the Gnormen had placed them; so it seemed that the potential spread across the planet would go as planned. All around the planet's surface they encountered the destruction that the recent holocaust had created. Huge numbers of the large beasts were dead or obviously sick from the continuing radiation; and the plants they consumed as food had vast areas of wilting, dying, and dead vegetation. Almost overnight, the lush planet teeming with life had started to become a desolate one; with much of its former dominant inhabitants obviously on their way out of existence.

"Say, Dort," said Zandor, "we haven't given this planet a name yet. What shall we call it?"

"You know, Zandor," replied Dort, "I don't think we should name it. Why don't we wait until our creatures have evolved enough to name it themselves, and then we can use the name they decide? After all, it is their planet!"

"I guess that's right; we can certainly wait," said Zandor. The Gnormen began their preparations for the long trip back to Mekan. They were anxious to make sure that their time warp mechanism would be able to control time well enough to have enough years pass by for their enhanced creatures to evolve a governing substance that could be used back on Mekan to continue the Gnor society's positive evolution.

Dort could not conceal his anxiety about the project. "There are so many things that could go wrong, Zandor. I wish we were on our way back instead of just leaving!"

"All in good time, Dort," answered Zandor. "I'm still worried about how the Prime Mover is fairing back on Mekan. We can't be sure exactly when we will return, even though we can get pretty close to the time we want thanks to our time warp mechanism. We will try to make sure enough time has passed when we return so that the evolutionary process will have created what we are seeking in our creatures."

As the Starship hurtled closer to Mekan the time warp mechanism was able to cause only about a year of time to have passed since they left their home planet. They prepared to land at the Prime Mover's well fortified landing strip atop one of the highest mountains on Mekan.

Zandor seemed puzzled. "What I can't understand, Zeltor, is how we will arrive back at Mekan a year in the future. Shouldn't we be about fifty million years into the past as we were when we were on the third planet?"

Zeltor smiled, "You're right, Zandor. If we landed on Mekan as we did on the third planet we just came from, we would be fifty million years into the past here. But here is where all the complicated calculations and the use of great quantities of fuel come into play. We use the ship's time warp mechanism and a great deal of energy to advance or reverse time's passage. If our calculations are correct we should be back on Mekan six months to a year from the time we left here. This time warp mechanism lets us advance and retreat time in large or small amounts, depending upon how much energy we expend. You see now why we were worried about having enough fuel to complete our mission successfully."

"Yes, I see now," said Zandor. "But will we be able to cause enough years to have gone by when we return to the third planet for the evolutionary project to be successful?"

"Yes," answered Dort. "Zeltor tells me that with some manipulation of the time warp mechanism, we can increase the output so that enough years will elapse to enhance the evolution of our creatures. We will obviously need to carry more fuel on the next trip than we did on this one, but that should be able to be arranged."

"I hope you're right, Dort," said Zandor. "Just a minor slip in calculations and fuel allotment, one way or the other, and everything we've worked for may be to no avail. It's a rather disconcerting thought!"

Zeltor motioned the Gnormen to their various landing positions as they approached their home planet, Mekan. He glanced quickly around as the Starship neared its destination and said with a wry smile to Zandor, "Well, I guess we'll soon know if we're back at the right time and in the right place." He snapped on the large telescreen on the forward wall of the Starship's bridge, and the Gnormen gazed intently as the wispy clouds of the Mekan atmosphere began to clear before them. The surface of the planet appeared in an area of high mountains with snow-covered peaks.

"Look, there it is!" exclaimed Zandor. He motioned to a small whitish area amidst the craggy peaks that represented the Prime Mover's mountain fortress and landing platform for the Starship.

"Well, Zeltor, at least it's the right place; good work!"

"That is a relief to know we are right on track so far," returned Zeltor. "We should be landing shortly. I think they know we are here as I felt the ship's navigation controls being partially taken over a short while ago. Let's try to contact the Prime Mover by telescreen." With that he manipulated the controls and the telescreen before them instantly revealed a visibly relieved Prime Mover in his library.

"Gentlemen, congratulations and welcome home!" the Prime Mover said warmly. "It's good to see you! We have you in our landing controls and will guide the Starship onto the landing platform. So sit back and relax while we complete what I'm sure has been a very long and arduous journey back to Mekan. We are all happy and grateful to see you and hope all went well with your expedition. We are anxious to see how you fared on that distant planet. You have come back not a moment too soon. Much has transpired since you left here a year ago."

Zandor gave Zeltor a quick look and mouthed the words "a year" and smiled.

"I will greet you in my study as soon as possible after you land to discuss your project and what has occurred here since you left. Again, we give you a heartfelt welcome home, gentlemen!" And with that remark, the screen went dark.

Dort glanced at Zandor. "The Prime Mover looked very tired to me. I wonder what has happened here."

"Well, we should soon find out," answered Zandor. "In the meantime, since we won't have to navigate the Starship in, let's just sit back and enjoy the ride."

As the Gnormen disembarked from the Starship they were amazed to see the whole area battened down as if prepared for a coming siege. All the Gnormen at the landing site and in several spots along the long corridors they traversed to the Prime Mover's quarters were heavily armed with lasers.

"I wonder why we aren't using a Portal to get to the Prime Mover's study?" remarked Zandor.

"Yes, it does seem odd," answered Dort. "These heavily armed soldiers are somewhat disconcerting as well. I guess we'll soon know what's going on; I believe this door is the Prime Mover's study."

They were ushered into a large room with no windows on three walls but with an entirely transparent wall at one end of the room overlooking the lower slopes of the mountain. There was a sheer drop of several thousand feet from this spot to a plateau below, and the Gnormen noticed several seared craters scattered at this level as though the area might have been under laser fire fairly recently.

The Prime Mover entered the room from a small door in one of the walls, accompanied by the elder Councilman, Zar. The two Gnormen statesmen wore troublesome frowns as they entered; but then smiled warmly as they greeted the returning space Gnormen.

"Gentlemen, it is good to see you back here safe and sound! We must know all about your expedition and whether your experiment in evolution on that distant planet was successful or not. You see, things have changed drastically back here on Mekan; and your work may now be the only possible way to save the forward evolution of our Gnor race! Tell me. Dort, was your experiment successful?"

Dort looked puzzled and troubled by the Prime Mover's obviously ominous remarks. "We won't know until we get back there, of course, but we do feel it will succeed, sir."

A great wave of relief immediately came over both of the Gnor statesmen's faces. The Prime Mover said with great earnestness, "It is so good to hear this, Dort. But before you give us the details of your expedition, we want to inform you about what has happened here on Mekan in the year that you have been gone. It has finally been established beyond any doubt that the synthetic Council members have openly started a campaign to annihilate all composite Gnormen other than the ones they wish to keep to staff the Life Factories! All of the remaining composites that weren't killed off by the poisoning of their nutrient supply or direct violence itself, have been forced to seek asylum here with me in what I fear is the last outpost of composite Gnor society. Apparently the Councilmen used a device like we used on Dort and Zandor to identify who the composites were and then went about systematically getting rid of them! As you may remember, most, like you, did not know they were composites; so they have been easy prey for these dastardly killers. Zar and I rounded up as many composites as we could when we clearly realized what was going on, and retired to the safety of this fortress. We are extremely fortunate that we have been able to save the cream of our composite Gnor society, including many of the surgeons that extract the living governing substance and reinsert it into the synthetic Gnorman's head, and many of the technicians that manufacture and assemble the circuitry of the synthetic Gnorman's body. Unfortunately, the totally synthetic Gnormen, led by the Councilmen, constantly attack us and have battered our force fields relentlessly several times already. They even tried to storm the one avenue up here from the plateau below, but we were able to repel them with laser fire. They have the ability to manufacture as many synthetic Gnormen in the Life Factories as they will need to eventually overwhelm us by sheer numbers. You can see, it doesn't look good for us at all!"

"Yes, I certainly can see that," said Dort. "That explains those seared craters we saw when we were arriving."

"I fear we are living here on borrowed time, gentlemen," said the Prime Mover. "It will not be long before we are overcome by the synthetic Councilmen. You probably noticed how we took over your ship and rather hurriedly brought you to land. We were afraid they might storm us when we lowered our force field to bring you in; but fortunately, they were not ready to attack and did not. We also have eliminated Portal travel, as it is one way entrance might be gained to our fortress. Sad to say, gentlemen, but what must be done now if we are to survive, is for us to leave Mekan with the tools and knowledge of our current society to set up a colony on another planet. Your Starship is a prototype that the synthetic Gnormen may never be able to reproduce with their limited governing substance; so once we take off, they should not be able to follow us. We have the best theoretical minds from the Life Factories with us and all the equipment and raw material we will need to keep us going and rebuild our society on a new planet. And if your creatures have advanced enough, we may eventually be able to design a synthetic governing substance with their help. Then one day we can return to Mekan with a race of synthetic men having a synthetic governing substance capable of continuing the evolution of our Gnor race. We may be able to eventually achieve complete individual immortality in a stable society where nothing like what is happening here now will ever happen again!"

Dort and Zandor seemed stunned. "You mean, sir, we must leave immediately? Can it be done Zeltor?"

"Possibly, yes," replied Zeltor. "Mr. Prime Mover, how many people will be traveling with us?"

"All that we could save," answered the Prime Mover, "fifty-one counting Zar and I. It should be enough to rebuild our new Gnor society on the new planet. We have a great deal of the necessary equipment, including raw material, machines, computer banks and laser weapons. There are also about thirty synthetic Gnormen that are unquestionably on our side that also will be coming with us. We have calculated it out; and the Starship, with modification of some of the cargo holds, should be able to carry everything and everyone without any trouble. We are prepared to start reconstruction of the Starship immediately so that we can get away as soon as possible. We have designed a new way of carrying almost twice as much fuel as you had before, and we fortunately have an almost limitless amount here at my fortress. I began to stockpile it right after you left on your expedition."

"Then," said Zeltor to Dort and Zandor, "I would say we should have no difficulty taking off when the ship is ready."

The Prime Mover appeared tired. "And now, Dort and Zandor, tell us all about your expedition before we get engrossed in the preparations for the return trip to your planet. Do you think we could set up on this new planet?"

"I don't know," replied Dort. "It might be exceedingly difficult if the creatures we treated have evolved into the numbers we think might be possible in the three areas of the planet we placed them.

The fourth planet beyond our third planet is smaller and might be a candidate for colonizing. It has a much thinner atmosphere than the third planet or our planet Mekan that is made up of about 95 percent carbon dioxide gas. Since we get the oxygen for our governing substance from our nutrient capsules and don't have to breathe it in, we could survive there if we could construct force fields to protect us from space debris bombardment and radiation. What do you think, Rol?"

"I think it might work out well," rejoined Rol. "It's close enough to the third planet with our Starship for transportation, and the creatures could be harvested from time to time as they are needed... perhaps without their ever becoming aware of us. But I have another suggestion. Remember how I told you the third planet's lone large satellite's back side never faced the planet so it couldn't be seen from the planet? This then, would be an ideal, close place to at least have a base, if not the actual colony itself. We could establish the colony on the fourth planet and use the base on the far side of the third planet's satellite for sorties to obtain the creatures' governing substances, and never be seen from the planet itself. Also, there is the drawback that the fourth planet has a much weaker magnetic field than the third planet has. This could make it more difficult for our internal magnetic electric-current-generating apparatus, which on Mekan generated enough electric current when passing through the planet's magnetic field to continually bolster and recharge our chest battery power packs. We might run out of power to function if there is not enough of a magnetosphere around the fourth planet. I actually believe there will be enough of a magnetic field on the fourth planet; but it will need to be checked out when we arrive there. The third planet's field is exactly like Mekan's so there will be no problem for power maintenance on its satellite."

"This sounds excellent, Rol," said the Prime Mover, "But we will have to talk about our policy concerning obtaining governing substance. We do not want to do what our ancestors did to their living creatures. I'm sure we can come to consensus about how and who we can utilize if these creatures of yours have evolved into a reasonably elevated state. We will obviously need to see how far they have evolved when we get there. Well then, the matter is settled; as we have no other choice if we are to survive. Come into the briefing room now and meet the remainder of our composite Gnor society. I'm sure that Dort and Zandor will recognize several of their colleagues from the Life Factories. We must all prepare now for a safe, speedy departure."

The day of departure dawned bright and clear on Mekan; as though the planet, by displaying her magnificent natural beauty in all of its splendor, were trying to dissuade the composite Gnormen from leaving their ancestral home. The Prime Mover, Dort, and Zandor stood apart on the landing platform while the remainder of the composites and thirty synthetic Gnormen filed slowly into the Starship to assume their assigned positions for the journey. As the early morning radiation from their star lit up the solemn faces of the boarding Gnormen, Dort noticed how conspicuous they would be on the new planet.

"You know," he mused, "we may have to develop some sort of camouflage to make us a little more like what our evolved creatures look like if we are to make clandestine visits to their planet."

"I'm sure our three plastics experts will be able to come up with something appropriate on that score," remarked the Prime Mover. "Jol was the original designer of our present plastic body cover, and his two younger colleagues have come up with several brilliant revisions on the present synthetic governing substance now used in the completely synthetic Gnormen. Do you remember, Zandor, when you asked about the early creation of two types of Gnormen to match our early ancestors with their strange 'pleasure' organs? Well, you'll be interested to know that Jol has the plans for designing and constructing those two Gnormen as well; although the smaller being probably should be called a Gnorwoman, as was called the smaller, round-shaped one of the two early living natural creatures."

"That reminds me of your brush with that huge beast back on the planet, Dort," said Zandor. "I hope there are none of those creatures left there!"

"According to the evolutionary trends I noted of both the life forms and the planet's geology," rejoined Dort, "the creatures whose evolution we enhanced should be of a size similar to our own by now; and certainly present in the greatest numbers. Because of their far superior governing substance, they should be the dominant creatures now present on the planet and a larger beast should be able to be handled by them very easily."

"Well, that is some measure of relief," said Zandor. "Say, Dort, I just had another anxious thought. What if there are advanced and hostile life forms already on the fourth planet? We never really explored that planet in much depth."

"It is exceedingly unlikely," rejoined Dort. "It is only about half as large as the third planet with very little water or protecting atmosphere. It seemed quite desolate secondary to our created cataclysm, and showed evidence of ancient and continued bombardment from space by our limited scanning of its surface."

As the last of the contingent of Gnormen entered the Starship through the ship's Portal, the remaining three Gnormen took a final long look around at the planet of their birth. The Prime Mover broke the silence with almost a whisper.

"Well, gentlemen, this may be the last time that we see our mother planet; or at least for a very long time. It is quite a sad time for me."

"I guess it is for us all," rejoined Dort. "But sir, I have been worried that the synthetic Gnormen may divine our plans and attempt to follow us to our new home bent on our destruction. Do you think they are aware of our plans or will gain access to them from documents at your mountain fortress as soon as we leave?"

"Have no fear, Dort," answered the Prime Mover. "They do not know our plans now, and fusion explosives have been so arranged that as soon as we are far enough away, the top of the mountain will be disintegrated with complete vaporization of my entire mountain fortress. Zar and I also worried about this and arranged the destruction of our fortress to occur just after we left. Well, gentlemen, let us be on our way to our new world!"

As the gleaming silver Starship majestically rose from Mekan and plunged into space, the four composite Gnormen all felt a physical twinge of pain as they witnessed the brilliant flash of blue-white light on the telescreen before them representing the destruction of the last composite Gnorman stronghold on their mother planet.

The Prime Mover whispered almost inaudibly, "Gentlemen; a last sad look at the old, and now a questioning, perhaps apprehensive look at our coming new world!" With that, the telescreen went dark.

The Starship became alive with activity as they entered the thin atmosphere of the fourth planet in their new star system home.

"The atmosphere on this fourth planet is certainly different from Mekan and the third planet here," remarked Dort. "Unlike the higher oxygen content there, this planet's atmosphere sports a 95 percent carbon dioxide, 0.13 percent oxygen content. The atmospheric pressure is only 1/150 of Mekan and the third planet here; perhaps because of its being only half as big as those two planets. The actual density of the atmosphere here is only 1 percent that of the other two planets, but there is a much greater concentration of the heavier rare gases. I believe that there was a much denser atmosphere here at some ancient time, but the lower gravity of this smaller planet has probably allowed the lighter gases such as oxygen to drift off into space, leaving the heavier carbon dioxide and rare gases behind. Now they make up most of this thin atmosphere. I noticed as we came through, however, that there is enough oxygen left in the atmosphere to cause a very thin ozone layer in the stratosphere here; but I'm sure it doesn't protect the surface of the planet as the ozone layer on Mekan and the third planet here do. We may have some difficulty taking in enough gas to be able to speak here; the Gnor body designers will have to come up with a solution for this. It may mean we might have to maintain a denser contained atmosphere within our cities; but this could be done by enclosing them in a dome or other such force field. Because this planet's axis has an inclination to its star and a very erratic orbit around that star, it has a winter and summer as we have on Mekan and as is present on the third planet. Since it is much further away from its star than the third planet, I imagine it is much colder here; especially during its winter. We have seen severe wind storms on the planet's surface here as well, and the carbon dioxide polar ice caps on the winter hemisphere of the planet appear quite cold and expanded. If we end up having to create natural living creature farms here, I'm afraid the cold, lack of oxygen, storms, and lack of protection from their star's radiation may present too much of a challenge to maintain them on this planet without great technological effort. No, I think Rol's idea of a base on the dark side of the third planet's satellite, out of sight of the planet below may be the best solution if we develop these farms. It will be easier to get their star's energy to heat that compound from the closer third planet orbit than from this more distant orbit here. Hopefully we will find that the third planet's evolved creatures will be sufficient for our needs so a farm of living creatures will not be necessary. I do think, however, that there will be no immediate problem to our synthetic bodies here on the fourth planet. If necessary, we have several experts with us that can come up with adaptations enabling our governing substance to tolerate this planet's climate. The mechanism we already have in place for tolerating the cold in Mekan's winter ought to be able to be adapted to the deeper cold here. Tell me, Zeltor, could we use the ship's force fields for a period of time as a defense against these storms and the occasional space meteorite bombardments while our new city is being built on the planet's surface?"

"I'm sure that could be arranged," replied Zeltor. "Actually, it was what I had planned if we built the city here. I do think, however, that we should build on a site that will be unable to be observed by anyone on the third planet. You see, Dort, I'm already confident that your experiments have born fruit!" Zeltor gave Rol a quick smile as he made the last statement.

"Quite right," said Rol. "I have calculated orbital motion of both the third and fourth planets, and find the least observable site for our city will be behind and at the foot of the mountains now approaching below as seen on the telescreen. I would suggest landing at this site."

The great silver Starship gracefully descended to a level plateau at the foot of the mountains that Rol had pointed out previously, and

Zeltor eased the ship's stabilizer landing pads gradually down until they made a sturdy engagement of the dusty soil of their new planet.

"Be careful when you walk on this planet," said Rol. "The gravity is only 0.4 that of Mekan and the third planet, so you can go some distance with a small movement." The four Gnormen leaders finally stepped out onto the exit stairway platform and looked around at their new home.

"It certainly is a desolate place," whispered Zandor with an almost involuntary shudder. "I'm not sure I'll ever get to love a place like this. It is really cold here and there is a pretty strong wind blowing as well. That little creature from the third planet we returned with to Mekan could certainly not survive long on this planet, that's for sure!"

"Still," the Prime Mover rejoined, "it can be a temporary place we can get used to that will enable us to gain the knowledge to get us back to Mekan with our superior synthetic Gnorman. If we can accomplish this breakthrough, I'm sure we should be able to wrest the planet back from the synthetic Gnormen in charge of Mekan now. I'm still hopeful we will be able to convince the synthetic Councilmen that racial advancement also will ultimately be better for them since there is a good chance that they will be able to be enhanced as well. Once we get the city finished we can start turning out more of our current synthetic Gnormen to help us build the base on the third planet's satellite."

"I agree it is the plan to proceed with without question," said Dort. "Let us all assemble on this level plain close to the ship and at the foot of that sheer cliff. It would seem to be a sheltered and almost undetectable site for the city; and we will only have to use force fields above and on three sides to protect us from space bombardment while we work building it."

The four composite leaders climbed down the exit ladder followed by the remaining Gnormen within the ship. They found that they sank into a several inch deep layer of loose dust as they mulled about on the plain the ship had landed on. Swirls of dust enveloped them as the wind started up, siphoning along the cliff's base. Zeltor took several of the synthetic Gnormen with him and went back into the ship.

Moments later a large platform descended from the ship containing Zeltor astride a vehicle that was carrying several large pieces of heavy machinery that they had brought from Mekan to help with the building of the new city. From several other descending platforms came the rest of the Gnormen that had reentered the ship with Zeltor; all carrying various pieces of equipment or building materials for the construction planned.

"I have set up the Starship's force fields to protect us while we start construction of the city," said Zeltor. "Later on I'll make forays out into the surrounding territory to get the raw materials we will need to help with the construction."

Several days went by as the machines and tanks of chemicals they had brought with them from Mekan began to turn out increasing amounts of building materials manufactured from the elements in the soil around them. Zeltor and Zandor made daily forays to the surrounding cliffs with their transporting vehicle and brought back huge slabs of rock. These were fashioned into basic building blocks that were used to construct the containing walls and ceilings of the buildings.

"Later," said Zandor, "when we have time to begin to mine this planet, we can start building the metal and plastic city we were used to on Mekan. I am sure, however, that I will continue to miss the use of wood and wood products. If it had been present in the past, there certainly is nothing like wood on this planet now. Of course we can simulate wood with plastic, but it's not the same to a realist fussbudget like me. I suppose for now we should accept these primitive stone buildings as our temporary shelters."

"Actually, they will help to conceal the city because of their likeness to the surrounding cliffs," remarked the Prime Mover.

Three months went by and the city began to take shape rapidly. In a few short months it was finally finished and functioning on its own utilizing several of the fusion power generators they had brought from Mekan, as well as solar and wind power generators they fashioned to utilize the available local energy forces. These generators took over maintaining the force fields from the Starship as well as supplying the power needed to run the city. A few of the fusion generators were saved for power for the base they would build later on the third planet's satellite. Life Factory equipment that they had brought from Mekan was being set up in the new city so that new synthetic Gnormen could be manufactured to help maintain the colony here. The gold that Rol had obtained from the asteroid belt had turned out to be absolutely invaluable in the manufacture of the new Gnormen's circuitry. Therefore, they planned to mine the asteroid belt for materials they couldn't find on this fourth planet. After the Life Factory was firmly established with enough appropriate composite technicians available to start the manufacture of new synthetic Gnormen, the Prime Mover suggested that they prepare for the trip to the third planet. Then they could start building the base on the dark side of its satellite and at last find out if Dort and Zandor's experiment had been successful.

The elder Zar was left in charge of the city while the Prime Mover, Dort, Zandor, Rol, Zeltor and Dr. Ran, along with several other Gnormen, including the composite Gnorman designer, Jol, reentered the Starship in preparation for their flight to the third planet's satellite. As Zeltor maneuvered the Starship smoothly away from the city's landing site, the Prime Mover said to the others, "You know, we have been so busy constructing our city that we have not named either it or its planet. What do you think would be appropriate? Mekan II, perhaps?"

Dort's reply was thoughtful, "This planet is certainly nothing at all like Mekan. Perhaps we should wait and see if our creatures on the third planet have evolved enough to have discovered this fourth planet and given it a name. Zandor and I have already agreed that we would wait to see if these creatures have given a name to their planet and accept that as its name for us as well. I'll tell you, gentlemen, I can hardly contain my excitement at the prospect of shortly being able to see the results of our handiwork on this third planet! Zandor and Rol should be able to adjust our scanners to enable us to see clearly what creatures are present below when we get a little closer to the planet."

63

The Starship circled the third planet on a high parabolic orbit, and put out an electronic screen to jam any possible device that might be present below that could discover their presence. They were thus able to get close enough to the planet to have the scanners effectively visualize almost everything on the surface in great detail. To their immense relief and very great excitement they found that Dort and Zandor's experiment had worked far beyond their wildest expectations! On the planet below was a highly developed society of obviously sentient beings with quite sophisticated technology; although not as advanced as the Gnormen's was. Not only were the creatures' governing substances highly enough evolved for use in the Gnormen composites; they had considerably greater capacity that the creatures' present bodies were able to use. It was just as the two Gnormen had hoped would be the case. Dort estimated that perhaps only 15-20 percent of the total potential functioning of their governing substance was being utilized in even the best of the creatures; obviously a great advantage for the composite Gnormen that would get such a governing substance! What was much more fantastic, however, was that the creatures bore a strikingly similar outward appearance to Gnormen, and looked a lot like Dr. Ran, the only remaining living being from Mekan. Their skin was of a fragile nature and had a somewhat different appearance than the Gnorman's synthetic skin. The ozone layer in the planet's stratosphere, however, was obviously sufficient to protect these creatures from the deadly radiation from their star. They also discovered there were two types of creatures; just as there had been with the original natural living creatures on Mekan.

"It should be an easy thing to make us look just like these creatures," said Zandor.

"Yes," agreed Dort, "comparing these creatures to Dr. Ran, it looks like they have evolved into beings very much like us. This similarity is probably reasonable since we did put genetic material into them that came from our own living lower animals on Mekan that we probably evolved from. I have often felt somewhat sad for Dik Ran when we learned that he was, quite by chance, the only surviving living Gnorman left on Mekan. Perhaps these creatures are similar enough to be able to give him some living companionship. We shall see! Also, gentlemen, I think it's time we stopped calling them 'creatures.' They are certainly not Gnormen; but they are definitely men. We must study their language and customs if we are to walk among them without discovery. I must confess that my mind is racing with the thoughts of all we must learn about them. It is extremely fortunate that we are able to advance and retreat time with the time warp mechanism on the Starship and its scout vehicles. It will help us enormously to study these creatures, I should say men, and decide how and probably more important, who, we will use for our composite Gnormen. I have already noted how many of them meet unfortunate ends in isolated parts of the planet in their somewhat primitive vehicles. It would be relatively easy to capture many of these men without any other inhabitants ever knowing it; especially since in almost all of these cases there is no hope for their survival or recovery. I also am appalled at how many of these men take each others lives, often for very frivolous reasons. They have a great distance to go before they attain our philosophy of peaceful interaction with one another."

Here the Prime Mover broke in on the conversation. "Gentlemen, we must decide now what will be the ethical principles that we will use for obtaining governing substances for use in Gnormen. We do not want to repeat the wrongful use of living people as our ancestors did on Mekan. Our Project is unfortunately a necessary evil that we will have to accept until we can design the synthetic higher governing substance that will allow us to have no further need of composite beings."

"I agree completely," said Dort. "Since we have the ability to advance and retreat time, I recommend that we only take men that we know have died. We can also make sure that the body, which will be changed by the removal of its governing substance, will never be able to be recovered so that discovering unexplainable changes on these bodies will not have a chance to change the timeline. Since they are obviously a sentient creature, we should also obtain their permission for them to be utilized in Gnorman creation as well. Remember, even though we can go forward and backward in time, past experience has shown us that changing the timeline can be disastrous. If these men decide they would rather go back into their position of certain death rather than committing to Gnormen creation, they must be made to realize that they will not remember us or our proposal when they resume the timeline we return them to. Thus, they will not be able to change what is about to happen to them."

Everyone nodded assent to Dort's ethical proposal and agreed that this should be the only manner in which they would obtain use of a man's governing substance. They decided to get closer to the planet during evening time so that they could get accurate visual recordings of the men below. This would enable the plastics experts to fashion a reliable identical plastic skin for them to complete their disguise when they landed on the planet to get more technical information.

After several weeks of studying from the data they had been able to obtain from their sensors, the time finally came for Dort and Zandor to descend to the planet's surface and begin their first hand surveillance of the current races of men and women, as the second type of creature was called. They had been able to determine that the inhabitants had several languages, and had realized that they would have to learn how to speak most of the seemingly important ones. English seemed to be the one most utilized by much of the "world" as the planet was called. Its formal name was Earth. They were in what the inhabitants called the beginning of the twenty first century in the year 2003; but the Gnormen had been able to travel backwards in time to learn most of their sentient history. They also squandered some fuel to go further back to learn how their originally placed creatures had spread. They found that the three sites that Rol had mapped out for them to place the tree creatures for easy spread across the planet were now called Europe, Asia, and Africa. The European descendants were called Caucasians and were white-skinned, the Asians were called Orientals and had slanted eyes and yellowish skin, and the Africans were called by various names, but mostly Blacks, and had very dark skin. Dort and Zandor were amazed how differently these same original creatures had developed. Excess star radiation, lack of it, and prevailing wind may have been the reason for the differences in their evolution; with lack of pigmentation in the decreased radiation area, eye changes and coarse hair in the prevailing wind area, and dark skin in the increased radiation area. Of course, nutritional differences probably had much to do with the appearance changes as well. The island continent they had left alone to evolve on its own was called Australia and had an interesting fauna of marsupial creatures that didn't exist anywhere else on the planet. The "human" (as the men were called) creatures in Australia were a smaller race somewhat similar to the black races present in Africa. There were many variations of outward appearance in the different races but the Gnormen's scanners showed that they were all actually quite similar internally; even the small black men in Australia.

All the continents had a mixture of the different types of humans from their proliferate spreading around the planet. The most obvious of their characteristics on this planet was the enormous numbers of them in all corners of the world, and their dominance over all the other creatures and plants. There was also subtle evidence that they were on the same course of destruction that had occurred on Mekan millennia ago; and the Gnormen wondered if that same reproductive urge and aggressive demeanor might eventually cause their demise here on Earth as well. The governing substances of all the different races of humans showed almost identical evolution. This part of their body composition was obviously their most important feature and raised them above all the other animals on the planet. They found that there was transportation on the ground in vehicles called automobiles and in the air in vehicles called airplanes, both jet- and propeller-driven. They discovered that most of these transportation vehicles had been invented in only the last hundred years, as was most of their medical science advances. They had ships that sailed on the seas and were propelled similarly as the other vehicles; although a few used the wind alone for locomotion. The fuel they utilized was petroleum-based, and was obtained at great cost to the environment of the planet. This was the start of the pollution that had doomed the

Gnormen's ancestors on Mekan in a similar fashion. The humans, however, had discovered non-polluting alternative energy sources using the wind, water, radiation from their star, and electricity from fuel cells that held promise that they might be able to escape the Gnormen's fate. Unfortunately, it appeared that men in the petroleum industries presently in positions of great wealth and power were trying to suppress, or at least slow down, progress in these alternate energy areas. This similar repression had occurred successfully in the past on Mekan. The Gnormen were excited and a little apprehensive to see that there was already a small contingent of early space rocket vehicles that had sent unmanned spacecraft to some of the other planets in what they called the "solar system." They had been able to land on their satellite, which they called the Moon, in 1969. This reinforced the belief the Gnormen had that bases on the fourth planet and the Moon would have to be disguised or cloaked to prevent discovery. Most of the developed areas of the planet figured time from the birth of one of their highly respected religious leaders. Many of their religions enabled them to feel comfortable in a Universe that they could not completely understand as well as they wished. They called their star the Sun; the first planet, Mercury; the second, Venus; the fourth that the Gnormen were now on, Mars; the giant gaseous fifth, Jupiter; the sixth, Saturn; the seventh, Uranus; the eighth, Neptune; and the ninth, Pluto. The belt of asteroids, created from the original fifth planet by the Gnormen, lay between Mars and Jupiter.

It was obvious to the Gnormen that their bases on Mars and the Moon would have to be disguised or cloaked if they remained in this time because a future space probe might be able to see them. Of course, they could always go back further in time to accomplish what they wished to do and not need the disguise. They did not wish, however, to chance losing any of the excellent evolution that had occurred up to this time of the present governing substance or "brain" as humans called it. Also, if they had to remain here for any length of time to accomplish their research on development of the synthetic brain they sought, early space travel would most likely eventually be present requiring disguise or cloaking.

The plastic skin developed in the Starship's laboratory had replaced Dort's and Zandor's former skin so that they were indistinguishable from the human beings, as they were called. They even had their own hair changed to more resemble human hair.

"You know," said Zandor with a smug look, "I think we look rather distinguished, don't you, Dort?"

"Well, we certainly look different," replied Dort. "I agree that this hair looks better than our own and there is a little more maneuverability to this skin that will enable us to be as expressive as the humans below are. I guess we're about ready to descend. We can land and conceal the scout vehicle in that secluded canyon in the mountains that is practically inaccessible, and use our gravity packs to reach the different areas we have designated to study. If we travel at night, and secure our gravity packs in safe spots at each location we visit; we ought to be able to record enough of the planet's inhabitants to enable us to learn their languages, customs, and mannerisms. It seems strange to wear such heavy and loose outside coverings, which they call 'clothes'; but I can see how they would be quite helpful to the fragile human skin in the heat and cold of the planet. Once we can discern their languages, we can learn a lot from their copious books that seem to be present everywhere."

The two Gnormen entered the scout vehicle where Zeltor was already at the controls, and it dropped away from the Starship into the night below proceeding toward their mountain canyon at the ship's most rapid speed.

"I'll be able to land here and pick you up when you signal me that you're ready to leave," instructed Zeltor. "Good luck on your mission. I hope it's as successful as your last one here." With that he directed his attention to the planet below and soon they were dropping gently down into the isolated canyon in the mountains.

Dort and Zandor had buried their gravity packs in their sealed containers beneath some boulders in a small dense thicket in a glen near the Potomac River, just outside of a city called Washington,

D.C. From this point they progressed on foot towards the city with their recorders concealed within their coats, and with thousands of yards of recording wire secured within each of their four extremities and trunk. The recorders transmitted audio and visual signals that were automatically picked up and captured on the wires within their bodies. Many hours of recordings were possible on the miles of wire within the two Gnormen. Whereas on Mars their great strength and the decreased gravity there made it possible for them to travel great distances with ease, here on Earth where the gravity was almost identical to Mekan, they found the traveling required more effort on their part. They made their way to several of the libraries and universities in the area and began the task of recording all the necessary information which would allow them to learn as much as they could about these humans they had helped to evolve into the creatures they now were. They did learn to speak enough English to keep them out of trouble with their interaction with the humans, but they avoided contact as much as possible until they could learn more about them. They had already made several runs back and forth from the Starship; and Zeltor jokingly said his pickups of them were becoming what the humans called a "milk run." It amazed and delighted them to see how well human evolution had progressed. As the weeks and months sped by they soon became thoroughly acclimatized to the different languages and customs of the humans they traveled amongst, so that at last they were quite at ease in their company. They had even learned how to copy the sound similar to what the humans created with their lungs and vocal cords when they spoke, so there was very little chance that they would be detected as aliens on the planet.

"Dort, how are the Life Factories progressing?" asked Zandor one day on one of their runs back to Earth. "I noticed you spent some time there last month when we had returned to the city with our tapes."

"They are doing remarkably well," answered Dort, "and have just about completed their first Gnorman. In fact, the Prime Mover told me just before we left that plans for another Life Factory on the dark side of the Earth's moon were in full preparation. He also told me that if we came upon any human being who was young and vigorous, and who was dying of a non-reversible disease not involving his governing substance, that we should bring that human directly to the Life Factory if it could be done with his permission and without revealing our presence on Earth. They will transfer his 'brain,' as the humans call their governing substance, into the just completed Gnorman body at the Life Factory. If it will help the subterfuge, and the changes from the Gnor surgery will not be identified, the body can be brought back to Earth for burial. You know, Zandor, with all the knowledge we have learned about our evolutionary creations, the comparative study of their brain with ours actually show a superior development in theirs; and in a time frame far less than ours took to reach this height. It is a pity that their clumsy bodies can only utilize such a small percentage of its total potential."

"And yet they do remarkably well with that percentage!" remarked Zandor. "Speaking of the Life Factories, you know it has always intrigued me why they always form this protuberance with double orifices on our face—all for those tiny two sensors for detection of harmful gases in the atmosphere. The sensors could have been placed flat almost anywhere and didn't really need the elaborate housing. I thought perhaps they might have been to protect our eyes or mouth; but I see now they were also used for breathing in our original ancestors and this was a means for the designers of Gnormen to keep that form alive. It is obvious when you perceive our human friends below. They even have sensors in their 'noses,' as they're called, that connect to their brains just as ours do; but they are not quite as sophisticated as ours are."

The scout vehicle was approaching the planet below under cover of the night when Zandor saw a light airplane that was on fire go crashing into a densely wooded mountainside just below them. The scanning sensors showed them that the plane was now practically consumed by flames and contained a single pilot that was still alive. Zeltor quickly descended, hovering just above the crash site; and Zandor donned his gravity pack and jetted to the burning airplane.

"It's a female!" exclaimed Zandor to Dort through his

71

communicator. "She has almost a 100 percent burn of her skin and is just barely alive!"

"Bring her aboard, quickly!" said Dort. "You will find a sustaining tank the Prime Mover had installed for this in the second cargo hold just before we left, and I'll help you place her within it. I'll call the Starship so they will have a surgeon ready just as soon as we can get there. After the surgeon has removed her brain and placed it in nutrient solution, we can return the charred body back to the remains of the airplane to avoid any suspicion of the inhabitants involved with this woman. There will be enough damage from the fire to cover any of the surgical incisions that will be used to remove her brain, and too much damage for the ritual of an embalming autopsy that we have seen them do to their dead. Then the Starship can return back to the Life Factory on Mars to transplant the living brain to the completed Gnorman body there that is now ready for a brain transplant."

As soon as Zandor was aboard and he and Dort had placed the still living woman into the tank of sustaining fluid, Zeltor rushed the scout vehicle at full speed to the Starship where all was ready for the surgeon there to remove the woman's brain. As soon as they docked, the sustaining tank with the still living woman within it was whisked off to the laboratory on the Starship and the surgeon was able to remove her brain without difficulty and place it within a nutrient solution that would keep it alive and functioning. The charred body was returned to the scout vehicle for transport back to the crash site, and Zeltor, Dort and Zandor quickly prepared to get underway to accomplish this. They used the time warp mechanism to time their approach to the crash site to coincide exactly to when they had extracted the woman originally.

"Find out as much as you can about this woman," the Prime Mover had instructed Dort and Zandor, "We must know these facts to be able to prepare her later. She obviously had no chance to decide her fate as we had hoped to do with all we were to use for this purpose. We will keep her eyes bandaged for a while with the pretense that they've been badly burned. This will give us a chance to see how she might take what has happened to her before we let her know the truth."

Dort and Zandor were able to get the woman's body back to the airplane and place it within the cockpit which was still burning. There was a briefcase of aluminum on the adjoining seat that they were able to remove before any more damage was done to it. They opened it up and found the woman's wallet containing information that would aid them in finding out more about her. After they copied this information, they placed the briefcase back in the cockpit that was now a raging inferno. The place on the mountainside was so remote and densely wooded that it would be hours before anyone would be able to reach the crash site. By the time the rescuers arrived there the woman's body would be burned beyond recognition. Zandor and Dort then proceeded to the town mentioned in the information in the woman's briefcase to gather information about her.

"I'll pick you up here as soon as you get the information the Prime Mover wanted us to get about this woman," said Zeltor. "Call me on your communicator when you're ready to leave."

Dort and Zandor went to the library in the town mentioned in the woman's wallet and were able to find out quite a bit about her in reviewing the local newspaper archives there. Her name was Ellen James. She was thirty-two years old and a well-known and respected young woman who flew her own airplane and was an associate professor of world history at a local university in the town. Although she apparently was quite attractive and had many friends, she did not have any permanent attachments to anyone, and her only family consisted of a maiden aunt. Apparently the accident occurred when she was flying to her aunt's town to visit her after her classes had ended for the summer.

"This couldn't have been a more perfect person to have this happen to in this way and from our ethical perspective," said Zandor. "We should call Zeltor and get back to the Starship and to Mars as soon as possible."

Ellen awoke to find that her eyes were bandaged and her hands restrained so that she couldn't release the bindings to see. She remembered her burning airplane about to crash into the mountain after being struck by lightning and presumed she had been rescued and was in a hospital. Strangely though, she felt no pain at all; in fact, she felt amazingly well. Her skin, however, felt queer to her; and her sense of touch, smell, and hearing seemed much more acute than they had ever been. Even in her restraints, the little ability she had to touch things close to her seemed very different; she felt she could almost see what she was touching. She sat partially upright and called to find out where she was and why she was restrained. Even her voice seemed very different, quite a bit lower in pitch than normal. Dr. Ran, who had been treating her, along with Gnorman designer, Jol, came into the room and moved quickly to her bedside.

"Now Ellen, please don't get excited," said Dr. Ran quietly. "You had a very bad accident in your airplane, with very serious burns. Your eyes are bandaged because of the burns, and we kept you restrained so that you wouldn't hurt yourself. You've been unconscious for about two months now and it's wonderful to see you fully awake and speaking. I want someone to speak to you before we remove any bandaging." With that Dr. Ran went to the wall intercom. "Please tell the Prime Mover that the 'patient' is now fully awake and in excellent condition, and **he** will be able to speak with him now."

He! thought Ellen. *Well, I must have had all my hair burned off, and this must be a new doctor on the case!* Her confusing thoughts were interrupted by the opening of a door and sharp footsteps advancing to her bed. Again, she marveled at the extreme acuteness of her hearing.

"Good day, Ellen!" said the Prime Mover. "As you have probably surmised, you had a very serious accident in your airplane which crashed in flames. We were able to pull you from the burning wreckage and brought you here for treatment."

"Is that why my eyes are bandaged, doctor?" interrupted Ellen. "Was I burned very badly?"

"Yes," replied the Prime Mover. "That is why your eyes are bandaged. As to how badly you were burned; we estimated that you had third degree burns to almost 100 percent of your body."

"What do you mean, almost 100 percent third degree burns? Isn't that percentage of a third degree burn almost always fatal?" Ellen was beginning to feel very apprehensive and her voice faltered somewhat. Her voice itself was unnerving to her because it didn't sound like her at all. It was too low and flat in pitch and seemed to lack the usual inflections she prided herself in having. She assumed that perhaps the crash had burned her throat and vocal cords to cause this. Another thing that caused her great confusion was that she didn't seem to breathe unless she spoke.

"What I am about to tell you," the Prime Mover began, "will be exceedingly difficult for you to accept; in fact, after studying your psychological makeup we are not sure how you will respond when you fully realize what has happened to you. Your profile is that of a strong woman who is intelligent and very stable; so we are hoping that this will enable you to accept what has happened to you."

Ellen's fears mounted rapidly. "What are you talking about, doctor?" she asked. "What is so terrible that you are restraining me and keeping my eyes covered?"

"All in good time my dear," the Prime Mover said gently. "First, tell me a little about yourself and where you were going in your airplane."

"My name is Professor Ellen James," she replied. "I was flying to visit my aunt in—oh my God! My aunt! She will be worried sick about me. She has always hated me flying my own plane, and always said I'd get into trouble someday with it."

"It looks like your aunt was right," said the Prime Mover. "I guess that is why she was so broken up when she learned about the accident and what happened to you."

"You spoke to my aunt?" said Ellen. "Is she here? Can I see her?"

"I'm afraid that won't be possible, Ellen," rejoined the Prime Mover. "You see, your burns were so bad she believes that you died in that crash and a ceremony has already been performed concerning you."

"What do you mean, she thinks I'm dead; and what kind of a ceremony?" said Ellen with a strange sound in her voice.

"I believe you call the ceremony a 'wake' and it was done many days ago," replied the Prime Mover.

"But…but that ceremony is for people who have died!" blurted out the now thoroughly frightened woman. "But I'm not dead, am I? I feel fine, I have no pain anywhere." Her voice had a peculiar quality to it that she or even the Gnormen had never heard before; obviously the first attempt at a tearful voice by a Gnorman.

"Here will be the difficult part for you to accept, Ellen," said the Prime Mover. "Most of you did die in that crash, burned horribly beyond recognition. We were able to save your brain, as you can readily attest by your memories and knowledge of what has happened to you and what is going on around you now. We have developed the technology to place your living brain into a totally synthetic body, and it functions in that body almost identically as it did in your former living body; except that this body is stronger, more durable, more agile and more sensitive than your old body ever could be. In addition, this body will survive for several hundred years. We have developed a nutrient fluid that nourishes your brain in the new body's head without needing blood vessels to do it. You are only required to ingest a capsule daily to keep your brain nourished properly."

Ellen was completely stunned. "Is that why I'm restrained and my eyes covered?" she almost sobbed (if that is what the sound she made might be called). "Am I some horrible robotic creature that will frighten even me when I see myself?"

"Actually," replied the Prime Mover, "everyone here except Dr. Ran is exactly like you, Ellen; and we don't think that we are horrible. Two of our people have been mingling with your people on Earth, and they have not noticed much difference between us as yet. Before I remove your eye bandages and restraints let me tell you the whole story of why we are here."

The Prime Mover then related to Ellen the entire history of Gnor civilization and the development of the synthetic bodies because of the pollution, wars and diseases that had devastated their world and necessitated their synthetic development. She was made aware that Dr. Ran, who was taking care of her, was the only living member of their society still present. She was told of the war with the totally synthetic men back on their planet that they were trying to deal with to keep their evolutionary hopes alive. Ellen saw the parallels between their two worlds; with the current air pollution, diseases like aids, mad cow disease, tetanus, malaria, and SARS; the wars and aggressive behavior, the preoccupation with sex and violence, and the continuing overpopulation. She had always been fascinated by the people involved with SETI—Search for ExtraTerrestrial Intelligence—so now she was torn between fear of these creatures that had done this to her and the excitement of being in the actual presence of extraterrestrial beings that actually seemed kind and concerned about her well being. There was also the fact that she now had a much better body that still seemed as much hers as the old body was; even though she hadn't really had a chance yet to fully explore it.

The Prime Mover continued explaining to Ellen how the experiment that Dort and Zandor had done in the distant past, thanks to their time warp mechanism, had been fashioned to aid the evolution of the current humans on Earth. It is true that they were hopeful of utilizing human brains for their composite Gnormen, but he explained that under no circumstances would they use any human brain unless the person gave permission to do so. He explained about the timeline and not being able to change it; and that people who were returned to the situation they were taken from if they refused transplanting, wouldn't remember anything that had happened to them. She was also told that only situations where the people would not be able to be recovered, such as ocean crashes, etc. would be considered. Ellen marveled at the story of the colony on Mars, where she was now, and the description of the destruction of the former fifth planet that killed off the dinosaurs to protect her ancestors was mind-boggling to her as well.

"As you can see, my dear," said the Prime Mover, "we did not have the luxury of discussing with you what you wanted to do. Dort and Zandor, who rescued you, came upon your crash quite by accident.

They only had minutes to get your brain out to safety; so we took the chance that you would like to go on living. Thus, you became the first transplantation of a human brain into a synthetic Gnorman body, and it seems to be doing better than the ones that used to be done back on our home planet, Mekan, according to Dr. Ran. Whether that is because of your brain specifically, or human brains in general, will have to be determined later."

When the Prime Mover had finished speaking, Ellen sat in stunned disbelief. "Is this all true?" she whispered. "Is it just a dream I'm having, or are you all just playing a horrible joke on me?" she almost sobbed. The noise that came out sounded more like a gasp than a human sob. "Oh God!" she exclaimed. "I just realized I'm not breathing!" Again she became agitated on the bed and Dr. Ran took her hand to calm her down. His hand felt warm and quite human to her; and she seemed to be able to discern its texture, shape and warmth far better than she ever could before. Dr. Ran told her that the oxygen for her brain was in the capsule that he had been giving her daily, so she didn't have to breathe. Air was only taken in and expelled in speaking from a bellows mechanism in her chest cavity linked spontaneously to her brain. She had vocal cords, a tongue, and teeth to facilitate that speaking, just as she had before.

"Doctor," said Ellen, "will you take off my restraints now and remove the bandages from my eyes please? I'd like to see what I look like."

"Of course," said the Prime Mover. "We installed human flesh-colored skin and long hair so that it would not be quite so alien to you. You also have been given back what is mostly your own face. We removed a scar and a mole that you had on your face." He reached over and removed her arm restraints. Dr. Ran then removed the bandages from her eyes.

Ellen looked down at her hands and arms, flexed the fingers and squeezed each arm with her other hand. "It...it feels perfectly normal!" she stuttered. "It even looks and feels quite like skin, but the sensation is much more acute to me."

The covers of the bedclothes had been covering most of her torso.

As she sat up one side fell away and she reached down to pull it up to cover her exposed breast—only when she glanced down she discovered there were no breasts. This was because the Gnorman that had been ready for the brain transplant was the usual male body! Ellen looked up and saw the Prime Mover and Dr. Ran with Dort and Zandor in the background. All had Earth type skin and hair so they did not appear too strange to her. The two Gnormen helped her to her feet and escorted her to a full-length mirror against the wall near her bed. As she gazed into the mirror she let out a shriek.

"I have no breasts! I have no sex organs!" she cried. "I'm not a woman and I'm not a man by how I feel in my mind! I'm a...a neuter!" With this she gave out another gasping shriek and fell to the floor unconscious. She regained consciousness later but lapsed into a catatonic state whereby she seemed to retreat into herself completely. It was as though she were alienating herself from her synthetic body and retreating into the last bit of human femaleness she knew—her mind. The only one who seemed to be able to elicit any response from her was Dr. Ran; perhaps because he was her doctor and a living being very similar to her former human form.

All of the Gnormen were bitterly disappointed over the failure of this first human-Gnorman combination and deliberated for some time in conference as to why it had occurred. Dr. Ran was certain that it was the drastic change from a vibrant female to what she called a "neuter being." As a living being who knew about and had as part of him such feelings, he could empathize with the young woman quite easily and understand her mental predicament.

"I am convinced, gentlemen," he argued, "that this woman is having great difficulty accepting her human death and the situation that has resurrected her without her female identity which she obviously reveres so much. It seems that some of the centers of the human brain that may not be present in a Gnorman composite are related to these sexual structures' neural connections. It may be that the rest of the brain will not function properly without these connections—at least in the initial conditioning at transplantation. You have existed so many hundreds of years without gender identity that you wouldn't miss it or even see its necessity. You know intellectually of the strength of these drives from your study of your ancestors; and I certainly can physically vouch for their existence myself. In actuality, you can certainly identify your affection and admiration for your close friends here among us, and that is really an expression of the same type of brain functioning. We know these human brains are slightly different than ours although not to any significant degree; but it may be that we will not be successful with them as transplant material unless we include this gender and sexual functioning ability in the Gnor-human's bodily structure. Without the cellular substances or organs to reproduce, the lack of that aspect of their sexual function will probably be accepted and gradually fade away as your gender identity has. In thinking about it, it would seem that these physical structures that are necessary to produce these pleasant feelings should be able to be designed and included in the Gnorman's body configuration and neural circuitry. In fact, I believe we actually have early designs of such configurations already." He turned to the senior Gnor designer, "Am I not right, Jol?"

"You are indeed correct, Dik," rejoined Jol to his doctor friend. "I do have the designs and have looked at them carefully and can add several neural circuitry features to these designs that will enhance them and make them work a lot better than the original designs did. You know, gentlemen, the original design says that the areas stimulated with these sexual structures are close to the same area in our governing substance that occurs when we utilize sensorchair relaxation. Is that not curious?"

"Indeed it is," said the Prime Mover. "Jol, can you get started on designing the appropriate structures for Ellen and installing them as soon as possible? If it works in her case we will probably have to consider it on all future composite Gnor-humans. It actually doesn't seem to be much of a problem as far as the race is concerned; in fact, gentlemen, we might want to be converted ourselves in time." All the Gnormen smiled at this last statement except for Dr. Ran who appeared quite serious.

"As one who knows and feels these sensations and appreciates their extremely strong effects," he said, "I can see that this addition to Gnorman structure, without the penalty of reproduction and disease induction, could well be a giant step forward in the evolution of our synthetic race; an actual great addition!"

Jol began immediately to design the smaller, more rounded, female shape for Ellen, including breasts, nipples, and a vagina with all their stimulating neural circuits. He also added more stimulating circuits to her lips as well. In all of these areas he fashioned copious neural pathways that were led to the brain end plate where it was believed the Gnorman circuitry would connect to the appropriate areas in Ellen's brain, just as the other connections had already done in her. After several days he was at last finished with the enhanced designs and was ready to install them into Ellen. Because Dr. Ran was her doctor and had established a physician-patient relationship and was able to communicate with her somewhat, he was able to break through Ellen's isolation from her surroundings and obtained her consent to the physical changes to be made to her synthetic body. The operation was done; and after the conditioning period of time was ended, Ellen had restoration of completely normal functioning of her sexual apparatus and a distinctly attractive human female appearance. It took her several days, however, before she began to take any interest in her surroundings; and the Gnormen were concerned that perhaps the human psyche could not handle this sort of mental trauma. If this were true, humans might not be amenable to brain transfer.

One morning, when Dr. Ran approached Ellen's bedside, he began his usual cheerful conversation, extolling her beauty and her new form. In the recent past she did not respond to this and remained unresponsive, usually looking absently around the room. This morning was different. Ellen gazed directly into Dr. Ran's eyes, reached up and threw her arms around his neck and began making unusual sounds that would have to be interpreted as sobbing as she clung to the good doctor.

"Oh Doctor Ran," she blurted out. "I'm so confused! I don't know whether I should live like this or have you reverse time and put me back into my burning airplane!"

"Ellen," said Dr. Ran with subdued enthusiasm. "It's so good to have you back! Only please let me go for a moment. You have the strength of a Gnorman now, and remember I'm still a living creature! I must say, though, as the only living male member of my race, it does feel good to be embraced this strongly by an attractive woman once more."

"Oh, I'm sorry, doctor," said Ellen, and she dropped her arms from the doctor's shoulders, but kept his hands in hers. "I have been looking at my new shape and am delighted to be able to look and feel like a woman once again; but it is still very hard for me to accept all I am now faced with."

"Of course it is, Ellen," answered Dr. Ran. "But remember, from your background in human history and interest in flying, you could be invaluable if you decided to take part and become a member of this Project. You would be able to help us find accidents in history where the people didn't survive and were never recovered. We could then solicit from them whether they wished to take part in our restoration and evolution of the Gnor race. If they didn't want to take part, we would restore them to their original timeline positions and let fate take its course."

"But, Dr. Ran," interrupted Ellen, "Why not save these people if you have the ability to do so?"

"A very good question," answered Dr. Ran. "When we first discovered the ability to go forward or backward in time we soon learned that it was disastrous if we changed anything in the timeline. If a person who wasn't supposed to survive did and reentered his former timeline, it often caused a profound change in the future of all the people in that timeline. We also noted that even recovering the person in secret, if the accident site was able to be searched, the missing body also often caused great disruptions in the future timeline as well. Therefore, our policy has become that if we rescue someone, it must be someone that history has shown to not survive, and their body never recovered or if recovered there must be no evidence of any unexplained changes in it. With our technology allowing us to go backwards and forwards in time, we have the ability to stay strictly within this policy. Thus, the timeline will not change perceptively as long as we don't interfere with it very much and change it only minimally. Ellen, with your knowledge of human history and your ability to research such information, you obviously would be absolutely invaluable to us in our quest. The other things you should consider is that you have an almost indestructible body that will live for hundreds of years. You have been given back your female shape and feelings. You know how much more acute your senses are now compared to your prior human senses. Of course, you will not have the ability to reproduce, except by manufacture in a Life Factory. Since reproduction has been developed by your 'Mother Nature' mainly to perpetuate your race, it is not necessary in Gnor society; and as the Prime Mover has already told you, it was the source in our early living years of overpopulation, wars, intractable diseases and death. You still have the neural connections now to enable you to have all the wonderful feelings obtained from sexual activities, without the drawbacks. You have seen how your planet is beginning to have the same problems we had; with overpopulation, pollution of the air and water, the greenhouse gas effect, aids, mad cow disease, SARS, other common diseases, and the aggressions of violence and war throughout your world."

"Yes doctor, I do see that," said Ellen. "But I have one problem with all this. If you have to use living brains to govern the manufactured bodies, won't you have to continue with living creatures that have to reproduce to supply the brains?"

"An astute observation, Ellen," answered Dr. Ran. "Yes, that is the flaw in our society at present. So you can see now, why the Prime Mover wants a continuing source of living brains. He knows that the only way to break this unfairness to living creatures is to continue with composite Gnormen who have the intelligence and creativity to be able to design and eventually build totally synthetic higher brain centers that function independently exactly as the living brain does. This will realize his dream of a totally synthetic race that may eventually be super intelligent, ethical and moral, essentially immortal, and have the required limited population to accomplish all

83

this! He feels that such a race will fit into the Universe like a key in a lock; remaining in harmony with it, rather than fighting it with the decimation caused by overpopulation. With what is happening to Earth now, and the fact that its history is uncomfortably mimicking ours, there is a good chance that Earth's races may want to do what we are attempting now at some future time. With the longevity of your new Gnor body you should still be around and able to help your planet immeasurably in the future!"

Ellen sat up on the edge of the bed, her new female Gnor body filling out the bedclothes she was wearing. She looked thoughtful as she contemplated Dr. Ran's words in her mind. She suddenly gave the doctor another big, long, hug.

She said now quite enthusiastically, "Dr. Ran, you and the others are right! I see it all now quite clearly. What a fool I've been! I will be glad to help in any way I can. I realize now how extremely grateful I should be to all you Gnormen that have saved my life and given me an almost fairy-tale opportunity to make a great deal more out of my life than I ever could have before. Oh, I'm sorry; I keep forgetting my strength," she said as she sheepishly withdrew her arms from around the red-faced doctor.

"Thank you," said the doctor with a smile on his face. "Remember, I still have to breathe, although sometimes it is a nuisance. They have to keep the oxygen level in the buildings elevated unnecessarily just for my benefit."

"Why don't you transplant your brain into another Gnor body, doctor?" asked Ellen.

"Actually, Ellen," the doctor answered, "I have considered it many times, but I worry that they may need me to reproduce if something happens to this Project. It would seem that I would be compatible to mate with a human being, and the failsafe to this Project might turn out needing me in that way."

"That is very noble of you doctor," said Ellen. "I find myself hoping for your sake that the project doesn't fail and that you can become a composite as you would like.

"Doctor," Ellen said hesitatingly, "I hope you don't take offense about some questions I'd like to ask you about yourself. I have had a great curiosity about your people the Gnor society has depended upon for so long. I presume you are a doctor somewhat like our human doctors, but there must be little need for such a person for the almost indestructible Gnormen."

"Quite correct, Ellen," rejoined Dr. Ran. "Most of the problems with present day Gnormen are handled by the technicians like Jol. My function had been to take care of the living Gnor people at the satellite farm on Mekan. Although there were little disease problems there at this time in our history, there was still the need for trauma care, aging problems, and, of course, the delivery of infants. Now that I am the only living Gnorman left, there is little need for my services at this point; except for my use with the human patients we will encounter in our present rescue Project. I have studied your medical school teachings extensively, and have made the discovery that your anatomy, physiology, and illnesses are remarkably similar to that present in the Gnor race of living people like me. Dort tells me that I should not think it to be so unusual if I realize that the genetic influences he placed into your ancestors were taken from the lower animals on our planet, Mekan. We, of course, evolved in time from these lower creatures as you did from yours on Earth. Thus, the genetic patterns could easily be similar. At any rate, human physiology is definitely very similar to mine, and that makes my physician knowledge once again valuable."

"Doctor Ran, can I ask you a question that embarrasses me, but I confess it seems to be very important for my mental well being?" asked Ellen.

"Certainly, my dear," replied the doctor. "How can I help you?"

"Well," Ellen again began hesitatingly, "Since you are similar to a human male physiologically, I was wondering if...that is, do you think you could be...doctor, am I still attractive to males as I was before? My skin feels the same to me, and I have the same sensations in my sexual areas, but I'm afraid it still seems important to me that I am attractive to the opposite sex. I'm sorry doctor, I don't mean to embarrass you, and if I could blush, I know I'd be very red faced at this time."

"To answer your question, Ellen, as a person who hasn't been with a fellow creature of the opposite sex for some time now, it would be a lie for me to deny that you are indeed an extremely attractive woman. Yes, Ellen, you are very attractive, and I'm sure you would be back on Earth as well. Unfortunately, there is the possibility that this strong need in you now may dissipate in time, although I'm not sure about that yet. The new sexual neural connections Jol has now put in the current Gnor male and female bodies may keep this function alive. I know this function worked in my people to cause greater creativity and satisfaction in life, and it wasn't always the reproductive need that caused it. Many people that never reproduced were benefitted by its power. As I have said to the others here, I believe the presence of these new structures and neural circuits may further enhance the Gnor race."

"Doctor, you have made me feel like a human woman again," said Ellen, and she put her arms around him and kissed him on the cheek.

In the days that followed, Ellen's complete change of heart and direction led to great optimism on the part of the entire company of Gnormen concerning the probable success of Dort's and Zandor's experiments on early Earth and their coming Project. Being the first Gnorwoman with a human brain, she found herself to be quite a curiosity, even among the seasoned composite Gnormen. Because of her interest in history and flying, for the next several months she requested instruction in the history of the Gnor civilization, along with the functioning of the Starship and scout vehicle. Also, with her piloting ability, Zeltor took it upon himself to teach her how to run both the Starship and the scout vehicles. He found her to be a quick and able learner and soon she was flying the scout vehicle herself. She occasionally would escort Dort and Zandor to their missions on Earth when Zeltor was not available to fly the ship.

One day Ellen was summoned to the Prime Mover's study; and when she arrived there she found all of the senior Gnormen present as well.

"I've called you to our temporary Council meeting today, Ellen," the Prime Mover began, "because we now have about thirty Gnormen and Gnorwomen bodies ready for brain transplant. You see, we all have already adopted 'brain' from your language instead of the more complicated phrase 'governing substance.' We are all extremely happy and relieved about how well you are doing, and we would like to elicit some extremely important help from you now if you are willing. With our ability to move forward and backward in time, and your knowledge of human history; we are hoping you will be able to find situations where people of some mental stature have been killed and their bodies never recovered. We can then proceed to these encounters, rescue the people and have their brains for transplantation if they will allow it. As we all know, we will not transfer any person's brain that does not want it to be done. We must make it clear to them, of course, that we cannot change the timeline; and that if they are restored to the position they were in just before we rescued them, the timeline will erase all memory of their encounter with us and they will go on to their death."

There were audible acceptances and positive nodding all around the room. Ellen smiled broadly at the Gnormen seated around her.

"Of course, sir," she said warmly, "It will be my pleasure and privilege to do whatever I can. My gratitude for everything you all have done for me is hard to express adequately; especially when I compare my extremely enhanced body to what I had before. Your quest for intelligence and immortality, along with order and peace for all, is without question the noblest of goals. I will be proud to be a part of it, no matter how small. Now that there are Gnormen waiting for brain transplantation, I should be able to assist with finding appropriate well-known deaths throughout history that we could utilize. For instance, there was a famous young anthropologist I have always been interested in who drowned when a ship sank that he was taking passage on. It was sailing from San Francisco to China when it was lost at sea. He was working on his theory that the races of man had evolved from three different sites in the world; and not from what everyone else said was a single site in Africa or Asia. The ship went down somewhere in the Pacific Ocean, and his body was never recovered. With what I have been told about Dort's and Zandor's successful placement of my ancestors at three locations in Earth's early evolution, I suspect this man should be one you would all like to rescue. I can give you the details and we could proceed to that time and place and see about saving him."

"That is exactly what we had in mind, Ellen," said the Prime Mover enthusiastically. "You know it's interesting when you contemplate that you will be helping an alien society to rescue itself. Still, with what Dort and Zandor introduced into your ancestors many, many years ago on early Earth; maybe we're not really alien to you at all! Dort, Zandor, Zeltor, Dr. Ran, and Ellen—please start preparing for the journey back to Earth to the proper time to rescue this anthropologist!"

It was 1932, and John Scott, a 33-year-old anthropologist from Harvard University was taking a sabbatical from his teaching schedule in order for him to study the areas of the world from where he felt the different races of man had originated. He had always found it difficult to understand the current accepted theory for a single site of origin for the races of man in Asia or Africa; especially coupled with the presently available knowledge of geology. Instead, it had appeared to him that man must have evolved from at least three different areas of the world at almost the same time to account for his present racial and geographical distribution pattern. He had written several well-presented papers on this theme and had been promptly redressed by most of the anthropological world and his department head at Harvard for his departure from conventional opinion. It was at this point that he had decided to take a leave of absence from his Harvard teaching assignments to travel the world in hopes of discovering something that might reinforce or dissuade him from his present controversial theories of the origin of the races of mankind.

After taking leave of his Harvard department head in Cambridge, Scott flew to San Francisco and decided to take a tramp steamer from that port to China to begin his explorations. Early one evening while out at sea and still several days from any port, the ship encountered a severe typhoon. The old ship was not able to withstand the constant battering of the waves and began to leak badly in its lowermost cargo holds. The storm passed by after an interminable period, but the overworked baling pumps became severely overheated in the forward hold which apparently contained some leaking gas. There was a sudden explosion that blew a hole in the port side and the deck itself where Scott had been standing watching the aftermath of the storm on the sea. A fire started which rapidly was raging out of control, and Scott had been knocked unconscious and pinned down by a large beam across his chest. His right ankle was bent at a grotesque angle, and he was bleeding from cuts about his arms and legs. Many people in the forward section had been killed or severely injured in the blast; and the ship began to settle to the port side into the sea. As the flames licked closer to where Scott lay pinned down, the ship's captain called to abandon the ship, and the remaining passengers struggled to the ship's stern where all the lifeboats were lashed. They were immediately launched as the ship began its slow slide into the deep. Unfortunately, the blast had destroyed the ship's radio so that no S.O.S. went out to any possible nearby vessels.

When Scott regained consciousness he found the ship at a steep angle to port and sinking rapidly, with a fire raging around him on all sides. After several frantic futile attempts to free himself from the beam, he glanced around the littered deck of the ship and found he was perhaps the only remaining person on board. It appeared that the lifeboats had left earlier; and several shouts he made attracted no one to help him. It was obvious to him that this was his final hour on Earth; but he curiously seemed much calmer than he ever thought he would be when death approached. He thought wryly that now he would never find out if he or the establishment was right about the origin of the races of man, unless he was to learn it in another life. He could not know how prophetic the last part of this final thought was to become.

The scout vehicle skimmed close to the waves as it approached the burning, sinking ship.

"Stay far enough away from the light thrown by the fire so that the scout vehicle won't be seen by the people in the lifeboats," Dort instructed Zeltor. "Ellen, please help Zeltor keep the ship in position while Zandor and I use our gravity packs to go over and get him. Dr. Ran, you may have to resuscitate and support him to enable us to get him back to the Starship alive. Remember to have oxygen available at the appropriate levels for his needs when we get back here with him."

"Right!" rejoined Zeltor, "but you'd better hurry; that ship won't stay afloat much longer, and the fire may be getting close to him."

The two Gnormen quickly donned their gravity packs and laser sidearms, while Zeltor and Ellen maintained the scout vehicle at hover several yards from the sinking ship on the opposite side of where the lifeboats were. Dort and Zandor then jumped from the scout vehicle and jetted rapidly over the waves towards the flickering lights from the burning ship.

Scott looked up and saw two figures making their way towards him across the littered deck.

"Hurry! Hurry!" he shouted. "The fire's very close and the ship won't stay afloat much longer! I'm mighty glad to see you two!"

Zandor reached Scott first and was unable to extricate him from beneath the beam that was pinning him to the deck. Even when Dort rushed to help him they were unable to move the beam enough to get Scott free. The water was over the deck now and beginning to wash toward them. Dort drew his laser and disintegrated the section of the beam that had jammed into the bulkhead, trapping Scott against the deck. They were then able to pull Scott free, but the injured man immediately crumpled to the deck as he put weight onto his very painful right ankle.

"I think my ankle might be broken," said Scott, grimacing with pain. "Thanks for pulling me out from under that beam; but you probably should have saved yourselves. It looks like the ship is about to go under, and now it may be too late for us to escape!"

Dort spoke quickly to the injured man. "We are about to transport you to our ship in a way that will seem unbelievable to you. The ship itself is something you will also find difficult to comprehend. Since time is urgent, let me just say that we are visitors from another planet in another distant galaxy, and have desperate need of you. Your safety is absolutely essential to us, and we mean you no harm. We will explain everything in great detail to you when we reach our mother ship and transfer you to our city on the planet you call Mars. But hurry! We must leave this dying vessel now! Zandor, take his other arm!"

With that the two Gnormen took hold of each of Scott's arms, and the three men jetted upward away from the burning ship and back over the darkened waves to the scout vehicle.

Scott was completely amazed at what was happening. He began to think that he was imagining all of this prior to his sinking beneath the waves to his death. Impulsively he looked back toward the burning ship; just in time to hear the rushing hiss of the sea quenching the fire aboard the ship as she slipped beneath the waves. He turned back to his two rescuers just as the three of them arrived at a ship floating silently just above the waves. The ship was nothing like he had ever seen or heard of before.

"Who in God's name are you?" Scott gasped as fear mounted within him. He was beginning to believe Dort's statement about the two men being aliens. "What do you want with me?"

"Please don't be afraid," Dort repeated. "We truly could not mean you any harm. When we get back to our mother ship we will try to explain everything to you."

The three men entered the open hatchway into the ship. When they were safely aboard Zeltor set the course immediately for their rendezvous with the Starship, and the scout vehicle flashed upwards at full speed. The three men entered the scout vehicle's control room and Dort and Zandor placed Scott gently down upon a cot at the edge of the room. Scott gaped in open wonder at his surroundings and noticed a man and a woman at the controls up front. All of these creatures had the same body configuration of a human being and actually looked about like he did; although they were bigger than he, but the man who was piloting the ship had a skin color that was a different hue than the others. The woman was slightly smaller than he was, however, and he felt better for that. The startling observation he made, that was quite unnerving to him, was that none of them appeared to be breathing except for one of the men. It seemed that they only took a breath to speak. Ellen slid away from the controls and approached Scott on the cot.

"Well, who would have thought I'd get to meet the famous Dr. John Scott, lost at sea in 1932!" she said amicably. "How are you feeling, doctor? Dr. Ran, could you take a look at our distinguished visitor's wounds. Some look pretty nasty, and Dort says he may have a fractured ankle."

"Of course, Ellen," answered Dr. Ran, and proceeded to examine Scott. He rapidly bandaged his multiple lacerations and placed a splint on his ankle after injecting him with a pain killer. Scott noted that the doctor was the only one on the ship who was breathing as he was.

"Thank you very much, doctor," said Scott. "I feel much better now." He turned to Ellen, "Do you know me, miss? I'm afraid I do not know you. And why did you say in the past tense, 'lost at sea in 1932'?"

"I know of you, Dr. Scott," said Ellen. "I was a history teacher at the university level, with a secondary interest in anthropology. Your theories of the origin of the races of man are of great interest to the people on this ship. I know it's all confusing to you now, but when you are given all the facts it will become very clear to you; and I wager you will be quite proud of the justification of some of your theories. You will have a decision to make; but fortunately, unlike what happened to me, there will be time for you to make it with your ship now sunk and unrecoverable in uncharted waters."

"I am confused, greatly impressed with everything I've seen, and a little scared, I must confess," said Scott. "I used to pride myself with being able to pinpoint where a person was from by their accent, but yours is unfathomable to me. Where are you from? Your English is excellent. Are you all really aliens from another planet as the older gentleman who rescued me said?"

Dort broke into the conversation. "All in good time, Dr. Scott," he said. "I want our leader to talk with you and apprise you of all the facts of our history before you make any decision. You can take as fact that we are from another planet, except for Ellen, and desperately need your help. We are in control of a time warp mechanism that allows us to go forwards and backwards in time, so there is time to decide. You may wonder why we didn't then save the ship with this ability; but let me tell you we cannot change the timeline without disaster occurring, except in certain specific instances. Our leader will make it more understandable for you when we reach our city on Mars. Please just try to relax and rest for the time being."

Scott turned to Ellen, "He said Mars again; your city is on Mars? Amazing!"

"Yes, they are amazing," returned Ellen. "And they have ethics and morals that are far superior to that of mankind, so don't have any fear of them. You could say that they actually feel for humans as a human grandfather feels for his own grandchildren."

"It is all so unbelievable to me," said Scott, "especially in that all of you appear almost the exact image of human beings."

Dort and Zandor glanced at one another and smiled broadly. The other Gnormen did the same and finally broke out into laughter. Because of the puzzlement this laughter caused to Scott, Dort decided to impart some explanation of the Gnormen's presence on Earth to him.

"Yes, Dr. Scott," he said. "We are from a distant planet, and our skins, except for Zeltor's, have been modified to look human like you. Our skin, as you see on Zeltor, is actually a plastic substance that is quite a bit more durable than your living skin; we wouldn't have been as badly cut up on that ship as you were. Our bodies are made up of non-living metal, plastic, and other chemical substances and we have no blood vessels; but our governing substance, or brain, as you call it, is living organic matter just like yours. We are also much stronger and more durable than you are as well. All this was developed in us because of changes in our planet that made it impossible for us to survive without some way of protecting our bodies that were once fragile like yours. Sad to say, in some of our time travels around your planet we have detected very similar changes starting to occur here as well. There is a distinct possibility that in the future you might need to do just what we have done on our home planet, Mekan. Let me just say for now that we are composite beings with a living brain in an almost indestructible body. We usually live close to 900 years. Our Life Factories, where our bodies are designed and manufactured, have arbitrarily decided to change our facial countenance every one hundred years. That is why I look older than Zandor over there, and of course, I actually am. The design of our bodies is done to preserve the image of our once living ancestors, who, like you, lived about one hundred years. Most of the bodily configurations are similar attempts to preserve our once living countenances. Our faces are those of the living Gnormen whose brains we have in our synthetic bodies. Over the centuries, our synthetic bodies have been perfected in the Life Factories so that they now function extremely well. As for us being in 'almost the exact image of human beings'; that is what caused the laughter among us, Dr. Scott. You see, it is you humans that are like us; not the other way around. When we arrive at the Starship and you are stronger, we will be able to discuss it further. Suffice it to say, however, that your current state of evolution was directly set up and helped by us about 70 million years ago during your age of dinosaurs. Our time warp mechanism has enabled us to do this. Now, please, lay back and rest; that fragile body of yours has taken quite a beating and will require some time to recoup itself."

Scott lay back on the cot mulling over what Dort had just said. He felt he had more questions than he had heard answers; but he was feeling much more relaxed, thanks to the pain medicine that Dr. Ran had given him. The scout vehicle was approaching the Starship when Scott suddenly caught a glimpse of the huge gleaming silver vessel in the distance through the front view port. *A monstrous flying ship for traveling to distant planets and with the ability to change time,* he mused. *I must be dreaming or delirious or maybe even dead!* With that he drifted off to sleep.

Once aboard the Starship, Scott was taken by Dr. Ran to what was obviously a hospital ward and put to bed there. Ellen accompanied Dr. Ran and glanced around the room with a look of nostalgia.

"I was in this section not very long ago, Dr. Scott; and Dr. Ran took great care of me as well. After you've had your briefing with our leader, who we call the Prime Mover, I'd like to come and tell you about my experience and how I've come to be quite dedicated to the Project of these people. Yes, even though they are mostly synthetic, they are 'people.' They are sentient, and have living parts; and as far as that goes, who says life can only occur in a carbon-based form? Their manufactured neurons reach out and combine with their living brain in pretty much the same way as our human brains connect to our spinal cords in the very early stages of our development. In fact, because of the advanced engineering of the neurons in their bodies over the centuries, their brain-neuron and neuron-neuron connections are much improved over ours. Acetylcholine, dopamine, or any other chemical is not needed by them to make neuron connections except in their living brains; it is all done electrically. I keep saying 'ours' when I must tell you that I am a composite being as well; only my brain is a living human brain and theirs are all from living Gnorman brains like Dr. Ran's. The doctor is the only living Gnorman left on their planet today. The Prime Mover will relate why this is and other things about their race, when you two meet after you're feeling better. I can tell you now that my physical abilities are infinitely better now than they were before I was pulled back from death in a burning plane crash and changed. I don't want to be indelicate, Dr. Scott, but they redesigned their usual male Gnor body into a human female one for me; as I had to do a great deal of mental adjusting to what happened. All of my erotic female parts were constructed for me; and I must admit that they work better than they ever did before. I know this is a lot for you to understand at this time, but wait until the Prime Mover has had a chance to speak with you. After that we can get together and discuss everything. But now, you must get some

95

rest. Good night! Sleep well! And yes, the Gnormen must also sleep to rest their brains, just as you do. Dr. Ran tells me it is for the same reasons physiologically. Apparently, all living brains must get some relief from the constant electric flow needed to maintain an awake body. Good night, Dr. John Scott! It is very pleasant for me that we were able to rescue you; since it was my research that allowed us to find you."

When Scott awoke the next morning his ankle, it turned out, was not fractured but just badly sprained and would probably be well in a few more days. It amazed Scott that Dr. Ran knew how to treat human injuries as well as he did. This Gnorman, as he learned to call these beings, turned out to be very similar to him. Both had soft, warm, pink flesh; both breathed oxygen; and both had a similar facial appearance. The doctor had told him that most of their internal organs were similar, including those of reproduction, and that he wouldn't be surprised if the two races might have the ability to mate successfully. He smiled at that statement, as he said that since he was the last living Gnorman in these times, it wouldn't be long before his genetic material was massively diluted by the human gene pool. Still, he admitted that ever since he had observed the close compatibility his anatomy and physiology had with humans, he had begun to feel the old yearnings for female companionship he had had on his home planet. He told Scott that those same yearnings mutated in the single sex Gnormen over the centuries into feelings of friendship, loyalty, admiration, and respect for one another. This was similar to the human situation of homosexuality although the sexual part of that relationship was not present. He stated that even in the living male and female Gnorman couple, after their reproductive age passed, often had much of their feelings turn into the same kind that the composite single sex Gnormen felt for one another. The doctor mused that if they continued to fashion male and female Gnor people, there would be a noticeable change between how the sexes interacted here. He had noted that female humans were not given as much respect or reward on Earth as the male humans received. Gnor people have always had the same respect and reward given to any individual based on merit alone and that has been their ethical and moral custom for centuries now. The Gnor-human women would thus receive exactly the same respect and reward that the Gnor-human men receive here on Mars. The doctor had told him that the Prime Mover would give him a much clearer picture of all these things when they spoke. As to why he knew so much about human anatomy and physiology, Dr. Ran explained how Dort and Zandor had secretly entered and extracted a great deal of information from two storehouses of medical knowledge in the United States; the Countway Library in Boston, and the Armed Forces Institute of Pathology in Washington, D.C. He said that he had studied this data extensively; and because of his more evolved mental abilities, he was now able to do essentially anything human doctors could do. He did say that in his dissections and studies of human brains obtained from accident victims' bodies, he was able to conclude that these brains were almost as advanced as the Gnorman brain, and perhaps had a better potential for further evolution. He thought that Dort's and Zandor's experimental introductions 70 million years ago here on Earth may have been the reason for the similarity and actual enhanced comparison now found.

"Tell me, Dr. Ran," said Scott, "a little about Ellen. She is a remarkably attractive young woman!"

"She would be happy to hear you say that," answered Dr. Ran. "She was very emotional about that loss originally, until we redesigned her back into a human female. That body configuration had been available from designer Jol, but had been discontinued centuries ago as only the male Gnorman was eventually manufactured in the Life Factories. Jol restored her human female parts and it has enabled her to recover and become an integral and important part of our race at this time. Ellen was flying her plane when it was struck by lightning and set on fire, and she crashed. Dort and Zandor pulled her from the burning airplane and brought her here almost dead, and her brain was the first human-Gnorman transplantation. I hope I haven't spoiled it for her; I think she wanted to tell you this herself. I'm sure she'll give you much more detail when you speak with her later. Try to get some rest now; I'll visit you in the morning."

"Yes, thank you, doctor," answered Scott. He lay back on his bed and the thoughts of the past twenty-four hours happenings whirled dizzyingly through his mind. Finally, he slept.

Dr. Ran came briskly into Scott's room the next morning and stood at the end of his bed. Scott was sitting on the side of the bed, having just sat down after testing his right ankle with a few steps around the room. He had found the ankle well enough for him to limp on it with very little discomfort if he were careful and progressed slowly.

"How is your ankle this morning, John?" the doctor asked.

"Quite navigable, Doctor," said Scott. "I hope you don't mind me calling you that. Whatever you put on my cuts, bruises, and burns has worked miraculously. They are almost completely healed already!"

"That was not actually human medication," rejoined the Gnorman. "It was a compound I devised that would instill wound growth factors to enhance your healing ability while blocking the growth of bacteria in the area. From my study of the current state of your medical knowledge I have noted that you are just beginning to recognize the use of these growth factors in healing wounds and soon you should have similar compounds like what I used on you here. Your earthly bacteria have a cell wall structure that is quite simple and easy to couple with chemically. We had much the same problem in our early days on our planet until we discovered a way of blocking our bacteria so that our plastic skin wouldn't be constantly attacked by them. We did it by changing the chemical structure of the skin itself, not by putting anything on it as we must do with you."

"Well, whatever it was, it is working fine and I thank you for it," said Scott. "Tell me, what do you have planned for me today?"

"Since you seem so well," responded Dr. Ran, "I will inform our leader on Mars that you are able to meet with him as soon as we arrive there. I'm sure you will be able to go to your new quarters on Mars tomorrow. You will be staying in my building where proper oxygenation is maintained in the atmosphere." With that the Gnorman left Scott's room.

I wonder what the "other quarters" are going to be like, thought Scott. *And they're on Mars at that! Well, I'll find out soon enough, I guess! It's quite exciting that I'll be the first **awake** human being to get to Mars! I guess just Ellen's brain itself made the trip here before me.*

The following day they docked at the Gnormen's new city on Mars. Scott had to don a helmet and suit that delivered oxygen and heat to him on his transfer from the Starship to his "quarters" with Dr. Ran. The quarters were pleasant and bright and had an extensive library of Earth literature which he found comforting. Dr. Ran joined him in the library and told him that he would see the leader and the temporary Council the next day.

"In the meantime, Dr. Scott," said Dr. Ran, "Ellen wondered if she could come over and talk with you about her experiences since her transplant. Incidentally, since you and I will be living here together in this complex, please call me Dik, not Dr. Ran."

"Thank you, doctor…Dik," said Scott. "And please call me John as well. I would be delighted to have Ellen come and talk to me any time!"

"I'll call her and she should be right over shortly," said Dr. Ran. He left the room to make the call to Ellen.

Ellen very shortly arrived in the library and John sprang gingerly to his feet as she entered the room.

"I haven't seen that for some time," smiled Ellen, remarking about his standing up to greet her. "It gives me a pleasant warm feeling, Dr. Scott."

"Please," said John, "Call me John. Dr. Ran and I decided first names are appropriate so he is now Dik and I am John. I hope you and I can also be on a first name basis as well."

"I would like that, John," said Ellen. "You should call me Ellen then, as well. Actually, almost everyone is on a first name basis here; I'm not even positive that the others have a second name. I only know that Dr. Ran has one for sure."

"Well, Ellen," began John. "What should we talk about besides my million questions?"

"I'd like to tell you about my rescue and change to my present state, if you're interested," Ellen answered. "Dik told me about how much you knew about me. First of all, I am extremely grateful for them saving my life. Their goal of a totally synthetic society that is super intelligent, moral, ethical, immortal, peaceful, and population limited is an extremely noble one to say the least. Like the functioning of the Universe, these people do not compete, they fit in and cooperate! I am proud and happy to be able to help and try to advance this Project as much as I can. I have only a maiden aunt as a relative, and am able to be helpful in this quest because of my former occupation as a history professor. We actually rescued you because of my secondary interest in anthropology and my being able to do the research necessary to find where and what time you died. I have several more projects waiting to be done from research on famous people who have perished with no recovery of them ever having been accomplished. I know it sounds ghoulish on the surface; but we will be able to keep alive brains that could not only be helpful to the Gnormen's Project, but also to projects that may be very helpful to the human race in the future. I won't say any more about it now as the Prime Mover will tell you everything you'll need to know tomorrow at the Council meeting. I'm sure you realize that they will ask you if you would consider transplanting your brain into a Gnorman's body. It is a big step; but they have now fashioned the Gnorman body with all the male organs and circuits that will make you have a body that will function better and more sensitively than your old one ever did before. This new body will also contain sexual organs and sensory neuronal hookups that will be very much more enhanced than your prior ones. Believe me, they work much better!" Ellen sheepishly lowered her glance with her last remark. "I hope you will consider joining us, John. I would hate to lose you now, just when I found one of my anthropological heroes and was able to rescue him!"

"It's a lot to take in one swallow, Ellen," said John. "But your eloquence and passion remind me of a young woman I once knew who died of a violent crime. She was attractive like you, and very committed to her projects like you. She also wouldn't have been killed in a society these Gnormen are trying to create; and I probably wouldn't be the academic bachelor I have turned into. I will think long and deep about this, beautiful lady; I appreciate your interest in talking to me. I guess I'll see you at the meeting tomorrow." With that John stood up and took Ellen's hand and led her to the exit door of the library. Ellen smiled, squeezed his hand and departed through the door.

The next day the Council meeting was held in a large room in the same complex John lived in, because of his and Dr. Ran's need of oxygen in larger amounts than available from the 0.13 percent in the Martian atmosphere. The room John entered contained a large oval table. Sitting around it were Dort, Zandor, Zeltor, Dr. Ran, Ellen, the chief designer, Jol, Rol, and the Elder Zar. At the head of the table stood a tall, athletic, intelligent-appearing older Gnorman that John presumed was the Prime Mover as the leader was called.

"Ah, good day, Dr. Scott," welcomed the Prime Mover. "You know most of the people in the room. The Gnorman on my left is Zar, and on my right is Jol, our chief Gnorman designer. Please take your seat between Dr. Ran and Ellen and I'll try to enlighten you on what we Gnormen are all about and what we want from you. I am the Prime Mover and head of our temporary Council here on the planet you call Mars. You know, it's interesting that when we first arrived I was thinking to call this planet, Mekan II, after our own original planet. Dort and Zandor, however, convinced us that we should wait and call it what your people called it; they were convinced you would have been evolved enough to have discovered and named it. And so you have; and you have evolved far more than we had hoped for! Let me tell you about our society; and the aspirations, hopes, and dreams for it, and why we are here on Mars and Earth."

The Prime Mover then went into the same amount of detail that he had done with Dort, Zandor and Ellen concerning the Gnor society. He discussed its history, the background for the need of a synthetic body, the war back on Mekan, and how they hoped to accomplish the development of a totally synthetic brain with their research here with the Earth people's help. Much of this had already been told to him by Ellen.

"We hope," continued the Prime Mover, "to eventually return to Mekan and convince the synthetic race there to accept our improvements which will benefit them as well as the race as a whole. It is entirely possible, however, that some of our people may wish to stay here on Mars instead, and they certainly can do so with our blessing. Our Project is to continue to save irretrievable human deaths using our time warp mechanism. Thus, we will increase the composite Gnor society here on Mars while continuing our research to develop a totally synthetic brain. We have placed our first city here on Mars at the head of what your astronomers have called the Candor Chasma, in the Valles Marineris or Canyonlands. Stretching out for hundreds of miles are canyons, craters, and channels where we can build additional cities that we will conceal from Earth. As we create more Gnor people, we can build appropriate space for them in these cities. If it becomes necessary to place our cities in one spot where they will be absolutely concealed from any observation from outside Mars, we can place them within a giant extinct volcano which you call the Olympus Mons. This volcano probably is the largest one in your solar system and is fifteen miles high; occupying land about the size of your Texas in the United States.

"As I said before, at some point in time, we hope our research will enable us to develop a totally synthetic brain and we can become the population-stable race we have dreamed of creating. In gratitude for Earth's help we would act as a consultant to all Earth's peoples encountering the same problems we have already worked through. It seems prudent to everyone now, however, that we should remain hidden from Earth until we are much further along in our research. As far as staying on this planet, there are many ways to make Mars more hospitable to our durable Gnor bodies. We could make the atmosphere more dense by melting the carbon dioxide polar caps with solar space mirrors and/or fusion generators. This increased density would make it easier to speak, even though Jol has enhanced our bellows mechanism within our chests to improve speaking in this less dense atmosphere. We could also mine the asteroid belt for the proper material to create additional gases to add to the planet's atmospheric density under our cities force field domes. Those same orbiting mirrors could be used to heat the cities by directing solar radiation onto heat collectors outside the cities. The heat could be piped into the cities from these collectors during the day and force fields could be utilized to retain the heat at night as they are now doing. The constant wind storms we have already used for powering wind generators. And, of course, we have the fusion generators we brought from Mekan as the basis for most of our power and heat supply here.

"Eventually we could leave Mars and find a more hospitable planet to live on if our home planet's current synthetic inhabitants refuse us reentry there. So you can see, Dr. Scott, we no longer feel we absolutely have to return to our home planet, even though we are planning first to try to go back there in the future. Many of us are becoming quite attached to you humans and are enjoying being able to continue saving people who otherwise would die. It allows them to continue living, and of course, enriches our new Gnor-human society at the same time. Which comes to the question we shall put to you now—will you join our composite society and allow us to transplant your brain into what we now call a Gnor-human body?"

"Sir," answered John slowly, "I am completely overwhelmed by your narrative right now, but I recognize your quest as the dream of several of the most highly civilized humans on Earth. Your goal is not foreign to many of our philosophers; and I must say that I have been quite favorably impressed by my conversations with Ellen and Dik Ran. I, too, like Ellen, am extremely grateful for your saving my life. I would like to think it over just for tonight; I will be able to give you my answer in the morning if that is satisfactory. I know, and accept, that you will have to return me to the sinking ship if I refuse; and again, I thank you all for your kindness to me."

"That is entirely satisfactory with us, John," said the Prime Mover. "We will look for your answer in the morning." With that the meeting was adjourned and John, Ellen and Dr. Ran returned toward the library while the others left the building and departed to their quarters in another part of the city. As Dort and Zandor walked along the street, Dort remarked to his friend, "I hope John joins us; he will be very helpful to us. He and Ellen should make a great combination!"

"Yes, they certainly will," replied Zandor, "and as the humans say, let's 'keep our fingers crossed' that he does join us."

Back in the oxygen quarters Ellen, Dik and John entered the library. John took Ellen's hand in his and said to her, "A big decision for me, I guess." He looked down at the hand he was holding and remarked, "This hand feels as human to me as any I've held in the past, but even though it feels alive, I know it is not. How much does 'being alive' count in the scheme of the creation of a moral, just, intelligent, and peaceful society?"

"As I have come to realize, John," said Ellen with a gentle squeeze of his hand, "who says an organic four-carbon structure is the only form of life? These people...me, are sentient, intelligent, moral, ethical, peaceful, and at least partially alive. Isn't that pretty similar to any totally living being? Sure a child is created in a woman's womb; but a similar 'child' is created in the Life Factories, and as much love and care is given to these creatures as is given to our human babies. The main difference is that the Gnor people mature faster, but they must learn just as our children do. Again, it is just on a more rapid time scale. But should you fault them for being quick to learn? Do you do that with your bright children? The composite Gnor people learn very rapidly; but remember, they have an already mature brain in place. The totally synthetic Gnormen on Mekan took several months to learn even a simple task; they were a lot like human children. I suspect that even when we have a totally synthetic brain with the higher centers present, that new brain will take time to learn as well. So you see, John, there really isn't that much difference between us after all." She gave him a quick hug and kissed him on the cheek. Goodnight!

Sleep well! I'll see you in the morning! With that she let go of John's hand and left the library and the building.

"I guess I'll sleep now also, John," said Dik. "You know how I feel about your joining us. Goodnight!" He also left the library to return to his quarters. John slowly walked to his room and climbed into bed. *Sleep may be hard tonight,* he mused, but soon drifted off anyway.

The next day found that John had pretty much made up his mind to join the group, but he had some more questions he wanted to ask. When the meeting of the Council had begun that afternoon he stood and addressed the Prime Mover.

"Sir, I have decided to join your society," he said. "I do have some questions I'd like to ask you if I could."

"Of course, John," answered the Prime Mover. "We are extremely pleased that you have decided this way. What are your questions?"

"Well, I see how well Ellen went through the procedure, and I suppose I really shouldn't pay much heed to how it will go since the other choice is death anyway; but what are the chances that my brain will accept this new body?"

"We would have been surprised if you hadn't asked us that, John," answered the Prime Mover. "There can be no guarantees since yours is the first human male brain to be transplanted. There were absolutely no significant problems with Ellen's procedure and we do hope the same will be true with yours. Dr. Ran and Jol both are extremely optimistic about it and we all hope they are correct!"

"Excuse me, sir," began John again, "but I find it hard to believe that Dort and Zandor could have started their evolutionary experiment here on Earth seventy million years ago if composite Gnormen can only live a thousand years at best. Can you explain this to me?"

"Your point is well taken, John," answered the Prime Mover. "Zeltor and Zandor, would you explain this to John?"

Zeltor proceeded to give a simplified definition of the time warp mechanism; and then Zandor explained his time warp optics device which had allowed them to scan distant galaxies to find a planet like Earth that could be satisfactory for their experiment.

"If only my detractors could know this!" exclaimed John. "It looks like my theories of the simultaneous multiple origin sites of man were right on the mark after all!"

"Yes," rejoined Rol. "I have read your papers, John; and your conclusions, based on the Earth's geology, were quite similar to my original calculations. I used those starting locales to get the best evolutionary spreading of the original arboreal mammal Dort and Zandor chose to treat."

"When will I have my 'operation'?" John asked the Prime Mover.

"Tomorrow morning is what we had planned if you agree," answered the Prime Mover.

"Then let's do it!" said John. There were smiles around the room and the meeting shortly concluded so that all could be made ready for the procedure the next day.

The brain transfer procedure on John turned out very well, and his brain's assimilation of his new Gnor body progressed faster than Ellen's had. All were very happy about this; especially Ellen, who had been extremely nervous about John's safety. Dr. Ran joked with her about her apparent attraction to John, saying that he wanted a first hand report of how their erotic apparatus worked if they ever got together. Ellen, of course, became somewhat flustered at this good-natured comment, but secretly she confessed to herself that John was very attractive to her. Indeed, she found herself hoping that he would feel the same towards her eventually. It was quite obvious to her that her human femaleness had not diminished one iota up to this juncture. Perhaps Dr. Ran was right when he said that it might never disappear, and this was certainly very acceptable to her.

John had been moved to new quarters since he no longer needed to breathe oxygen. These quarters were within the central portion of the Gnor city which lay against the sheer cliffs, and were at the highest elevation of all the buildings in the area. His room was quite comfortable, but of mostly glistening metal and plastics. Quite functional, John had thought, but not very warm or aesthetic. John learned that he was in the same complex as Ellen, who lived in her apartment at the end of his corridor. Dort and Zandor occupied the intervening apartment. The living rooms of these apartments opened out onto a magnificent common balcony which afforded them a grandiose panorama of the Martian landscape and the Gnor city below. The balcony was made out of the original Martian rock slabs that the Gnormen had first made use of as building material before they were able to mine metal and chemically formulate plastic building components. These massive sections of rough-hewn native rock were much more appealing to John than the plastic and metal appearance of the interior of his quarters.

John moved quickly from the balcony to answer a knock on his apartment door. Outside in the corridor stood Ellen, with a smile on her face.

"Hello, John," she said. "I wanted to stop by and see how you were getting along in your new quarters. Is there anything I can do for you?"

John smiled broadly at Ellen, "Come in, Ellen; but didn't you bring a housewarming cake?"

"I guess we won't need that custom anymore," Ellen replied. "But I'll never have to worry about watching my weight anymore and that used to be quite a chore for me."

"That's hard to believe if it's true what Dik told me about your body shape being just about what it was before you were rescued. He said it was attractive then, just as it is now."

Ellen's face looked a little embarrassed, but she was very pleased inwardly with John's remark. She went to the chair that John offered her and sat down. "You and Dr. Ran have the unique propensity to embarrass me, John; but thank you for your comment. But to change the subject, how are you getting along with your new body?"

"Ellen, it's fantastic!" he replied excitedly. "I am much stronger, and my senses are unbelievably keen. For instance, I would never have heard your knock way out on the balcony with my old ears. How long has it taken me to recover? They haven't told me how long it's been since the operation; I guess they don't think that's important."

"It's been a little over two months," replied Ellen. "They said everything has developed well without any problems and that your brain has accepted the Gnor body even faster than mine did."

"You see," said John with a smile, "Women always take longer to make up their minds."

Ellen gave him a wry look at this remark and then said with some embarrassment and hesitancy, "How did your...your...do you still feel like a human male?"

"As you told me about yourself a while back," John replied with a smile, "everything works far better than it ever did before. I honestly believe this transplantation has made me feel even more human than I did before if that's possible. You know we really could be considered a combination of the two races. Thinking about what wonderful creativity our human sexual expression has been responsible for in the past, I thing Dik is right about it being a very positive addition to the Gnor race."

Ellen seemed a little flustered. She rose from her chair and took the hand John offered her.

"I must get to a meeting shortly, John," she said. "I hope when you are fully recovered we can get together again. I know your expertise and information will be invaluable to our quest, and I am really looking forward to working with you."

John escorted her to the door, still holding her hand; and as she released his hand and left the room, she looked back at him with a warm shy glance, and then swiftly continued down the corridor.

The two Gnor-humans very quickly did get together to work on the Project for rebuilding the Gnor society on Mars, and made a formidable team with the expertise they brought to it. By now the bonds of respect and admiration between the Gnormen and Gnor-humans had deepened into a very warm, friendly relationship. John and Ellen had become the prime source of appropriate human candidates for rescue. They would pour through human history looking for intelligent people who met the criteria for their death and non-recovery; and then pinpoint the date and time when rescue could be accomplished without the Gnormen being discovered.

The first rescue set up by the team was for a heroine to Ellen, Amelia Earhart. In her undergraduate years at Smith College in Northampton, MA, Ellen had been intrigued by the famous aviatrix's life. Earhart had been a former Smith College student and had supposedly trained in auto mechanics at a home close to the college. Ellen had visited with Hortense Clapp, the current owner of this restored home, and been shown the garage where Ms. Earhart had been trained in this unusual discipline for a woman in those days. This had led to Ellen becoming interested in flying, and during her years at Smith she frequented LaFleur Airport in Northampton and eventually was able to get her pilot's license just before her graduation from the college.

Amelia and her co-pilot, Fred Noonan, had left Lae, New Guinea on their around-the-world flight on July 2, 1938, in the early morning at 0:00 hours on their way to Howland Island. The Coast Guard cutter *Itasca* was in the ocean off Howland Island and was keeping radio contact with the airplane, an Electra that had been bought by Amelia for what she called "the last trip of hers around the world." The brave aviatrix already had several world records for women flyers under her belt, and she had told the media that this flight was to be her last hurrah. She had no notion how prophetic her last statement to them would become.

The Electra had been loaded with one thousand gallons of fuel enabling her twenty to twenty-one hours of flight time. The last transmission to the *Itasca* had been at 8:14 pm; just twenty hours and fourteen minutes after her takeoff. She had said that they were running low on fuel and couldn't find Howland Island. The *Itasca* received no further transmissions and assumed that Amelia had ditched in the sea. U.S. President Roosevelt had dispatched nine ships and over sixty aircraft to search for her plane at a cost realized later at over four million dollars. She or the plane was never recovered and the search was called off on July 18th.

"Fred," said Amelia anxiously, "where is that damned island? We're very low on fuel and if we don't find it soon we'll have to ditch in the ocean! I just dispatched that message to the Itasca, and the connection was full of static. The radio now seems to have failed as I can't seem to raise them any more. Do you see anything?"

"Nothing but ocean so far, Amelia," answered Fred. "We do have a lifeboat aboard if we have to ditch, don't we? Wait a moment! What's that? There's some sort of ship flying up along side of us. A ship like nothing I have ever seen before! It's very big, Amelia; could it be some sort of new navy rescue ship?"

"I don't know, Fred," answered Amelia. "It doesn't seem to have any wings! But it is a sight for sore eyes to me since we're about to go down; there's zero on the gas gauge! I hope they can pick us out of the sea from that fantastic ship!" As she said this, she saw herself disintegrate in the cockpit, as did Fred; and seconds later they materialized on board the strange vessel.

Amelia grabbed Fred and gasped, "Fred! What happened to us; where are we?" They both saw a man and woman walking across the room to where they were standing under a device in the ceiling of the vessel that was still bathing them with a fading light. "Who are you?" asked Amelia. "How did you do that to us? Are you a new type of navy rescue ship?"

"Whoa, slow down, Ms. Earhart," said John. "I'm Dr. John Scott and this is Professor Ellen James. We came to rescue you. Your Electra was about to ditch in the sea and your lifeboat won't detach from its moorings, leaving you both to flounder and shortly drown."

Amelia looked incredulously at the two strange rescuers, "How do you know that? How can you tell that is about to happen?"

"Because we've already seen it happen," said Ellen quietly. "Now please, just be thankful that we have pulled you off that airplane in time for now. We will explain everything to you in great detail when we arrive back at our mother ship."

"You mean that there's a bigger ship than this that we're going to?" asked Fred. "How much bigger than this could it possibly be?"

"About 100 times this size," said Dort as he entered the room from the stairway above. "I'm Dort; and if you'll come with me I'll brief you on who we are. On our arrival at our city, our leader will tell you in great detail about our history and mission and what you may expect of us. It will be difficult for you to comprehend our ship's method of propulsion; but please rest assured that we mean you no harm, and actually are extremely dependent on your help." With that the two, looking at their surroundings in awe, accompanied the Gnorman up the stairs to the quarters set up for them on the scout vehicle.

"Well, John," said Ellen. "I really love this job! I'm getting to actually meet many of my heroes I've just read about in the past. And, I'm even helping to rescue them from certain death! Try to beat that for satisfaction!"

"That's easy," replied John with a wink. "But you keep telling me to keep it in perspective! Incidentally, you didn't give Dik that report he asked for did you?"

"John, you're incorrigible!" said Ellen with a frown. "Of course I wouldn't do that. Besides, it's already well known, and all the Gnormen have opted for the change. We will have to rescue a lot more women soon it looks like. Dik's idea that human sexuality will add to the Gnor race has been accepted widely. He told me it was because of how you and I have turned out so far." Ellen smiled at him demurely after her last remark.

"I'm sure it will prove correct," said John. "I have not lost even a small amount of my human feelings. I don't know about you, Ellen, but I am more and more attracted to you every day."

"You can't know how much I have wished you to say that, John," replied Ellen softly. She was close to him now, and they both embraced. "You know, I may be just intellectualizing, but I believe Dik may be right again about the procreation urge being able to fade away in our minds. I have been to the Life Factory, and can see how one could become attached to a new life that has been created. It is sort of like loving an adopted child. We both know how humans love their adopted children just as much as their own. We hopefully will do the same with our creations. Still, that is to be known only in the future.

"One thing that has intrigued me, John, is the possibility that perhaps the brain of a human child could be utilized with a Gnor body. Remember, the human brain is pretty much fully developed at birth and just needs to be programmed during the life of the child. Also, we all know how readily human children learn new things; why wouldn't the superior Gnor body be utilized with a fresh, growing child's brain just as well as an adult one? I have broached this with Dik and he says he is quite excited about this. He has been talking to Jol and he also is excited as well. We may get a chance to do this; especially if we approach large scale disasters like the sinking of the ocean liner Titanic. Of course, someone would have to 'rear' and teach these children; but if the maternity instinct doesn't dissipate, what a nice education job for a Gnorwoman so affected!"

"You're amazing, Ellen," said John. "I guess that's part of why I'm so attracted to you! Of course you're the only woman available at present." He absorbed an angry soft shove Ellen good-naturedly pushed against him and as they separated John said, "No, seriously, Ellen, I think you are right about the children. Who knows what will happen in the future? Maybe the world will become polluted and uninhabitable by the current humans on Earth. Maybe there will be an era when Gnor-humans will be the only salvation for the human race. Maybe there will never be a workable synthetic brain able to be developed by the Gnormen. Or maybe it will be developed and the Gnor race will leave for another planet, leaving us behind to try to save humanity. There are many 'ifs', aren't there? That's one good reason why I'm here and fully committed to this Project!"

"Me too," murmured Ellen; and she slid back into his arms and squeezed him tightly for a moment. She released him and stepped back. "Well, let's get up to the bridge. Zeltor said he'd let me fly the scout ship back to the Starship."

"Oh no," said John in fake horror, "a woman driver!" He dashed up the stairway just ahead of a shoe aimed at his back.

When they reached the Starship it was night of the next evening. John and Ellen were seated in the quarters they shared on the ship. They had recently taken up living together at their Martian quarters, and everyone treated them as a couple. "Just like an old married couple," John had said humorously. But he and Ellen were as much "in love" as any human couple could have been on Earth, and all of the other Gnormen recognized this and saw the real value of it. It was obvious that the work the two were doing was greatly enhanced by them being together.

"I hope those two will join us," said Ellen. "They have expertise that could help us enormously, what with the six new scout vehicles and another Starship that have been on the drawing boards now started into production. The base on the dark side of the moon has also been site planned as well. We must get more Gnormen available to help complete the infrastructure of that new base and the new city on Mars that we may need soon to accommodate the new Gnormen and Gnorwomen."

"From what you've told me about Amelia Earhart," replied John, "I think they will become part of the group. There isn't much more groundbreaking to a human being than brain transference; and Amelia has apparently been quite famous for female groundbreaking!"

"Yes," said Ellen, "she certainly has done that in spades! Well, John, I'm beginning to get a little sleepy; shall we sit in our sensorchairs for a while or just go to bed now?"

John smiled broadly, "You know I don't need the sensorchair with you in my arms, you little vixen! Let's go to bed." Ellen also smiled and led him by the hand into the bedroom.

Soon after they were in bed, John put his arms around Ellen and gently caressed her; which caused her to reciprocate his embrace and pull him over to her. The two soon began to make love up to a fierce crescendo which eventually came to an end in an ecstasy of passion and murmurs of "I love you so much" from both of them.

Afterwards they lay apart, reveling in the warm feelings of love they had for each other. Ellen was the first to break the silence.

"John, dear," she said, "I've made love before as a human but it was never like this! I sometimes wonder if it is the Gnor body's strength and neuron structure, or is it just you? I suppose it's probably both!"

"Well, I'd like to think it was me," said John with a broad smile. "But I agree; you are more than I have ever experienced before, and I'm afraid I love you more and more each day I'm with you. Ellen, I'm more human now than I was before, and I'm beginning to think we will remain human forever in spite of our synthetic Gnor bodies."

"I agree completely," answered Ellen. "And I must say, I love it!" She turned toward him with a loving look and caressed his face. "John," Ellen asked softly, "I hope you won't think me too clinical, but something has intrigued me for some time now. I can understand how they can 'wire' male and female erogenous areas to the 'sex' centers of the brain; and I can see how a vagina could be constructed to function as it did in a human female; but how can a male Gnorman sustain or even cause an erection to occur when he possesses no blood supply?"

"You will probably understand this better than me," replied John, "but apparently I am fashioned with an apparatus that is triggered from a small tube that comes from the bellows mechanism in our chest that also allows us to speak. Apparently there is a bead-filled pillow that is used in modern human surgical operations on Earth today, and Jol says he got the idea for his mechanism from this pillow. The pillow remains flaccid and moldable until some air is sucked out of it. This causes the pillow to become rigid to hold the patient in a certain position. When the air is allowed in again, the pillow becomes flaccid again. When I look at your beautiful body or touch your curves; or you or I—you is better—touch me down below, I get psychically aroused. My brain then automatically sends a message to the bellows mechanism which proceeds to aspirate air from my bead-containing male apparatus causing it to extend out and become rigid. You have probably noticed the 'bumps' in that apparatus; the beads are the explanation for those bumps. When our passion is over, my brain causes the bellows mechanism to pump air back into my male apparatus and it becomes flaccid again. You know, I'm amazed I'm not totally embarrassed by telling you this, but it is really quite fascinating to consider. Jol is really a mastermind; especially considering he has no practical experience in this problem!"

"I have noticed those 'bumps', John," said Ellen softly, "and I love them. Can I ask you one more question that Dik told me he had discussed with you? You know the raw material capsule we take daily for oxygen and nourishment for our brain; what happens to it? I know we put it in our mouths and push it forward and down somewhere with our tongue. But where does it go; and what happens to it? We don't have a stomach or intestines; how does it get to the brain?"

"Dik did explain it to me," John answered. "It is a marvelous mechanical device; and since there have been years to work out all its bugs it now works perfectly. The capsule is placed into your mouth, and your tongue, because of an involuntary neuronal reflex, spontaneously pushes it through a membrane in the floor of your mouth into a chamber under your chin. The membrane closes by itself after the capsule passes through it. You can actually feel it there transiently if you keep your hand under your jaw while the process is going on. This chamber contains a fluid that dissolves the capsule into a liquid which then flows into the main nutrient chamber in the head which contains the brain. Definitely a neat apparatus that Jol's designer group has perfected."

Ellen suddenly became serious. "But the one thing I have been very anxious about is God, John. Are all of these machinations we are doing blaspheming Him?"

John replied very quietly and thoughtfully, "His wisdom probably goes far beyond this; in fact, it may be part of His plan for perfection. It is easy to see that overpopulation is one of the commonest causes of the demise of many living things, both animal and plant. The Gnor society corrects this problem; with their ability to fit the population to the conditions available. Whether one believes in God or the Universe per se, I can't see that there will be any conflict with either in what we are doing. After all, we are just trying to understand the Universe and fit into it in the most acceptable way for our survival. Don't let this upset your pretty head Ellen, dear. Look what a wonderful gift God or the Universe has sent me—my life, and you!" With that remark Ellen pulled closer to him and kissed him gently on the lips. They both then rolled over to their own pillow and drifted off to sleep.

Amelia and Fred had both opted for becoming Gnor people but the operations had not been scheduled as yet. They were living in Dr. Ran's quarters where oxygen was present and were standing looking out of the large windows overlooking the city with its many lights.

"It certainly is a beautiful city," said Amelia. "The power need must be tremendous!"

"You know," said Fred, "I was talking to Dort earlier today and he told me that when they first landed on Mars they had to use the power from the Starship to run everything needed to build the city and protect it from meteor showers. Apparently the thin Martian atmosphere does not offer the protection from them that Earth's atmosphere does. Since that early time they have built what he called 'fusion generators'; and they supply the tremendous amount necessary to light and power the city and cover it with what he called a 'force field' that stops anything from passing through it and retains the city's heat. He said there are six more of the scout vehicles being built for use in their project to retrieve dying humans like we were. And he said that there is a great possibility that we will be taught to fly these ships ourselves on retrieval missions!"

Amelia's face began to light up. "Us?" she said excitedly. "We will be taught to fly one of these ships? I knew we made the right choice! I was nervous about our upcoming operation, even though Ellen and John have done so well; now I can hardly wait for it!"

The operation also went well for the two and they soon fit right into the rescue Project. It was left for Zeltor to train them to fly the scout ships as he had taught Ellen. At this juncture Ellen and John returned to their next recovery effort.

Ellen had always been a fan of a certain band leader who had revolutionized the use of many instruments in close harmony. Since he was too old to be drafted at thirty-eight years, he had enlisted as a captain in the Army Air Corps in WWII, and had formed a superb band from many of the military men that had played in several of the civilian bands before they were drafted for wartime service. This band was extremely helpful in the morale of the military during the war effort; and because of this, their leader received promotions from captain to major and several medals as well.

Major Glenn Miller took off from Twinwood Farr airfield outside London on December 15th, 1944. His destination was Paris, France where he was to make arrangements for his band to entertain there later on. He flew in a Norseman UC-64, with his pilot, Lt. John Morgan, and his business manager, Norman Baessell. The plane never reached Paris.

"John," asked Glenn, "how long before we reach Paris?"

The pilot turned around in his seat and was about to reply when they saw it coming right at them at supersonic speed and they knew they would be unable to escape it hitting them. It was apparently an errant Nazi rocket "buzz bomb" that was on its way to London. Just as it was about to strike the Norseman, the three men in the cockpit were transported via Portal directly into the reception hold of the nearby Gnor scout vehicle being piloted by Ellen. John was there in the hold and told the three men to grab the supporting rails and hold on, as Ellen banked sharply away from the exploding airplane. The three men saw the destroyed plane fall into the sea below; and realized they had just been saved from their deaths by this strange flying ship which none of them had ever seen before.

"Who are you?" asked Major Miller. "What kind of a ship is this? And please, don't get us wrong; thanks for saving our lives."

117

"Well, Major," said John. "My name is Dr. John Scott, and if you will accompany me to the bridge of the ship I will introduce you to the pilot who whisked you away from your certain destruction. She is a great fan of yours, Major Miller; and the things you are about to learn will be both incredulous and unbelievable to all of you. Suffice it to say that we rescued you for a certain purpose that you will hear about from our leader. You will be able to make whatever decision you want and we will carry it out according to your wishes."

"Did you say, 'she'," queried Major Miller. "You mean a woman maneuvered this ship like we just felt?"

"That's right, Major," answered John. They had climbed the stairs and entered the control room. "Major Glenn Miller, meet one of your fans, Professor Ellen James."

Ellen glanced towards the four men and smiled broadly. "Welcome aboard, gentlemen," she said. "Please take your seats and we will get you back to our mother ship where all of your questions will be answered by our leader. I look forward to chatting with you Major Miller. Your style of music is still revered by a lot of people, and is one of my favorites! You probably will have a lot in common with two other members of our people; you have probably heard of Amelia Earhart and her navigator?"

"You mean Amelia Earhart and Fred Noonan?" said the musician. "But their plane crashed in 1938 in the South Pacific and they were never recovered! And what do you mean by 'my style of music is still revered'; that's past tense!"

"You are correct," rejoined Ellen. "Just know that we mean you no harm and are indeed very dependent upon you as you will understand when you meet our leader. Now please relax and enjoy the ride!" With that she placed the scout vehicle into a rapid climb toward the Starship.

The three men were as astounded as all the previous humans had been when they reached and boarded the immense Starship. The awestruck trio was greeted by Amelia and Fred who were to escort them to their quarters.

"I enjoyed your new composition work in Chicago, Major Glenn Miller," said Amelia to the major as they were leaving the landing stage. "I was afraid there was war coming. My husband George was nervous about us flying where we did, as he was sure hostilities were about to break out in that area of the world as well. I know you know about our supposed demise. All will be understood after you meet our leader." With that the door at the top of the stairway from the landing area closed behind the six.

"You know, John," said Ellen, "do you think our chest bellows mechanism could be trained to blow a musical instrument? I know you can play your violin well with your Gnor fingers. Perhaps we could introduce big band, classical and other types of music to the Gnorman race. It probably would go along well with our gift of sex!" She smiled broadly at John.

"For a stodgy professor of history, Ellen James," answered John, "you're a little devil! Seriously, though, this is another of your great ideas. Yes, I do think it will be worth pursuing; and I'll wager the major will be all for it as well!"

"His musical composition was truly inspired genius for its time, John," said Ellen. "On our next trip to Earth I'll get the apparatus and records to let you hear his great music. His military band was marvelous, as he had his pick of drafted musicians that were the best of many different great civilian bands of the era."

"If you keep this up, Ellen," said John, "You'll change all of the Gnormen into humans!"

"There's no danger of that for some time, John," Ellen replied. "The Gnormen are so far ahead of us ethically and morally it may take an eternity for us to catch up to them. I have thought at some length about that, John. It seems to me that with human beings, technology is the easiest thing to make rapid strides with. But I believe that after a certain technological state is reached our society retracts some, allowing a catch up of what is slow to develop, an ethical and moral sense containing discipline and responsibility. If this doesn't happen, I think blatant, unsupervised technology can be the downfall of everything alive. The Gnormen have been through this already, and we must travel a considerable distance to catch up to them to understand it properly."

"As always, my beautiful lady," replied John, "Your thoughts are right on target, and I agree with you completely. But to change the subject to more mundane things, let's make sure we find Dort or Zandor as soon as we get back to Mars and see if they will approve our next Project. I'm pretty confident Amelia, Fred, and the Prime Mover will be able to convince those three new recruits to join us; and it will be another potential scout vehicle pilot with Lt. Morgan."

Back on Mars, John and Ellen sought out Dort with their new rescue Project.

"You know, Dort," Ellen began the conversation, "there are two persons that we had in mind for rescuing next, since the six new scout vehicles and the new Starship are well along in their construction. They both were excellent pilots in Europe in WWII, and their demise occurred on a secret mission that was reserved for their expertise. John and I think they would be excellent candidates to go after next. The main pilot's younger brother, who went through the same war safely in the South Pacific, became president of the United States after the war and had the misfortune to be assassinated. Obviously, no recovery of him would be possible; but his older brother's case was a different matter."

"The younger brother had a great first name also," said John with a wink. "We think these two pilots will be helpful for the new ships being built."

Dort and Zandor agreed with the two, so the rescue Project was begun.

It was August 12, 1944 and Lt. Joseph P. Kennedy, Jr., with his fellow pilot Lt. Wilford Willy were on a secret mission to blow up a rocket manufacturing plant of the Nazis across the English Channel.

Even though Kennedy had been due for transfer home because of extensive service already performed, he had volunteered for this dangerous mission. He knew they needed his expertise and that of his friend Lt. Willy; so he took on the assignment and was happy with the 50/50 chance they were told of completing the mission called "Operation Aphrodite". He had often told other pilots that he was always happy with a 50/50 chance in any endeavor, so this mission was no different to him. The plane he and Willy flew was loaded with twenty-one thousand pounds of high explosives, and was a drone plane; which meant its piloting could be taken over by accompanying planes and then piloted to fly directly into the target rocket factory. Because it was felt that it would be too difficult and dangerous to have the drone plane take off by itself and fly to the spot where it would be taken over; it was decided to have Lts. Kennedy and Willy take off with the drone plane and meet the two other planes that would then fly it across the Channel. The two men would then bail out there over southern England, and the two accompanying planes would take over and continue to fly the drone plane into the target on the other side of the Channel.

Everything started out well as Kennedy and Willy took off from Fersfield-Winfarthing airfield near Diss in Norfolk on the above date. They were piloting a B-24 navy Liberator four engine twin-tailed bomber, which Kennedy was very proficient in flying. On 6:20 pm, over southern England before they were to meet the takeover planes, their plane suddenly exploded; destroying them and the plane completely.

"We will have to get them out with the Portal before the other planes come into our view," said Zeltor. "Ellen, I will need your help on this maneuver while Zandor operates the Portal. John, when they materialize you'll have to convince them immediately that we mean them no harm and are not Germans; I read that Kennedy was a doer and he might be a problem if he thinks we're the enemy. If they have weapons and draw them you may have to stun them with your laser sidearm. I hope this doesn't happen, but be prepared!"

The two men materialized in the scout vehicle hold and John was relieved to see they carried no sidearms. As with the others before them, they were completely confused by what had happened to them and what they were witnessing

"Lieutenants," said John, "I'm Dr. John Scott, and we're not Germans; and if you'll accompany me up to the bridge we'll explain what has happened to you and you'll witness for yourselves why we removed you from your plane when we did."

Completely mystified, they accompanied John up the stairway to the bridge of the scout vehicle, where they were just in time to see their plane massively explode in midair on a large screen in front of the control panel of the ship.

"Who are you people?" asked Lt. Kennedy. "And what is this marvelous ship? You mentioned a bridge; are you navy, and is this a new type of navy airship? I'm sorry! Please pardon my manners. Willy and I are very grateful for your saving our lives!"

"Yes, Lt. Kennedy," said Ellen. "But now your brother Jack will have to be president instead of you!"

"Jack, president?" replied Kennedy. "President of what, and how do you know Jack? Oh, that's right; Jack is in navy PT boats in the South Pacific. So this is a Navy ship after all!"

"No," replied Ellen, "it's not a Navy ship; and I meant president of the United States, as your father had intended you to be after the war. I know this is all very confusing to you; but when we board our mother ship and fly back to our base city, our leader will answer all your questions. It will become very clear to you what our intentions are and how we would like you to help us. You will learn some troubling things about your brothers Jack and Robert that you will want desperately to correct but will be unable to do so. But you will be surprised that your kid brother, Teddy, will become a mainstay in the U.S. Congress for many years."

"Pardon me, ma'am," said Kennedy, "but are you the pilot of this marvelous huge ship? I didn't know the Navy had female pilots, and darned attractive ones at that!"

"I'm the co-pilot," answered Ellen. "Zeltor over there is the main pilot; and if you make the right decision back at our home city, he will probably be instructing you two how to fly this vessel yourselves. Also, I see you have the vaunted Kennedy charm, lieutenant." She smiled and returned to her position at the control panel.

"Gentlemen," said Zeltor, indicating two chairs, "please be seated over there. We should be back at our mother ship in a few minutes." With that the scout vehicle moved rapidly upwards towards the Starship.

Back again on Mars John said to Ellen, "You know I felt a little jealousy when you were talking to Lt. Kennedy."

Ellen blew him a kiss, "You were sweet to feel that way John, dear. But seriously, as we talked about the other day, this emotion is not present to any extent in the Gnormen, or it's under complete control. It makes me wonder how new Gnor-humans will handle their emotions, without the long period that the Gnormen have already had to understand, treat, and mature them."

"Without question," replied John, "it may become a factor. Our Gnor friends certainly abhor violence; although they have had to do it back on their home planet in the war that caused them to leave it. Still, it was forced upon them by a segment of their society that was relatively newly created; and perhaps hadn't had the time necessary to mature out of the violence. At any rate, we may get the chance to see what happens as we create more and more Gnor-humans."

"You know," rejoined Ellen, "I never thought of it before but perhaps we should try if possible to rescue people who might be more or less oriented towards peace and nonviolence. From what we've discussed, these people might fare better with the Gnormen. If we do this, I know just who should be our next rescue Project."

"And who might that be, professor?" asked John. "Do I know this one or do I get another history lesson?"

"This man is after your time, John," replied Ellen. "He was a marvelous, true renaissance man. He was very knowledgeable concerning French impressionist painting, and did some himself. He was an expert on Beethoven's music, a great athlete, wrote poetry, and was an outstanding student at his home country's Uppsala University, where he became an economics professor. He spoke four languages, and took important government positions in finance in his home country. He became Secretary-General of the United Nations in 1953 and was reelected in1957. The U.N. is an organization that is composed of all the nations of the Earth. He made the Secretary-General's office the site for operations for peace; and he won the coveted Nobel Peace Prize in 1961.

"On September 17-18th, 1961, he had flown to Leopoldville, The Congo, to aid the Congolese government that was having trouble with rebels in the north. He and fifteen others died when the plane they were in crashed. History is sketchy about why or how it crashed and who was recovered as it was in a remote area of the Congo. It might be prudent if we had the time warp mechanism on board the scout vehicle this time to remove him from the timeline and replace his body back into it later as they did me. I would be very surprised if he decided not to join our project."

"There's certainly no question in my mind that he would be an excellent candidate," said John. "Let's discuss it with Dort and the others and see if they agree."

The scout vehicle approached the plane as it flew low over the jungle. Scattered rifle and other hand held fire were aimed at the plane from below. Secretary-General Dag Hammarskjold sat by himself in the first seat up front in the plane, musing about what he would say to get the two protagonists to agree to a cease fire to the hostilities. There was no one in the first class area at this time as the only two others in that section had lined up behind the curtain in the rear of the section to use the bathroom. Suddenly, the Secretary-General dematerialized in his seat as the plane simultaneously was blown apart by either fire from below or an explosion on the plane.

"Where am I? What happened?" asked the Secretary-General,

who had been escorted by Ellen from the receiving hold to the bridge of the scout ship. "What kind of marvelous ship is this, and how did you get me over here this way?"

"Please don't be concerned, Mr. Secretary-General," said Ellen. "You're among friends... great friends. I for one am extremely proud to meet you in person; and I know you will become a personal friend of our leader back at our home city, who is much like you. He will explain what has happened and what we would like you to do for us if you decide it is right for you to do so. You just got the start of what happened to your plane as you were transported on board here. Look at the large screen up front now and see why we had to pull you out of there immediately." Zeltor ran the massive explosion and total destruction of the Secretary-General's plane on the telescreen for him to witness.

"Oh, those poor people!" exclaimed the Secretary-General. "There were 15 people on that plane besides me. Why couldn't you save all of them like you did me?"

"That is exactly what I thought you would say, sir," replied Ellen. "We couldn't save them because we don't know historically what happened to them afterwards. Your body will have to be placed back there itself after you have made your decision after talking with our leader. Please bear with us; you will get a complete explanation of the reasons from our leader back at our home city. It has to do with timeline changes which will also be explained. Now we are going to rendezvous with our mother ship which will take us back to our city for the answer to all your questions." The Secretary-General sat back and marveled at his surroundings in this strange ship that had pulled him from the jaws of death. Zeltor's attention became directed from the now-darkened telescreen to the control panel as he maneuvered the scout vehicle rapidly towards the mother Starship. When the Secretary-General caught a glimpse of the enormous Starship just before they docked with it, he was even more astounded.

"You people are extraterrestrial, are you not?" he said to Ellen with a slight quaver in his voice.

"John and I are not such beings, sir," said Ellen in reply. "We are human; at least the most important part of us is human. The other gentlemen are in that category. But there is nothing to fear from them; their ethics and morals are very much like yours, but infinitely advanced and matured. Again, please wait for explanation from our leader, who will meet with you when we arrive back at our home city on Mars.

"Mars, you say!" rejoined the Secretary. "Now I really don't know whether I'm asleep and dreaming, or maybe even dead! But lead on; my curiosity as always is outrunning my fear and trepidation!"

"As I knew it would from my studies of you, Mr. Hammarskjold," said Ellen. "That's why I related what I did to you; I knew you would be so interested that you would be more inclined to go along with us to learn the explanation."

When back on Mars, the Secretary-General soon met with the Prime Mover; and as Ellen had predicted, they had an instant friendly understanding of each other. The decision was made by the Secretary-General to join the project; so rapid plans were engendered for his brain transfer into a Gnor body. After the surgery they would return his body to the plane, since Ellen could not discern by her historical studies exactly what happened to his body after the explosion and crash of the plane.

"This will be tricky," said Ellen, "because we will have to get the body back into the plane just before the explosion. Otherwise there is the possibility that it might be noticed that the Secretary-General is dead in his chair if we return him too soon, and they may radio this information out."

"We should be able to accomplish it," said John.

The Secretary-General's brain transfer procedure turned out very well, so Zeltor, Ellen, and John soon were on their way back to Earth and the Congo, to place the Secretary-General's body back on the plane. They adjusted the timeline on the scout vehicle and flew in beside the plane. They were not worried about being seen as they knew the plane was about to be totally destroyed, obviating any possibility of signaling their detection. The body was sent back to its seat on the plane by the Portal; just as the two that had left before returned from the bathroom. They noticed that the Secretary-General sat slumped in his seat, and rushed over to see if he were all right.

"Mr. Secretary! Mr. Secretary!" exclaimed the first person to reach his seat. "Are you all right?" He examined the slumped man's pulse, looked at the other man and said in disbelief, "My God! The Secretary has no pulse. He's dead!" Just at that moment a loud roar ensued as the plane exploded and plummeted to the jungle below.

"Just in time!" said Ellen. "Let's get back to the Starship before we're recognized. Nobody to this day knows exactly what happened to that ship; it could have been shot down and was being monitored from below, and someone might be down there that could see us!" With that remark by Ellen, Zeltor engaged the scout vehicle into a rapid trajectory back to the Starship.

Back on Mars, Ellen suggested to Dort and the Prime Mover that perhaps it was time to consider going after more numbers of individuals all at once. This would make it possible to increase the number of Gnormen and Gnorwomen that could help with the expansion of cities on Mars, and the building of the base on the dark side of the moon on Earth. They could increase the oxygenated quarters on Mars to contain the people while their operations were being done. After that they could take their place in the concealed underground cities being constructed along the canals as was originally planned. The learning process necessary for them to acquire Gnorman facility in building took some time; so that if rescue could be done with numbers of people together, it would get more people up to speed in construction technique at the same time.

"This is obviously a good idea, Ellen," agreed Dort and the Prime Mover nodded his assent as well.

"But where will we find people together in an irretrievable death situation to accomplish this," asked the Prime Mover.

"There were several times in history," said Ellen, "when disasters have occurred to many people at the same time. In some of them we will have to be careful about whom we rescue. It will require good historical research but it can be done; the records are available. One such irretrievable death situation that has occurred frequently is the loss of undersea ships called submarines. Lt. Kennedy told me that there are naval records of fifty-two U.S. submarines that were lost in WWII without a trace. This means, of course, that their bodies were never recovered as well. We should be able to track them down and rescue the crews of each ship, which often numbered over 100 men. We could go after one ship at a time and set the crew members up here on Mars for their operation. Lts. Kennedy and Willy, both military men, have said they believe they would be able to get the Navy records that would help us to locate the submarines. Amelia, Fred, John and I could work with them by utilizing several of the recently completed scout vehicles together. This would make it easier to make the retrievals quicker from each ship."

"This sounds like an excellent plan, Ellen," said the Prime Mover, "as was your suggestion to rescue the Secretary-General. He is an outstanding person as you said he would be, and will be invaluable to us, I know. Dort and I will meet with Lts. Kennedy and Willy and get this Project started."

"The time warp mechanism gives us plenty of time to plan all our rescues," said Ellen. "After we have finished with the WWII submarines, there are two I have known about that would also be great candidates for rescue. The U.S.S. Thresher that went down in 1963, and the Russian submarine Kursk that exploded on maneuvers in 2000; both received worldwide attention when they were lost.

"On April 10, 1963, the Thresher was out on deep dive maneuvers 220 miles east of Boston, MA. Something happened and the ship dropped 5500 feet to the bottom of the ocean where she broke apart into six pieces with loss of all hands. There were 129 people on board the submarine; 16 officers, 96 enlisted men, and 17 civilian technicians. The ship was nuclear-powered; but the Navy determined that there was no radiation threat from the area. I doubt that there would be much of a problem for us anyway. Our Gnor bodies have been built to withstand such things from the past ancestral pollutions that made it necessary to design such protection in the first place. There has been no attempt at recovery of any of the bodies, and the site is now designated as a memorial to the sailors who died there. As a human being, I think we should consider returning the bodies to all the submarines after the brain transfers to honor this naval tradition for all those who have drowned there at sea."

"That is certainly agreeable," said the Prime Mover. He looked around the room and smiled. "It was certainly fortunate for us that Zandor and Dort came upon your plane crash, Ellen. Your insights have been continuingly extremely valuable to us, and we thank you for them."

"The Russian submarine, Kursk," continued Ellen, "was on maneuvers in the Barents Sea on August 12, 2000. They were testing a new on board weapons system when two torpedoes exploded killing all on board and sinking the ship. This was also a nuclear-powered ship; but again, apparently no threat of radiation was present here either. One hundred eighteen sailors lost their lives, and ultimately some of the bodies were left there as a memorial as well. All the appropriate information concerning this is available, so rescue and return should be able to be accomplished with ease. We should retrieve them just before the explosion; but we can put them back any time later when discovery can be easily avoided."

"Yes," said the Prime Mover, "our scout vehicles can maneuver under water and remain undetected without any difficulty. Well then, let's get together with your navy men and start the Project as soon as possible!"

The submarine project was as good as Ellen had imagined; and soon several new additions to the city had to be constructed for the increasing Gnor population. Once the new Gnormen were successfully trained, the construction of the new underground city additions on Mars and the base on the dark side of Earth's moon began to progress much more rapidly. The retrieval of the drowned victims was progressing without any serious problems thanks to the utilization of the new scout vehicles. These ships were flown by the Gnor-human pilots that had been successfully trained by Zeltor.

It was on a trip to Earth by Ellen, that the first mishap on the planet to a Gnor person occurred. Ellen had decided to get the CD record player and Glenn Miller records as a surprise for John to hear. She finally procured what she wanted in a small city in the same state where she had taught history at a store located in one of the less desirable sections of town. On the way back to where she had stashed her gravity pack for her rendezvous with Zeltor in the scout vehicle, two rather large young men accosted her and obviously had evil intentions for her in mind.

"What have you got in the bag, darlin'?" leered one of them as he dashed in her front of her blocking her way. The other man came up quickly behind her and wrapped his arms around her.

"What are you doing?" shouted Ellen. "Let go of me!" She struggled to free herself from his grasp.

"I guess," said the second man, "we'll have to see what this pretty lady has for us; in that bag and under this dress!" And with that he started to attempt to tear off Ellen's dress while pushing her to the ground. Ellen used her great Gnor strength and smashed her assailant unconscious with one blow of her right fist to his head. The other man pulled out a knife and was coming at her with it raised when a police cruiser screeched to a halt just behind them. Two officers jumped out with their revolvers in their hands and shouted for the man to drop his knife and put up his hands. He was quickly subdued and handcuffed; and he and his unconscious companion were placed in the cruiser and taken along with Ellen to the local police station.

When they arrived at the station, a woman detective questioned Ellen about what had happened. She repeated the story of her attack by the two men and asked if she could leave to get to where she was supposed to be meeting someone. The detective suggested she make a telephone call to let the person know she was all right. Ellen thought quickly and informed her that she didn't know the telephone number where the person was and that she would be OK just going there now. The detective informed Ellen that since the officers who had brought her in had seen the man attack her with the knife that she would not have to stay and prefer charges. However, she might have to appear in court later to identify the men when they were arraigned. She asked for Ellen's address and telephone number so they could contact her at the appropriate time for the trial; and she offered to drive her to her friend. This turn of events threw Ellen into a panic, but she managed to say that she was visiting and staying in a downtown hotel and had stopped to pick up a record player and records for her friend. She told the detective that she had forgotten the name of the hotel, but knew how to get there where her friend was waiting for her. The detective obligingly quoted the name of a hotel on Main Street, and Ellen quickly agreed that that was the one. She then gave her the old address and telephone number from the city where she had lived before she'd had her plane crash. As the detective was escorting Ellen out of the station to her cruiser for the ride to the hotel, they passed by the man who had wielded the knife as he was being placed in a cell.

"Man," he was saying to the officer locking him up, "you should have seen it! She cold cocked my buddy with one blow to his head. And she was on the ground when she threw the punch!"

"Yeah, yeah," said the officer, "I'm sure that attractive little lady must be a real powerhouse. Now get in that cell and shut up!"

Ellen looked anxious as she and the detective passed by and heard that comment.

"From what he just said, Ms. James;" the detective said to her, "maybe the officers saved him by getting there when they did!" Then she winked and smiled at her as they continued out to the car. Little did the detective know how true that might have been had they not arrived when they did!

The detective dropped Ellen at the hotel and Ellen thanked her for all her trouble.

"No trouble at all," said the detective. "It's always a pleasure to be of service, Ellen. Are you sure you're OK? Do you want me to come in with you and call your friend for you?"

131

"No, thank you detective," she replied. "I'm fine. Thanks again for your help."

"When they call you for the arraignment, if you have any questions, please ask for me; Detective Sarah Jones. I'll be glad to help you any way I can."

"Thanks again, Detective Jones," Ellen answered. "You've been most kind and I appreciate your concern." Ellen mused, *I wonder what she'll think when she calls my old number and ultimately learns that I'm dead! It should be interesting.*

She waved goodbye to the detective and hurried through the lobby and out the rear entrance of the hotel with her record treasures, and made her way rapidly back to where her gravity pack was stashed. She signaled Zeltor who shortly picked her up. After she told him what had happened to her he was quite anxious about what had transpired, but was relieved that she was all right.

"Actually, Zeltor," she said half seriously, "one of my assailants thought I was a terror, and told the police that I had knocked his partner unconscious with one blow. The detective that took me to the hotel kidded me saying that perhaps it was lucky for the two men that the police arrived when they did!"

Zeltor became somewhat anxious about Ellen's remarks. "Do you think they suspected anything, Ellen?" he said with some concern.

"I don't think so," she replied. "But it will be interesting when the detective calls my old number and ultimately finds out that I'm dead! She seemed to be the kind of a policewoman that might consider checking me out. I realize now that giving my real name and old telephone number to her might not have been the best thing to do; but she caught me by surprise and I panicked and gave them to her without thinking. I'm still feeling a little shaky."

"No," said Zeltor, "giving your real name and number probably came out more credibly than made up ones would have. She may have become suspicious and detained you longer if you seemed to be making up the name and number. We will have to wait and see what becomes of her telephone call when and if she makes it; or at least avoid this area in the future."

"Actually," said Ellen, "she probably won't make the call at all. It will most likely be done by a clerk in the department. But she offered to help me with any questions I might have about the arraignment. I have an uneasy feeling that Detective Sarah Jones will possibly be inclined to check out the mystery of a live dead woman! She impressed me with both her competence and compassion, Zeltor; I actually liked her very much!"

"Let's get you back to base," rejoined Zeltor, "I suspect John is going to be upset at what happened to you just because of you getting him a present!"

John was indeed visibly upset about what had happened to Ellen when she related the story to him. "You might have been hurt; or at the least discovered as an alien," he scolded her. "You and I sometimes forget that humans are not as advanced ethically and morally as our Gnor friends; and some people are downright primitive! The next time you do something unrehearsed make sure you take me with you! I don't know what I'd ever do if I lost you, Ellen." With that he took her in his arms and kissed her firmly on the lips.

Ellen pushed away from him a couple of inches and said demurely, "Yes, master! Whatever you say, master!" She embraced him tightly and returned his kiss; and as they separated she said soberly, "You know, John, this incident has made me think about the possible danger we may be getting into if we put the wrong human brain into a Gnor body. Even so-called normal people may harbor problems within their subconscious minds that could be disastrous in a powerful Gnor body. We keep forgetting that the Gnormen have had centuries to advance the civility that humans have yet to learn. I wonder if we may run into trouble with all these sailors being recreated in a Gnor body. You and I have not lost our human desires at all. Will these new powerful beings misuse their strength? Will we need police to keep them in check like we do now on Earth? I think we should at least discuss this with Dort and the Prime Mover and maybe we should be a lot more selective in the brains we transfer."

"Yes, my darling," said John. "You're right again, as usual. We'll talk to them first thing in the morning! Now come with me and we'll listen to these records you obtained for me at such a price!" He put his arm around her waist and they walked into their bedroom where Ellen had set up the recorder and records. She started the recorder playing, gave John a shy glance and started to disrobe.

"I'm going to take a long shower now after my messy encounter," she said to John with a knowing glance. "You can come and scrub my back if you are of a mind to." With that the last article of her clothing dropped to the floor, and she moved slowly and voluptuously toward the bathroom door, looking back at John who was quickly shedding his clothes.

"You are a young temptress, woman," he said with faked disdain, "but I love you for it!" He dashed after her into the shower.

The conference with the Prime Mover and Dort took place the next midmorning in the complex's library. Ellen expressed how her incident on the planet had made her realize that not all human brains might be ethically and morally safe in a powerful Gnor body. She worried that perhaps some of the sailors they were rescuing, though proficient as navy men, might prove to be found wanting as regards ethical and moral character. Would they have to develop a Gnor police force to reckon with them? Might not it be better to be much choosier in what kind of person we rescue, rather than just any human per se that dies unrecoverable?"

"Ellen," answered the Prime Mover, "your fears are well justified. Dort and I and the rest of the original Gnorman Council considered this problem at some length because we knew that even if the human brains were compatible with our Gnor bodies, they would not have the benefit of our long maturation history. We developed our peaceful ethical and moral character not just by gradual understanding alone. Inculcated over the centuries into the fluid that our brains float in and are nourished by, have been added different chemicals that keep our aggressive tendencies in check, allowing reason to triumph over emotions. We haven't destroyed our emotions; they are too valuable for life's total happiness. But we have learned with the help of these chemicals to choose the peaceful, non-violent, negotiable way to solve a problem. That is why what has happened back on our home planet has so saddened us and caused us to leave it. The same chemicals are in the nutrient fluid of the Gnor-humans, and we train them for several weeks in the Life Factory before we let them graduate to working on the construction complex. So far it seems that violence and aggression have not been a problem with any of the sailors we have assimilated. In fact, a couple of them have complemented each other on how easy to get along with they were now, compared to how they were before. We are aware of this possible problem, Ellen and are monitoring for it very carefully. For now, though, it doesn't seem to be a problem."

"Mr. Prime Mover," said Ellen, "You have made me feel much better about it with your words. John and I will rejoin the navy men and the other pilots to see if we can assist them with the many rescue missions coming up. I can think of two other famous ship sinkings that have historical records of the survivors that will garner us many more Gnorman candidates. They are the battleships Bismarck and Hood; and the ocean liner Titanic. With your time warp mechanism to get us there, we should have enough sinking ships to keep us busy for a long time and the navy men will enjoy being able to rescue more of their own. And considering sunken ships; if we need more gold metal for the Gnorman neuronal circuits and other body part connections, we should be able to get it from the several galleons that sank during the days of the pirates in the earlier centuries. I'm sure there are many thousands of gold coins on the bottom of the ocean in many sites in the Caribbean Sea. There is a pretty good history available to be able to track some of the ships that were lost to hurricanes and other mishaps. It will be difficult for you to understand why, but humans, from childhood stories of pirates, are very excited about finding sunken treasure. Especially enjoyed are stories about the old galleons that carried the gold plunder back to Europe from the new world recently discovered. I'm positive searching for any needed gold would be very enthusiastically undertaken by us humans!" Ellen smiled broadly at John after her last remark and he nodded assent with a smile on his face as well. "Well, sir, thank you again for your reassuring words." With that she and John rose from their chairs and left the library to find the others.

Lt. Kennedy was the first person Ellen and John encountered to offer their assistance with the rescue Projects.

"Professor James," said the lieutenant, "I was just going to call you to ask for your historical help in our next rescue project; that of the Russian submarine, Kursk. I believe most of the bodies were recovered eventually, so it would be nice to determine which ones we have to return, and which we do not. We should be able to do this either way; as from what I've read there was enough of a time lag in the rescue attempts for us to get in and out easily without being discovered. Incidentally, the scout vehicles perform extremely well under water; if we'd had submarines like this in WWII, we'd have dispatched the German U-boat fleet in short order. There is a 'dead zone' if one stays in the shadow of the other sub where it can't detect your vessel. So far in many of our rescues we have used that maneuver to come close enough to the ship without detection to transfer men to our ship via the Portal. It has worked out very well so far!"

"Well, lieutenant," said Ellen, "The final word on the Kursk is that eighty percent of the crew were killed within three minutes of the first explosion noted seismographically by the rescue ships. To this day no one is entirely sure of what caused the tragedy; but the accepted speculation is that another foreign monitoring submarine collided with the Kursk and distorted her torpedo tubes, causing a detonation that went backwards into the ship and caused further detonations. The Norwegian ship Normann Pioneer, and the British ship Seawell Eagle were the ships in the area that Russia accepted help from initially. The Norwegian diver specialists were the first able to reach the sunken submarine and open the lower hatch of section nine of the ship, finding it flooded and offering no further hope that anyone survived the mishap. The Kursk carried twenty-four guided missals and the same number of torpedoes; and even though they were engaged in war games, they were part of the main

Russian naval defense force and had live torpedoes on board. There were five staff officers, one military certification officer, and one civilian technologist on the ship; along with 111 seamen. There were lists published concerning the men on the ship which I should be able to recover. The ship was found at 330 feet on the jagged rocks of the Barents Sea bed. Some information that may be helpful in the rescue maneuvering—there were strong two knots currents at that depth, and only one meter visibility because of drifting silt that could be used for cover. The last bit of interesting information is that there were two other submarines in the area that were monitoring the war games and could have possibly been involved in an underwater collision with the Kursk. One was the British ship HMS Splendid and the other was the USS Toledo. Neither country honored the Russian request to show the physical status of those two submarines after the tragedy. If they had shown them and no damage had been found, it certainly would have led to much more cooperation in naval interactions between the three countries. That's about it for what I know about the history of the Kursk, lieutenant. I can get the list of what happened to the men on board so we will know who doesn't have to be rescued. John and I would like to accompany you if you are to be the pilot of the space vehicle; as we have learned Russian well and can help with the men we rescue."

"That would be great," answered Lt. Kennedy, "I am honored that you are offering to come aboard. My next mission project is the Kursk, so we can get started within the week!"

Lt. Kennedy skimmed the scout vehicle at night low over the waters of the Barents Sea and plunged under its surface, slowing the ship to a cruising speed of fifteen knots at about twenty-five meters depth. He was easily able to pick up the position of the Kursk a few miles ahead on the scout vehicle's sensors, and called to Ellen and John in the receiving hold.

"We should be in position to use the Portal to transfer the men to our ship in about ten-fifteen minutes," he announced to them over the intercom. "Wait a minute! There's another sub close to the Kursk, riding in its shadow zone, and it's too close for safety's sake! Oh, my God! Ellen, John! That sub has just collided with the Kursk and it's limping away. Now an explosion has just happened in the stern of the Kursk and it's diving at a dangerous angle! The sub has hit the bedrock at the sea bottom and now two more explosions have occurred on board! We will have to use the time warp mechanism to go back in time a few hours to get the on board people out before this mishap occurs. A large number of the men on the submarine are already dead at this juncture; we will have to go back in time if we're to get the ones we can rescue. I suggest we do that and then return all the bodies back to the submarine by Portal after we have affected their brain transfers at the Life Factories on Mars."

"We both agree with you lieutenant," said Ellen. "John and I will start the proceedings now." The two rapidly made the shift in time; and the scout vehicle was able to get all the appropriate men on board the Kursk off the submarine without detection by what turned out to be at least three other submarines that were apparently all monitoring the exercises. There were apparently at least two American and one British submarine present, but they were not able to say which sub had been involved in the later collision; or even if it had been one of them at all.

"It might be nice to go back and solve this problem that has never been resolved," said Ellen, "but we have more important things to attend to right now, so let's get back to the Starship and Mars! The Russian sailors are all pretty confused but they eventually responded positively to our explanations of their imminent demise. The telescreen showing of their ship's destruction was sobering and very helpful in convincing them to wait and listen to the explanation by the Prime Mover when we get back to Mars. They all seem incredulous but excited to be traveling to Mars!" Everyone agreed they should start for home at once and Lt. Kennedy put the scout vehicle into a rapid climb back towards the Starship. When the Russian sailors, in great awe of their surroundings, were all safely on board in their oxygen quarters, Zeltor proceeded to take the Starship back to Mars at a rapid pace.

Most of the Russian sailors from the Kursk chose to live as Gnormen and so underwent brain transfers. There were a few that did not choose that way; and they were returned to the ship along with the bodies of those who did join the Gnor society by brain transfer. The return was done by Portal just after the collision of the two submarines; but they were still unable to determine which submarine was responsible for the mishap.

The following evening Ellen and John were discussing their next rescue mission which was another submarine disaster, the sinking of the American ship, *Thresher*.

"That's an interesting name for a submarine," said John. "Is it true that the subs were named for sea life?"

"Yes," answered Ellen, "my research showed that a thresher is a type of shark with a tail longer than its body and head combined. Thus, it 'threshes' that tail around when maneuvering giving it its name."

"What happened to this submarine anyway, Ellen?" asked John. "I read that it was the newest, best ship in its class for some time. It apparently introduced a lot of new technology that advanced submarine capability tremendously. How did such an advanced ship go wrong?"

"The ship was launched in July, 1960," rejoined Ellen. "By March, 1962, she had taken part in many different trials and testing along the eastern coast of the U.S. as far as Puerto Rico, and was doing very well. She returned briefly to her New England launching port and then traveled to Florida for more testing. I believe a significant thing may have occurred when she was moored at Port Canaveral, in Florida. She was accidentally struck by a tugboat which damaged a ballast tank. It was supposedly repaired at Groton, Connecticut; and she did take part in more tests without incident later. On April 10th, 1963, the *Thresher* put to sea with the submarine rescue ship *Skylark* for deep-diving exercises which she hadn't done before. There were

17 civilian technicians aboard to observe the deep-diving tests, along with her 96 enlisted men and 16 officers. About fifteen minutes after reaching the first test site depth there were messages sent to the *Skylark* that some problems were occurring. The statements became garbled after that. A final rushing noise was heard by the *Skylark* over the underwater telephone communication and then nothing! No contact was ever able to be reestablished with the *Thresher* again, and it was only later on that the submarine rescue ship *Recovery* found bits of debris from the sub. The submersible bathyscaph *Trieste* showed that the *Thresher* had broken into pieces killing all those on board in 5500 feet of water about 220 miles east of Boston, Massachusetts. It was decided, after a court of inquiry, that a possible welding failure may have flooded the engine room causing electrical failures. This shut down the nuclear reactor which led to total power failure and loss of the ship. Fortunately, there have been no radiation problems from the monitoring of the site. Apparently the submarine lies in six pieces on the ocean floor, and the site has become a memorial for the people who lost their lives in the mishap. I wonder if that repair of the ballast tank injury when she was struck by the tug in port may have been at the root of the problem encountered in the deep dive. There may have been some hidden defect that only became a problem at the deep depth pressures. At any rate it should be a straightforward rescue mission, since no one was ever recovered and the crew we pick up will know their death is imminent. No body will have to be returned either; but I feel we should do it anyway, to honor the people who died there."

"Yes," said John. "I certainly agree with you there. It seems that we'll never lose our humanity after all, Ellen; at least the good part of it. The nutrient brain chemicals may keep us calm and introspective, but it looks like certain emotional parts of the human psyche are indestructible!"

"Actually," returned Ellen, "the Prime Mover agrees completely with honoring the dead. He feels that with humans having such a short lifespan, it should be important to memorialize people when they expire. He feels it will help the persons remaining behind to keep the ones who have perished in their memories. John, I believe we and the Gnormen think alike because we have some of their DNA; I wonder if what will develop in this new Gnor-human society will be what may have been predestined all along. There certainly has been some awfully coincidental history in both societies. We are beginning to have some really serious problems on Earth as they did on Mekan that could lead to our critical need of what the Gnor society has to offer—controlled population, a body that can live with pollution, and a psyche that thinks cooperation rather than competition. Add to this the discipline and responsibility now inherent naturally in the Gnormen and you have the makings of a pretty fair society. When it is right to do so, the ability to put another person's welfare before your own is becoming more and more lacking in a growing number of people in power on Earth today who are motivated by greed and self-interest! Maybe a Gnor-human society is the one and only way we can survive, seeing the path we seem to be heading along at this juncture. It is one of the main reasons why I want to make this Project successful!"

"As usual," said John, "everything you are saying, my darling Ellen, seems to me to be absolutely correct and I agree with it all. Maybe this is what the Universe has had in store for the human race all along. Our physiological evolution and much of our education has directed us to struggle against our environment in order to succeed. Maybe that has been wrong; maybe we should have been trying to understand and cooperate with the Universe around us and fit into it, not compete with it! Overpopulation and wrong choices technologically coupled with our 'competition-not-cooperation' mentality may be racing us down the path to extinction. This almost happened to the Gnormen until they realized the problem and changed their society. They controlled their population, learned how to create the ability to live and survive in their environment, went to the mandate of cooperation, not competition, and provided for everyone on their planet. They are still trying to fit into the Universe even more closely with our current Project. If successful, they will create a race that is an integral cooperating part of the Universe, not one that is fighting its dictums as some of Earth's peoples are doing now. It might be interesting to go ahead in time to see just exactly where the human race is going. Maybe changing the timeline might not be the bad thing that our Gnor friends seem to think it is! I gathered that when they were first experimenting with doing just that some dire consequences occurred. It could be possible that under different circumstances changing the timeline might create a much better future for the human race. I definitely think that we could consider an exploratory jaunt into the future later on when our daily activities aren't quite so hectic! Well, enough of this heady rumination, Ellen, I'm ready for more basic activity if you are. Let's get some rest; we have a big day ahead tomorrow with the Thresher rescue coming up."

They rose from their chairs and headed to the bedroom, John with his arm around Ellen's waist and her head leaning against his shoulder.

Using all the newly constructed scout vehicles and their recently trained Gnor-human pilots, the Thresher rescue went along without a hitch, and all 129 people on the submarine agreed to brain transfer. After this surgery was accomplished, all of the bodies were returned to one of the intact compartments remaining in one of the pieces of the vessel that enabled them to be sequestered from the creatures of the deep. It was very moving to all of the Gnor-human pilots when Lt. Kennedy played a choir singing *The Navy Hymn* over the communication intercom; after the last body was returned.

Eternal Father, strong to save,
Whose arm hath bound the restless wave,
Who bidd'st the mighty ocean deep
Its own appointed limits keep;
Oh, hear us when we cry to Thee,
For those in peril on the sea!

And when at length our course is run,

Our work for home and country done,
For all the souls that for them sailed
Let not one life for Thee have failed;
But hear from Earth our sailor's cry,
And grant eternal life on high!

Ellen, on the bridge of her and John's ship, was visibly moved by the soulful music.

"You know, John," she said softly, "if I had the ability to cry, I'd be bawling like a baby right now."

"I know how you feel," John answered. "It caused me to shiver all over. The words and music of that hymn are indeed extremely moving! That convinces me of two things. One, that we are still very much tied to our human emotions. Perhaps we always will be, in spite of these calming chemicals in our brain's nutrient fluid. And two, there could be a problem with some Gnor-humans wanting to get back and rejoin their loved ones. Of course, it's impossible for them to do so, but I know the Prime Mover has been concerned about this as well. He told me that this potential problem is discussed with each new Gnor-human transplant in the Life Factory, and fortunately there have been no transgressions as yet.

There is one other thing that this music brought to mind," he added with a grin. "We really must pressure Major Miller to get busy with his Gnor orchestra! Music would be wonderfully relaxing for us back on Mars in our apartment. His records are fine, but live music would be much more entertaining!" Ellen smiled broadly at the latter remark as she headed the scout vehicle back to the Starship. When the Starship arrived back on Mars John made good his suggestion and was successful in convincing Major Miller to think about forming an orchestra. The most convincing argument to the Major was the well-known fact that his band's music had been a very great morale-builder for the servicemen and women of WWII; and, of course, these people being rescued and transplanted were servicemen and women! He agreed that such music would definitely be morale-boosting to these people and promised that he would start the band formation project immediately! He had been told by Jol that apparently the chest bellows mechanism could be utilized in playing musical instruments by the synapses already present in brain-transferred musicians. He soon was able to find that many of the new Gnor-humans had musical skills, and the creation of the band was rapidly formed. This band was to become a source of extremely great entertainment and relaxation for both the humans and Gnormen, with the latter growing to love it as much as their human friends.

The next big rescue project was a massive undertaking! On her maiden voyage from England the ocean liner, HMS *Titanic*, was lost at sea off the coast of Nova Scotia on April 15th, 1912. At 2:20 am on that date the ship hit an iceberg and rapidly sank; losing one thousand five hundred twenty-six people to the cold North Atlantic Ocean. This time the people able to be recovered on this Project were no longer adult naval men and women, but instead were civilian men, women and, for the first time, children. At last Ellen would be able to work with Dr. Ran, Jol, and some of the Gnor-human health professionals on her suggestion that they attempt to create Gnor-human children and raise them to adulthood. She had felt that the responsibility to raise such a child would be beneficial to some of the Gnor-humans coping with their new lives and identities. The unknown factor present was that the children's brains would be in adult bodies, which they would have to adapt to while they matured into adulthood mentally. In theory, the children would properly mature mentally with guidance by surrogate older individuals acting as "parents" to them. This, of course, had never been considered before by the Gnormen, and its success was certainly unable to be guaranteed. Dr. Ran had suggested to Ellen that he and Jol might be able to construct a child-sized body that could be updated in size and form from time to time. And there was already present in the Life Factories the Gnormen precedence of aging an adult Gnor face every hundred years to mimic their ancestors changing form.

"I feel confident that we could accomplish this, Ellen," he had said. "It would mean more work for the Life Factory, but I'm sure they would enjoy the challenge. Besides, it is becoming clear that the emotional patterns that have formed in human brains cannot be dismissed very easily, as you are all showing. It took centuries for some of these feelings to become subsidiary in Gnor society, so there is no reason to think it will be any different in Gnor-human society. The intellectual process of logical thinking eventually will take over and run most of your actions as it does with us, but even we Gnormen still relish our emotions for the pleasure they bring to us. We haven't lost them; they just are secondary to our logic. It is obvious that most humans at this time are sometimes motivated by their emotions to their detriment; but some of them, like Secretary-General Hammarskjold, are motivated mostly by their logic as we are. Ellen, I am beginning to believe more and more that we should plan on emotions remaining in Gnor-humans. As such, Gnor-human children may be helpful to fill the emotional need for raising them that some Gnor-humans may require. As time passes this need may dissipate and its loss not be a problem as it might be now. I'm all for starting child rescues now and progressing with their education. We have garnered a few seafaring medical professionals already, but we shall have to look in earnest for some teachers like yourself and John now."

"Dik," rejoined Ellen, "we should get several teachers that were traveling on board the Titanic when she went down, according to my research on the sinking. I am excited about the prospect of rescuing children. Humans all seem to have the propensity to want to aid all children; I suppose it may be part of the procreation instinct developed to preserve the race. Perhaps I can give Jol and you some insights into human children's foibles to help you with their construction."

The devastation of the sinking of the *Titanic*, with the myriad of unidentified people struggling on the sinking ship and in the freezing water, would have made it almost impossible for them to make the appropriate rescues. Ellen suggested that she and John could transfer on board and try to locate and identify people known to have died and not been recovered. They both had studied the passenger list with pictures of the passengers extensively and could fairly accurately identify the ones that were going to come to an icy end. She suggested that if they were on board and could complete this location and identification before the iceberg hit the ship they would be best able to transfer the appropriate people using the Portal to the different scout vehicles. Even if they couldn't get to all the people that were never recovered, they could pick out ones that would probably be good candidates for transplantation. Otherwise, it looked like a nightmare of multiple forward and backward movement of the timeline to be sure they were getting the right people. Not even the Gnormen were anxious to encounter that much terror, pain and suffering repeatedly as they pulled people from the icy waters of the North Atlantic. The Prime Mover and the Council agreed with Ellen's suggestion, so plans were made for Zeltor to fly she and John to the *Titanic* on the evening of April 10, 1912 and transfer them to the ocean liner via the scout vehicle's Portal.

"We'll be back with all our ships the night of the sinking," said Zeltor. "You'll have to transfer as many people as you can on that fateful night. Don't forget yourselves, either. You know how many each ship can hold. Change your Portal's coordinates to the next ship when you fill one up. If you make a mistake of one or two people it won't be a problem. I'm going to transfer you now with your portable Portals to that large lifeboat on the aft deck. It might be a good place for you two to stay while you're on the ship. No one ever looks there, and if they do you can pretend to be lovers." He smiled broadly and said, "You see how humanized I've become? Well, good luck, you two; I'll see you in four nights!" With that he activated the Portal and Ellen and John found themselves in the back of the aft deck lifeboat on board the HMS *Titanic* four days before it was to hit the iceberg and go to a watery grave.

The two emerged from the aft lifeboat after concealing their two Portals there and began to wander around the ship, mingling with the passengers. They found, as they had read, that there were several different "classes" of passengers on the ship that had staterooms befitting the amount they had paid for their transit across the ocean. The poorest passengers were situated on the lower decks and obviously were the ones that didn't have a chance to escape when the ship went down. Because this was the maiden voyage of a new class of ocean liner, there were several rich and famous people on board. In the end, great heroism was shown by many of these individuals in sacrificing themselves to make room for the women and children on board the small number of lifeboats on the ship. Ellen and John tried to identify and mark the location as rapidly as possible of the people that were to die without recovery so they would be able to transport them by Portal to the scout vehicles on the night of the disaster.

On their wanderings through the lower decks Ellen came across a pretty little girl that she confessed to John looked exactly like she had looked when she was about that age. She started a conversation with the child, who had an English accent, and found out her name was Molly. She said she was six years old and was traveling to America to live with an aunt that she had never met in Halifax, Nova Scotia. Her mother and father had died of the pox recently; but her mother had arranged for her to go to this relative if she and her husband did not survive their illnesses. Molly was a friendly, sweet little girl and Ellen fell in love with her almost immediately. Review of the historical listings revealed that Molly would not survive the ship's sinking. For the next couple of days Ellen found herself being drawn to the lower decks whenever she could to be with the little girl. Molly reciprocated Ellen's affection and the two of them quickly became fast friends. Ellen was worried that Molly might not be able to get up from the lower decks when the ship was sinking as the lower deck people were not allowed to visit the upper decks where the wealthy people resided. The connections from the lower decks were often locked for that reason so Ellen tried to arrange by subterfuge some way for Molly to be where Ellen could get to her so she could transfer her. By the third night on board, John and Ellen realized that only the upper decks people would be able to be positively identified and located by them. They were able to identify only a small number of the below decks individuals, including Molly, for transfer. It would be relatively easy to transfer the upper deck people as it was expected they would all congregate in the Great Hall and could be transferred en mass by the Portal. They knew that they would have to travel around the ship as it was sinking to locate other passengers for transfer over to the scout vehicles. They decided it would be necessary for them each to split up with a separate Portal to be able to get as many as possible of these other passengers transferred.

"Please remember, my dearest Ellen," said John, as they were discussing their last minute transfer plans in the aft lifeboat, "just make sure that *you* get aboard the scout ship in time. We can always manipulate the time warp and do this again if we have to. I don't know what I'd do if anything happened to you!" He drew her to him and kissed her firmly on the lips.

"I'm just as worried about you, darling," answered Ellen. "Just make sure you do the same! John, there is one thing I must discuss with you about some of the people we are to transfer. At my current time in history there are many corporate business leaders who have piled up tremendous amounts of money by various dishonest schemes that have put millions of people out of work and caused trillions of hard-earned investor's retirement life savings to be lost in order to accumulate obscene sums of money for themselves. The leaders of five such companies; Enron, Global Crossing, Tyco, WorldCom and Health South Corporation have been singled out for investigation with possible jail sentencing depending upon the outcome of the investigations. The CEO's of most of these companies have been educated with the economic concept that a CEO of a company should accept a salary no greater than twenty-five times the lowest salary of the company. Current studies in my time in history have shown that many CEO's take home salaries over five hundred ninety times the lowest salary in their companies. I am convinced that ruthless and greedy people such as these should not be considered for our brain transfer; and there are some present on this ship. I really feel that a transfer of one of these individuals could become very dangerous if the greed, dishonesty, and selfishness in that brain is allowed to reside in a powerful long-lived Gnor-human body. John, would you please check my list where I have identified some of the ones I feel will not be good candidates for transplanting and tell me if you agree with my assessment of them and my suggestion not to transfer them."

"You most assuredly are right about this, Ellen," said John after reviewing her list. "We both know that there are humans out there that will have to evolve much more to get even close to the ethics and morals that our Gnormen friends have evolved to already. And Gnor-human longevity could work very detrimentally in greedy, criminal hands, even with the calming chemicals present now in our brain's nutrient fluid. I agree with you, and I concur with your list. We won't take any of the ones you've identified. We may have to get some of them out of the Great Hall when we transfer that group en mass, but we should be able to do it by suggesting a special lifeboat is available just for them at another place. Their self-centered ego will probably make them leave quickly. We better get some sleep now; we'll still need to look below decks for people tomorrow, the last day of our preparation!" John put his arms around Ellen and drew her to him, and they settled down in the aft lifeboat "apartment", their arms intertwined.

On the night the iceberg hit the great liner, pandemonium broke out all over the ship as people raced about seeking passage on one of the too few lifeboats available. Ellen and John were able to get the large number of people that had accumulated in the Great Hall transferred over to the scout vehicles with very little trouble. They had been able to remove the ones from the Great Hall that they had decided not to transfer by telling them that a special lifeboat was being prepared for them in another area of the ship. Then the two of them split up to try and transfer as many of the targeted men, women, and children that they had researched were eligible to be rescued. Ellen immediately went to the area where she thought she had told Molly to be but when she arrived at the place the child was not there.

She searched around and shouted her name but was unable to find the little girl anywhere. The water pouring into the lower decks forced her to abandon the search for Molly, so she again concentrated on locating the other passengers on her list to transfer them over to the scout vehicles with her Portal. Finally, with the cold sea water continuing to pour in all around her, she could not locate any more of the people listed for her to transfer. She decided to try one more time to find Molly and went lower into the sinking ship. She didn't find the little girl and suddenly found herself trapped below deck as someone had locked the escape door; presumably to seal off the rising water in that compartment. She was forced with a heavy heart to conclude that Molly was probably drowned, and she set the coordinates of the Portal to Zeltor's ship where she and John had agreed to transfer to.

She arrived on board Zeltor's scout vehicle amidst a large crowd of frightened, confused people and looked around anxiously for John. She saw his head above the crowd over in the corner and made her way toward him with great relief and joy. As she got close to where he was, he spied her and pushed toward her through the crowd. When they met they threw their arms around each other and John said, "I brought along a little friend who's almost as glad to see you as I am, my darling." He moved aside and there was Molly, who Ellen immediately picked up and gave her a big hug which the little girl returned.

"I was so scared, Ellen," the little girl sobbed, "the water was pouring in all around me, and then John came and took me over here by magic! I'm so glad that you were rescued too, Ellen." And she gave Ellen another big hug.

"Yes dear," said Ellen with her eyes sparkling, "that John surely is pretty magical, isn't he?" The three of them stood together in the middle of the milling crowd with their arms around each other.

Ellen and John had been able to rescue about one thousand people from the Titanic. That had included a few teachers and several medical personnel; which, for one thing, would certainly prove useful to help with the increasing number of transplanting operations that would be needed as the Gnor-human society continued to grow. They would also be needed for a time to help Dr. Ran with any human medical problems; since all the rescued people would have to stay in his "oxygen quarters" until they were able to have their operation and no longer need to breathe it. Major Glenn Miller and Lt. Jack Morgan had been able to capture the entire ship's band with most of their instruments to their ship; as they had all opted to give up their seats in the lifeboats to the women and children. John told the pilots jokingly that he had arranged the transfer to help with the Major's orchestra quest. These men had bravely continued to play appropriate hymns even though they knew the ship was carrying them to their deaths. Hence, all their instruments came with them in the transfer. Major Miller was very proud of these men and knew they would add considerably to the new Gnor-human orchestra he was developing.

Surprisingly enough everyone rescued opted for the brain transplantation rather than death at sea. A good deal of that decision was helped by the presence all around them of the previously rescued Gnor-human seafarers. Ellen and John's passionate discussions with them about their feelings and hopes for the kind of society envisioned by the Prime Mover and the other Gnormen also helped a great deal. Many of the wealthy famous people on board had sacrificed themselves and given up their seats on the lifeboats so that their loved ones and other women and children could be saved. These were the first to see and agree to the vision of the Prime Mover and Secretary-General Dag Hammarskjold. They were to become ideal candidates for leadership roles as the Gnor-human society and its cities on Mars continued to increase in size and number.

Jol and Dr. Ran had designed a child-sized Gnor body for Molly that was a little bigger than her present human one. They would design succeeding Gnor bodies at appropriate intervals that would gradually let her mature into an adult size in a natural way. The sensation and coordination in this smaller body, however, would have to be as effective as an adult one; it would be too cumbersome to fashion changeable neuron control to mimic a growing human child. Molly would have to get used to being able to do things physically as well as an adult even though her body was smaller. They were both confident her brain would be able to do this and that the transfer would be very successful physically. But how would they broach it to the little girl so she could understand what was going to happen to her? They knew that she adored Ellen and that only Ellen would be able to convince her to have the operation.

Ellen had been going over daily to the oxygen quarters to be with Molly. On this day she decided that she would start to teach the little girl about the Gnor-humans to get her to understand that no serious changes and no harm comes to people who have the operation. She sat in the library where she had first fallen in love with John, awaiting Molly's entrance.

"Hi, Ellen," said the little girl, entering the room. "Where's John? What are we going to do today?"

"Well, Molly," answered Ellen, "John has a meeting and may not be able to make it today; but I thought I might tell you a little about John and I and what we are doing way up here on Mars!"

"Where's Mars?" asked Molly. "Is it anywhere near Halifax, Nova Scotia?" The girl's lower lip began to tremble a tiny bit and her eyes began to fill up with tears.

"Why, what's the matter, Molly," said Ellen, and she went over and picked her up and placed her in her lap. "Tell me what's troubling you, dear."

"Well, Ellen," and Molly was crying now, "I really don't know my aunt at all, and I love you and don't want to leave you! I know my mommy arranged for me to go live with my aunt, but I'm sure that she would much rather I stayed with you, Ellen."

Ellen gave the little girl a hug and kissed her on the cheek. "Molly, you know that's just how I feel about you, too. I'm glad you want to stay with me and we're going to do just that! You won't have to go to your aunt, and you can stay with me and be my little girl if you want to." Molly's eyes lit up immediately and her tears stopped like a faucet had been turned off.

"Do you mean it?" she almost squealed. "I can stay with you and be your little girl? Oh, Ellen, I do want to stay with you. I do!" She threw her arms about Ellen's neck and hugged her.

"Well then, it's all settled," said Ellen with a broad smile on her face. "You are now officially my little girl! And dear, I feel very lucky to have you!" Just then John walked into the room.

"Oh John!" exclaimed Molly. "Ellen's going to let me stay with her forever and ever, and be her little girl!"

"Hey, that's wonderful, Molly!" said John. "But can I have a little piece of you too, honey? You know, I don't have any children either." Molly ran to John and hugged him.

"Sure you can, John," she said. "Say, since my mommy and daddy aren't with me anymore, could you and Ellen be my new mommy and daddy?"

John looked at Ellen who was beaming at the both of them. "If it's OK with Ellen, honey; it's certainly OK with me!"

"Well, Ellen," asked Molly, "is it OK?"

"Of course it is, darling," answered Ellen. "It's certainly not hard for me to love both of you very much."

"Well then, it's all settled," said Molly. "Can I come and live with you in your quarters now, Ellen? I like the kids and the people here but I'd much rather be living with you two." Ellen glanced over with an apprehensive look at John.

"Molly," said Ellen slowly, "right now you won't be able to come live with us. It's not because we don't want you to come right now, but where we live there is no air for you to breathe. John and I have a special body that doesn't need to breathe the way you do. That's why you're over in these quarters where there is air for you to breathe. As soon as we can fix you up like us so you won't have to breathe air, you can come live with us and travel all around everywhere with us. Would you like us to do that for you?"

"How will you do that, Ellen?" asked Molly. "Will it hurt?"

"Oh no, dear," Ellen answered, "you won't even know it's being done; and afterwards it won't hurt and you can live with us for many,

many years."

"It's an operation, isn't it?" said Molly. "I heard some of the people here talking about it. They said it didn't hurt at all. Can you be with me, Ellen, if I have it?"

"Of course, dear," answered Ellen. "I'll be right in the room with you and you can stay in John and my quarters afterwards when the doctors will allow it."

"When will they do it?" asked Molly.

"Soon, dear," answered Ellen. "I'll speak to Dr. Ran and he will arrange it sometime next week. OK?"

"OK," said Molly. "Will you finish reading me that story we started the other day now, Ellen. John can stay and hear it too if he wants."

"Unfortunately, John has a meeting he has to go to, dear," said Ellen. "See, he's already acting like a daddy and is going off to work. But you and I will stay and enjoy the story, won't we?"

"Sure we will," answered Molly. "Bye, Daddy," she said to John as he went out the library door with a big smile on his face. In the outside corridor he ran into Dik Ran.

"My Ellen has done it again!" he said to the Gnorman. "Your operation on Molly is all set for next week!"

"That's great!" said Dik. "Molly will be the pioneer who will help the other children decide for the operation!"

"Just like her new 'mother' Ellen did for the rest of us!" rejoined John.

Ellen went into the OR with Molly the day she had her operation, and left just before they started the procedure. The neurosurgeons removed the little girl's brain without incident and installed it carefully into the Gnor head and child-sized body that Jol and his colleagues had fashioned for her. Her Gnor head was only slightly smaller than an adult head as human brains were pretty much as large as they would ever be at Molly's age. She tolerated the operation well and was transported into the special care unit where many transplant Gnor-humans were recovering from their recent operations as well.

Ellen went in to visit her, but was greatly distressed when the little girl remained unconscious with no seeming responses at all to any outside stimuli.

"Dik," she queried Dr. Ran anxiously, as he had just entered the room to check on Molly, "what's wrong? Molly isn't responding at all. Is she all right? She acts like she's...she's dead! Didn't the operation go OK?"

Dr. Ran took Ellen by the hand and sat her down in a nearby chair.

"Ellen, relax!" he said to her. "Of course Molly won't respond yet. Her brain has to link up with her lower Gnor body before you'll see any response, and that takes some time. Fortunately, she won't remember much of the linking up time; but we will just have to wait to see how good her linking up functioning develops. It took you a couple of months to link up; and John about five weeks. Some of the others have varied from five to twenty weeks with an average of twelve weeks. Human children have the propensity to grow fairly rapidly so I would anticipate that Molly will break the speed record for link up time. We'll just have to wait and see." He went over to Molly's bedside and activated a device near her head.

"No, Ellen," he said, "everything looks great! Molly's brain is alive and responding appropriately. Why don't you go outside and comfort John; he's out there pacing like an expectant father. Boy, I haven't used that phrase in a long time! Go ahead, Ellen; Molly's doing fine!"

Ellen was obviously very relieved and went out into the corridor and caught John as he was pacing by.

"Well," he said anxiously. "How is she? Is everything OK? What did Dik say?" John was visibly upset and worried about the little girl. Ellen put her arms on his shoulders and smiled.

"She's fine, Dad," she answered, "Dik just checked her and said everything is going along as they had hoped. It apparently takes some time for the brain to link up with the rest of the body. We will have to wait and see what will develop. Dik says you took five weeks and I took eight weeks; but that Molly may do it quicker because children grow faster than adults do. They were pretty much able to preserve her face and hair the way it was before. She looked as sweet as ever lying there in the bed. Like Sleeping Beauty waiting to be awakened by a kiss from her Prince." Ellen smiled and gently caressed John's forehead to smooth away his wrinkles of concern. "You're already acting like a good father, my dear. It's just another clue that our human emotions are still very much alive!" John's frown eased on his face and changed into a smile. He put his arms around Ellen and embraced and kissed her; now visibly relieved by her words. His face suddenly clouded up again.

"But how will she get her daily oxygen and food capsule if her circuits aren't connected yet?"

"That's why she stays in the special care unit, silly," replied Ellen. "They will feed her until she can do it herself, just as you and I and the others have done. Now stop worrying and come help me get Molly's room ready for when she comes to live with us." Ellen took his arm and steered him toward the exit from the special care unit.

"I'll tell you, Ellen dear," said John, now much more relaxed, "Molly and I are sure lucky to have you to love." And he gave the arm with which she was steering him a squeeze as they exited the unit into the outside corridor.

Molly came along very rapidly as Dr. Ran had predicted and was soon able to join Ellen and John in their quarters to live with them. She was delighted with the room they had prepared for her and seemed to be progressing nicely. She was handling her adult sensations and coordination remarkably well. She proudly announced to Ellen that she was "really very strong for a little girl" and loved it! She also seemed to take her much keener sensations in stride as well and was obviously happy to be Ellen and John's "little girl" and be living with them. Ellen realized that she would have to start teaching Molly both human and especially Gnor history and philosophy if the little girl were to make a smooth transition into adulthood. She was grateful that Jol had not put adult erotic area neurons into Molly as yet; that would be done later when she was more mature and had another more adult sized body made for her. Ellen remarked that Jol was becoming quite an artist as he continued to design a step up series of increasingly older children. This would allow any children they transplanted to gradually ease physically into adulthood as their minds matured. She was glad that she would be spared the need to have to teach the delicate instructions concerning reproduction to Molly; but it occurred to her that it might be more difficult to explain to her why it wasn't needed anymore. Obviously, the Gnor-human condition must be explained to the little girl as soon as possible; the rest of her teaching would flow much more easily after she accepted that.

When the Prime Mover saw how well Ellen was doing with Molly's teaching he asked her if she would set up a school for all the children and help to recruit teachers from the Gnor-humans that had had some experience in that field. Ellen was happy to do this, and became the principal of the new school for the children they named the "Mars Institute".

"It's very appropriate that you be the principal," said John teasingly. "After all, Professor James, you did teach history at the college level."

"Seriously, John," said Ellen, "with the children possessing adult Gnor bodies, it is imperative that we teach them the Gnor ethical and moral standards immediately. We both know the highly competitive state that many human children get into. I believe that could be very detrimental to their mental development and eventual happiness. We must teach them the Gnor values of cooperation, not competition. I hope the calming brain nutrients we Gnor-humans all now have will aid us in getting the children to accept this way of life. If one child is more athletically gifted and another a little smarter, we must teach the other children not to be jealous of that individual; but they should compliment that person for their gift and be happy for them. And we must teach the gifted children to be humble about their superior abilities and look to help the other children to improve in the areas that they are so well skilled in. Cooperation, not competition! Thinking of the other person or for the good of the whole group before yourself! It's going to be a tough job, John! Up to now humans have all been schooled in competing to gain for themselves, not in cooperating to help others as the Gnormen do. A majority of the corporate business and legal leaders of my time laugh at and look down on people who think of the other person before themselves. They champion the concept of getting everything you can for yourself at the expense of any one person, group, or environment in your way; and they don't hesitate to try any kind of underhanded, fraudulent activity as long as they think they can get away with it. When they are successful in one of these endeavors, they look upon it with great admiration; and brag about it in their boardrooms closed to the public. There have been scores of dishonest, fraudulent dealings by corporate business leaders recently, at great detriment to thousands of people; and it looks like the trend in young people today is towards more of the same! Our entertainers, sports heroes, and a rapidly developing class of immensely wealthy people don't even come close to what they should be doing to help those less fortunate than they are. First of all they certainly don't deserve the enormous sums of money they accept in salary. The Gnormen laugh at the concept of getting a salary for doing something; they work at their special skills for the betterment of all the people in their society; not for a select few as we do. The growing gap between the very wealthy and a burgeoning group of less fortunate people now occurring in my time will most assuredly lead to disaster if this trend of selfishness is not reversed. The United States continues to consume most of the world's goods with only a modicum of its population. Many of these corporate business leaders have already destroyed many of the planet's life forms and environment with their selfish greed in developing the world for their profits. This has led to the U.S. being hated all around the globe—a sad byproduct of a successful competitive philosophy. There are several new non-polluting alternative energy sources available to everyone if people were encouraged to develop them. Unfortunately, the petroleum industry continues to suppress their rapid introduction to keep its highly polluting energy source as the main supply for the world's energy needs while they are maneuvering to gain control of the technology for their own profiteering. This will guarantee their continued obscene wealth. Yes, John; we already have some very detrimental concepts influencing our children now and it will be a great task to clear them from their minds."

"Granted, it will be a difficult job," returned John, "But who better to do it than you, darling. You know, sometimes I think you are more Gnorman than the Gnormen themselves. It makes me love you that much more. And just think, I have about 900 plus years to continue that love!"

Ellen smiled at John's last remark, and it made her feel very warm inside as usual. She loved the way he could lighten up a serious conversation between them with a few words that would totally defuse the discussion and make her feel good about it.

Molly's recuperation from her operation was complete now and she was progressing very well in the school Ellen was teaching at. The school now had five children in it from the Titanic disaster. Amelia and Fred were sponsoring one girl, and three other Gnor-human women were sponsoring the other two boys and another girl. The school was run on an as available basis until more teachers could be recruited to be there all the time. Ellen still continued with her Gnor-human rescue sorties with John and Dr. Ran, which often caused the school sessions to be discontinued until she returned. Finally, she was able to get enough permanent teachers on a regular basis to teach the program she had created. Three Gnor-human women had come forth and volunteered to become permanent teachers at the Institute, much to Ellen's relief. All three had excellent credentials to do the work and felt privileged to have such a job in their new life which allowed them to continue what they had done back on Earth. Ellen's program included Gnor and human history; and espoused cooperation rather than competition, along with the ethics and morals of the Gnor race that she felt were critical for the children to understand and accept as their own way of life. Ellen felt it was very important to remove all possibility of the children adopting any of the selfish, greedy, amoral attitudes that were rampant today in many of the human leaders in business, law, sports, entertainment, and the different governments. This allowed Ellen to have more time to be with Molly and John and to do the historical research and various rescue missions that she loved. She kept control of the institute as its principal and had time to keep up to date on the progress of the school and what it was teaching.

Molly was out of school session at this time and was insatiably curious about Ellen's various trips to Earth for research or rescue missions. At first Ellen was reluctant to take Molly with her to Earth, but finally relented to the little girl's very frequent appeals to go with her "mother" on her trips to the planet. On this mission Ellen was planning to look up some data on an accident that had occurred in the state she had lived in. The only available data was in the library of the city where she had had the altercation with the two hoodlums about a little over a year ago. The necessary information was in an old book that was the only copy still extant, and it could only be read in the library and not taken out. Ellen had the recording setup of extremity wiring that Dort and Zandor had used originally to gather information about humans on the planet, and she planned to copy the book for its list of people that had perished. She was worried about Detective Sarah Jones, to whom she had given her old phone number and address for contacting her when the arraignment of the two hoodlums who had attacked her was to be done. The detective had impressed Ellen with her competence and compassion, and if she had called that number and checked that address she would have found out that the woman she had serviced was actually dead! She wondered if the detective might have become curious about this and looked further into her history. Because of this she hopefully planned to avoid the detective during Molly and her brief stay at the library. Dr. Ran was to accompany Ellen, Molly and the pilot, Zeltor as he wanted to get some medical data from another city close to Ellen's destination. He said he would wait with Zeltor for Ellen's mission to be completed and would stop off at the other city on the way back to the Starship. As it turned out later it was fortunate that he had planned it that way and was on the ship with Zeltor when Ellen signaled to come back on board.

Ellen and Molly had no problem entering the library or receiving the book to read in a special protected-environment room. The librarian explicitly described the particulars of protecting the book from any damage while reading it. Ellen wanted to get started copying the book and get out of town as quickly as possible, so she told her that she was a professor of history at college and would be very careful of the book. The librarian eyed Molly with some anxiety and suggested to Ellen that perhaps Molly could play out on the swings in the library's courtyard so she wouldn't harm the book inadvertently. Ellen agreed that it would be OK for Molly to do that as she wanted to get rid of the librarian who remained in the room apparently to protect the book from the little girl. She told Molly to stay in the courtyard and she would pick her up there after she had read the part of the book she was interested in. With this the librarian and Molly left the special room and Ellen began to copy the book. After she had obtained all the information she needed, she signaled the librarian to retrieve the book and thanked her for her time and effort. She then went out into the courtyard to retrieve Molly from the swings, but they were all empty and the little girl was nowhere to be seen! Ellen looked around frantically but Molly was gone! She rushed back into the library and asked the librarian if she had seen her.

"Why, no!" answered the librarian. "Isn't she outside on the swings? I left her there a little while ago." She rushed to the courtyard door and they both went out and looked all around the building inside and out, but Molly was nowhere to be found!

"Oh my God!" exclaimed the librarian. "She's been kidnapped! I'm going to call the police at once!" She rushed to the phone and dialed 911. "Hello, police? I'm reporting a young girl about six or seven years old who we think has been kidnapped from the Green Street city library about a half hour ago. Please send someone up here right away!" She returned over to Ellen, whose mind was racing as to what she would do next. They were some distance from the site where she had stashed the gravity packs and communication device to call Zeltor to pick her and Molly up. By the time she arrived there to get Zeltor to use the sensors to try and track Molly she might be too far away for them to be able to sense her. As she dashed out of the library to search the surrounding area, a police cruiser pulled up at the curb in front of the library and out stepped...Detective Sarah Jones.

"Hello, Madge," said Detective Jones to the librarian, "what's going on here? You say a little girl has been kidnapped?"

"That's right, Sarah," answered the librarian. "This is Ms. James, her mother."

"James?" said the detective, peering closely at Ellen. "Not Ellen James? Yes, I recognize you now. About a little over a year ago you had an altercation with two men with long criminal records. We were unable to convict them because we couldn't find you to testify against them. Their shyster lawyer got them off because of it. You must have given me the wrong phone number because our secretary said the woman was dead who had had that number when she called it. The address was also incorrect as the person who had lived there was also dead and the room was occupied by a different person. What ever happened to you, Ms. James?"

"Well, Detective Jones," answered Ellen, "when I didn't get a telephone call I assumed I wasn't needed for the trial. But right now I'm desperately afraid that my daughter has been kidnapped! Can you help me Detective Jones?" Ellen's tone and the look on her face caused the detective to start thinking about the little girl's possible plight and she looked up and down the street to see if anyone was around who might have seen anything suspicious. She noticed an old woman sitting on a porch across the street from the library and hurried across to her with Ellen right on her heels.

"I'm Detective Jones from the police department, ma'am," she said to the old woman. "Did you see a little girl about six or seven around here recently? This woman with me is her mother, and we think her daughter has been kidnapped."

"Why yes, detective," answered the old woman. "You say she was kidnapped? A little girl came from the swings around back of the library holding the hand of a blonde man. They got into an old black 1990 four-door Subaru Legacy sedan and drove up the street. I know the car well as my son had one just like it, only his was blue."

"Did he have a big blonde handlebar mustache ma'am?" asked Detective Jones.

"Why yes, he did, detective," she answered. "Do you know him?"

"I think so ma'am," said Sarah. "If it's who I think it is, he lives in the last house a couple of miles up the road in the direction you saw them going. Thanks very much for your help! Come on, Ellen! We've no time to lose. This is a bad egg if it's who I think it is!"

"What do you mean, 'bad egg', detective?" asked Ellen, hurrying along beside the detective. They reached the cruiser and both jumped in.

"His name is Carl Jenkins," said Sarah. "He has a long rap of abusing children along with many other crimes of passion as well. And please call me Sarah, Ellen. Detective seems too formal for what we're engaged in right now."

"Thanks, Sarah," said Ellen. "What do you plan to do?"

"We're in a little trouble right now, Ellen," answered Sarah. "I can't call for back up because my radio is down. Carl lives out of town, away from the department and I'm afraid time is of the essence if we're going to save your daughter from any trauma he might inflict on her. That's his house up ahead! I'm going to go in and corral him and see if he has your daughter. You stay here; hopefully I'll be back shortly with your daughter. If something happens, take the cruiser back to the station and get someone out here as fast as you can!" She drew her revolver and rushed to the front door of the house. She knocked on the door, announced it was the police, and called for the man within to open up the door.

The door opened and a blond man with a large mustache fired a revolver point blank at Sarah's chest. As she was falling she fired two shots into his chest, and he dropped to the floor of the porch and lay immobile there. Ellen rushed to Sarah's side and saw she was still alive but gravely injured. At that moment Ellen heard a cry from within the house.

"Mommy, mommy," called Molly. "Is that you? Come and untie me. That bad man lied to me about some kittens he was going to show me and tied me up!" Ellen rushed into the squalid house and freed her daughter and carried her outside.

It was obvious to Ellen that Sarah was dying from the chest bullet wound. They were only a short run from where she had stashed her gravity pack and communicator.

"Molly," said Ellen, "you stay here with Sarah and hold her head up so she can breathe better. I'm going to call Zeltor to come at once to pick us up. We must get Sarah to Dr. Ran on the scout vehicle so he can stabilize her and save her life. Can I trust you to help Sarah?"

"Of course you can, Mommy," answered Molly. "Now hurry, this lady looks awfully sick!"

"That's my good girl," smiled Ellen and dashed off into the woods to the communicator. "Zeltor, bring the ship to these coordinates immediately, and have Dik ready to treat a human woman who has been shot in the chest saving Molly. It is the same detective I ran into here a little over a year ago and she remembered me! Hurry, she is dying!"

The ship quickly arrived and both Zeltor and Dr. Ran came down with gravity packs and resuscitative equipment to get Sarah up to the ship. Ellen took herself and Molly up with her pack and Zeltor and Dr. Ran carried Sarah up between them. On the ship Dr. Ran was able to stabilize Sarah and she regained consciousness. She looked around in astonishment at the scout vehicle and then caught sight of Ellen standing beside her bed.

"Did we get your daughter out OK, Ellen?" she murmured.

"Yes, you did," answered Ellen, "Here she is. This is my daughter Molly, Sarah." Molly came up to the bed.

"Thanks for saving me, Sarah," said Molly. "You're very brave for a pretty lady. You're a lot like my mother!"

"You're welcome, dear," said Sarah. She fell back on her pillow and then drifted off to sleep from the sedative that Dr. Ran had given her.

"Did I do the right thing, Dik," said Ellen. "If I had let her die, there would be no chance of her tracking me down and discovering our Projects here on Earth. But I couldn't just let her die; she had just saved Molly! I knew I'd never be able to get her to a hospital that I didn't know the whereabouts of in time to save her. I just thought of you and how many times you had stabilized and saved so many, so I opted to bring her here. And besides," she trailed off, "I really like her."

"You did exactly the right thing, Ellen," said Dr. Ran. "She might or might not have died, so we will have the dilemma of transplanting her or keeping her alive with me in my oxygen quarters. For now I will try to save her and let her remain with us as a living human woman. We can work out the exigencies later. I do know that with our present situation she probably shouldn't ever go back to Earth! What may happen in the future we will have to wait to find out? On the lighter side, it will be nice to no longer be the only totally living being in the Gnor society on Mars presently choosing to stay in that state.

Sarah awoke in a hospital bed at the Gnor home city on Mars; of course she didn't know she was on Mars! The problem of her oxygen need was handled by the fact that oxygen was present in the Life Factory atmosphere where it was needed for the many surgeries done on living humans in that facility. Even on Mekan the Life Factories there also had oxygen since it was present naturally in the planet's atmosphere. She was being administered extra oxygen through a nasal cannula and, except for some serious discomfort in her right chest, and profound weakness, she was amazed that she was still alive. Presently Dr. Ran entered the room and approached her bedside.

"Well, how are you feeling this morning, Sarah?" he inquired cheerfully. "You're looking much better after your surgery. It was touch and go for awhile there, but you have rallied well and are now most certainly out of the woods. Of course, you'll be weak and pretty tired for awhile yet, but that will improve with a little more time."

"Thank you, doctor," said Sarah. "I guess I have you people to thank for saving my life; I am very grateful to you all."

"Actually, it was probably Ellen who was most instrumental in saving you, Sarah," said Dr. Ran. "If she had tried to find a hospital in a city she didn't know very well instead of calling us, you most assuredly would have died."

"What do you mean, doctor, by 'us'?" asked Sarah. "Who are you people? Am I not here in City Hospital? If not, then where am I?"

Just then Ellen, John, and Molly entered the room and approached Sarah's bed.

"Hello, Sarah," said Ellen. "It's good to see you looking better. You had us worried for awhile there, but Dr. Ran tells us you are over the critical period and should recover fully in a little more time. That's good to hear." She turned to John and introduced him, "Sarah, this is my husband, Dr. John Scott; and you remember my daughter Molly."

Molly moved closer to Sarah and took hold of her hand; Sarah noticed the little girl's hand was cool to the touch. "I'm so happy that you're better, Detective Jones. I'm awfully glad you didn't die saving me from that bad man." She stretched way over and kissed Sarah on the cheek; Sarah noted that Molly's face was also cool like her hand.

"That's OK, Molly," said the detective. "I'm real glad I didn't die too; and I guess I have your mother to thank for that." She looked at Ellen and smiled. Then she turned to John and said, "I'm happy to know you, Dr. Scott; you've got a remarkable wife!"

"I'm glad to meet you too, Detective Jones; Ellen has told me about how you saved Molly with little regard for your own safety. I'm so grateful Dr. Ran and his colleagues were able to save you, and restore you to normal." He took Sarah's hand and gave it a gentle squeeze; she noticed that his hand was also cool like his daughter's was.

"Ellen," said Sarah, "Dr. Ran tells me I am not in City Hospital. If not there, then where am I? I don't have any relatives to contact, but the department will want to know how I'm coming along. I was scheduled to go on leave right after my shift ended the day we rescued Molly; so the department might think I just took off. I'm sure they're wondering what happened to me if you haven't told them. They certainly will wonder about the abandoned cruiser and Carl's body on his porch."

"We knew that would be true," said Dr. Ran, "so we sent someone back to return the cruiser to the station and inform them of what had happened and your immediate transfer to our facility for emergency care. You can consider talking to them later on when you're stronger; now you need rest." He picked up Sarah's hand and she noticed his hand was quite warm; different from the other two hands she had felt. "We can talk about all this later on but now you should rest, young lady! Ellen, John and Molly will be back to see you later on when you're stronger; and I'll be seeing you right along, probably more than you'll want!" Sarah smiled at the doctor and said with obvious emotion, "There's no way that will ever happen, doctor." And she squeezed the doctor's hand. With that all smiled, took their leave, and left the room. Sarah mulled over everything she had been told, but continued to wonder where she was and about the mystery of Ellen James. Finally, she drifted off to sleep.

Sarah mended very rapidly under Dr. Ran's excellent care and soon began to think about contacting her police captain to tell him about when she would be able to return to duty. She had decided to ask the doctor about his predictions for when she could leave the hospital. She felt a little twinge thinking about leaving; acknowledging to herself that she would miss Dr. Ran a great deal. She secretly hoped he was not married and wished that by some miracle he might consider dating her after she was able to leave. Little did she know that the doctor actually felt very much attracted to her as well and wanted to tell her so; but felt it might be inappropriate because of the doctor-patient relationship between them.

Dr. Ran entered Sarah's room that morning fully realizing that she would soon be ready to be discharged from the hospital and that he had to tell her the truth about what had happened to her. He had decided to have the Prime Mover and others relate to her more completely the Gnor history and the reasons for their project here on Earth. He would give her some preliminary explanations and then take her to the hospital conference room where the Prime Mover, Ellen and John would be in attendance to further explain to her why they were here on Earth. Deep down he admitted to himself that he was very much attracted to this human woman, and secretly hoped that she would stay here on Mars for the present as a living woman. He knew, however, that the most logical outcomes would be to either have a brain transfer, or go back to the planet and try to survive in an Earth hospital. He would broach these possibilities with her this morning before the conference with the others. He entered Sarah's room and found her standing by her bedside.

"Good morning, Sarah," he said cheerfully. "Are you feeling as good as you look today?"

"Yes, Dr. Ran," she answered, blushing slightly. "I actually feel quite strong today and walking around the room seemed almost effortless for me in spite of my recent surgery. I was told by the nurse that it was a fine day, although there are no windows in my room so I really don't know what it is like outside."

"You seem stronger," said Dr. Ran, "because the gravity in this area is only 0.4 as much as you are used to. It has helped you to recover from your surgery. Please, Sarah," said Dr. Ran, "I'd like you to call me Dik, as Ellen and John do. We have known each other for some time now, and I would like for us to be on a first name basis if you feel the same way."

"Oh, I do doctor...Dik," Sarah answered. She hoped her voice didn't betray how excited she was over his request!

"You know, Sarah," said Dik, "you haven't ever told me much about yourself. You did tell us you had no relatives. It's hard to believe such an attractive, competent, compassionate woman like you has no husband or family."

Sarah felt excitement rising within her at his words, "Why thank you, Dik. You're too kind! Actually I was married for almost eight years. My husband, Jim, was an assistant district attorney and was killed in the courthouse about a year ago by a felon who had a gun. I have only recently come to terms with this; my job has helped me. We didn't have any children as he had had a severe case of mumps in childhood and we were never able to conceive."

"Sarah," began Dik, "we haven't been exactly truthful with you since you arrived here. Since you are almost completely well, I feel it is time now to tell you the truth about everything."

"I have been very curious Dik," said Sarah. "Where are we exactly; and who is your Ellen James? I chased down the fact that an Ellen James was a professor of history in college and had died in a plane crash. The phone number and address your Ellen gave me were the same as that dead professor's. Why has she taken her identity? I must say, though, I really like her very much in spite of her mysterious demeanor."

"I'll start with where we are first, Sarah," said Dik. "Come with me across the hall where there is a window to the outside. It will back up my next statement." He opened the door to her room and escorted her to the window. Sarah looked out the window in amazement at the sprawling Gnor city below and the stark landscape of Mars in the distance. "We are on Mars, Sarah," he said. "And you must remain in this sealed complex as I do to be able to breathe the oxygen we both need. The atmosphere of Mars is about 95 percent carbon dioxide and only 0.13 percent oxygen. We are thankful that there is still enough oxygen to form an ozone layer to protect us from the sun's radiation here. You said that you seemed much stronger than you thought you should after surgery. This is because Mars is only half as big as Earth and, as I just said, has only 0.4 the gravity of Earth."

"But Dik," exclaimed Sarah, "I see people walking around down there without oxygen masks. How is that possible with that small percentage of oxygen in the atmosphere?"

"And that explains your mysterious Ellen James," answered Dik. "Ellen actually is that professor you checked out. She also did die, in a fiery plane crash; at least most of her did. Her brain survived and has been transplanted into a synthetic body; one that doesn't have to breathe oxygen and can tolerate a 95 percent carbon dioxide atmosphere. All those people you are seeing down below have had their brains transplanted as well."

"That would explain the mystery," said Sarah, "and her flattening that hoodlum with one punch; but this is fantastic! How long have we had a base on Mars? I don't ever remember reading anything about NASA having a base on Mars. Is it a secret U.S. base for deterring terrorists? And how long have you been able to transplant brains into a synthetic body? I can certainly see how it would come in handy with the diseases and pollution now present on the Earth."

"Your last statement will give you some insight into why we are here," rejoined Dik. "We are not a NASA space project; and this is not a U.S. base here on Mars. We are an alien race from deep space that has come here in hopes of humankind being able to save our race. We were here 70 million years ago and altered your ancestors' DNA so that you have evolved into beings very similar to us. That is why your brains are compatible with our synthetic bodies. I have arranged for our leader, called our Prime Mover, to explain our history, ethics and morals to you this morning so you will clearly understand why we are here."

Sarah was dumfounded by the doctor's remarks, but began to have paranoid thoughts that these aliens only wanted her brain and would kill her to get it! Her attraction to the doctor suddenly changed to fear, and he immediately sensed the abrupt change in her demeanor.

"Please, Sarah," he said softly, "it pains me to see how distressed you are. After you hear the Prime Mover's explanation you will lose all your fear and distrust. The Gnormen, as we are called, have ethics and morals that are far, far beyond that of humans. I realize what you are probably thinking—yes, we can transplant your brain if you decide to help us out and allow it to be done. If you decide you would like to go back to Earth and take your chances with your gunshot wound at your hospital on Earth, we can restore you to that scenario as well. We can restore the timeline, but cannot and should not change it for what that can do to the future. When you are restored to Carl's front porch with your chest gunshot wound, you will not remember anything that has gone on here. We will arrange for an ambulance to be right there to take you to a nearby hospital so you will have a chance at survival. I can't say whether or not you will survive there on Earth. It was certainly touch and go here for awhile. But you will have the chance to make whatever decision you wish to make and we will honor that decision. The only reason we received you in the first place was because Ellen thought you would die if she hadn't mobilized us to save you. She thought about letting you die, thus eliminating your discovering our project on Earth; but couldn't do it. Instead, she saved you; a credit to the human ethics and morals present in Ellen. She agonized a little about whether she had done the right thing, as she believes passionately in our Project; but I relieved her by telling her that it was exactly what any Gnorman would have done as well. Sarah, please don't prejudge anything until you have heard the Prime Mover and other humans that we have rescued from certain death. If you feel up to it we can proceed to the conference room right now. Ellen and John, who are both rescued human transplants, will be there as well to answer any questions you may have after the Prime Mover's narrative. The two of them have been absolutely invaluable to our Project on Earth."

"I feel, Dik," said Sarah, "that I should be very anxious and frightened about my situation here; everything is so unbelievable. But somehow, I believe you are just thinking of my best interests, and would never knowingly do me any harm. So let's get to the conference; I have to admit, I'm almost as curious as I am frightened. It's almost like I'm dreaming that I'm part of a Star Trek television show." She took the hand Dik offered her and they proceeded down the corridor to the conference room at the end of the hall where the others awaited them.

As they entered the room, Sarah was astounded to see familiar famous people who had perished in various ways on Earth seated around a large conference table. An imposing tall older man, who she assumed was the Prime Mover that Dik had spoken about, stood at the far end of the table and beckoned her to take one of the empty seats beside him. Next to that empty chair sat Ellen; John was across from her.

"Welcome, Sarah," said the Prime Mover, "please sit down here and let me introduce you to everyone here before I explain to you who we are and why we are here. You know Ellen and John already, of course. Major Glenn Miller is seated next to Ellen and next to him,

Lt. Joseph Kennedy. Across from them you may recognize Ms. Amelia Earhart; and next to her my new and good friend, Mr. Dag Hammarskjold. The remaining men in the last four seats are all Gnormen; Dort, Zandor, Zeltor and Jol."

Sarah had entered the conference room holding Dik's hand tightly, and took the seat indicated for her next to the Prime Mover at the head of the table. Dik smiled warmly at her and squeezed her hand as he released it and took the empty seat across from her.

"Sir," said Sarah, looking around the room, "I am absolutely dumbfounded at what I am seeing and hearing here. All of these people died on Earth at different times. You mean you rescued them all and transplanted their live brains into synthetic bodies? How could you do that?"

"Sarah," said the Prime Mover, "We have the ability to move back and forth along the timeline, allowing us to accomplish rescues of people just before their deaths. We are not allowed to change the timeline, and hence the future, except in certain minimally defined ways. But let me tell you the story from the beginning; all about us, our planet's war, and our Project on Earth to help us create an almost perfect society and solve our problem back on our own planet which we call Mekan."

The Prime Mover then proceeded to unfold the narrative to Sarah that he had similarly told all the others before they had made their decisions. Ellen and John also contributed much from a Gnor-human point of view that helped Sarah understand the relationship of Earth's apparent current course into trouble as the Gnor race also did on their planet. Sarah could see how such a body might also become necessary to save a dying Earth's population; and she understood why Ellen was so passionate about the Gnormen's Project on Earth. Zeltor, Jol, Zandor, and Dort were called upon to explain the design of the synthetic bodies, the time warp mechanism and optics, creation of the asteroid belt, and the evolutionary experiment with the introduction of Gnorman DNA into her human ancestors 70 million years ago in the age of the dinosaurs. Sarah was fascinated by how the dinosaurs had been destroyed to allow her ancestors to survive and evolve. When they had finished, the Prime Mover addressed her again.

"We are able to tell you all this, Sarah," he said, "because if you decide to go back to Earth and take your chances there as Dr. Ran has outlined for you, you will not remember what has occurred here. You will be returned to that timeline and continued there with Ellen and Molly gone and only another mystery for you to try to unravel. We cannot tell you if you will survive or not in the Earth hospital since it will be on that timeline that hasn't been created yet. If you decide to return to the Earth hospital, and you die there; we will be able to rescue you again at the former timeline on Carl's porch and save you again here. If you then allow us to, we can transplant your brain into a Gnorwoman's body. This will change the timeline only the acceptable minimum. All this macabre discussion needs to be said and understood by you since we should get your decision for what you want to do now and also later if you go back and die on Earth. We need to know if you would rather die than have your brain transplanted into a synthetic body. If you decide you would rather die than do this, we will not pursue you again if you die in the hospital on Earth; or, of course, if you live." The Prime Mover smiled and then said, "If you live, and we wish you well, we'll all hope you won't pursue us either!"

"Mr. Prime Mover," said Sarah slowly, "I would like to go back and take my chances at surviving on Earth. I still cling to my living human form, even though it is a short-lived one compared to a Gnorman's. It's too bad that I won't remember any of this because I would not ever want to harm your Project here on Earth. I believe it to be a very noble and wonderful Project, and I wish you well with it. I would use all my effort to try to keep it a secret; for as Ellen says, there is a good chance, the way the people of the Earth are going, that your technology may be needed to save the Earth's population in the future. As for transplanting my brain if I die in the Earth hospital; I would welcome that with open arms." She looked meaningfully at

Dr. Ran and continued. "You have been so kind to me here I must confess I hate to leave you, but the urge to cling to my living human form is too strong for me right now. In a way I regret not being a part of this grand endeavor; but I hope you understand that I must go back to Earth and try to survive there."

"Your decision will be respected Sarah," replied the Prime Mover. "Zeltor, Ellen, Molly, and Dr. Ran will take you back tomorrow and remain to see how you do in the hospital. They will have the time warp mechanism on board the scout vehicle to be available if needed. If you die there they will return the timeline with the time warp mechanism back to Carl's porch again, and bring you here for brain transplant. As much as you would seem to be a valuable addition to our project here, we all respect your wishes. As explained to you earlier, you really didn't qualify for our project in the first place; you were placed in this situation by Ellen's kindness. We wish you no harm; but if things don't work out in the Earth hospital, we will be very happy to welcome you back here with us!"

"Thank you, Mr. Prime Mover," said Sarah; and looking directly at Dr. Ran, "I look forward to seeing you again if I don't make it on Earth." The conference ended and Sarah mingled with the people there for a while, asking them questions and joking that she probably should be getting all their autographs. Everyone finally filed out of the conference room and left the hospital for their own quarters, leaving Dik and Sarah alone sitting next to each other at the conference table. Dik reached out and took Sarah's hand; and she was glad that his hand felt warm to her touch.

"Sarah," said Dik quietly, "I'm not so sure that you would have to have your brain transferred right away if you do poorly on Earth. There's no reason why you couldn't stay in the oxygen quarters with me until whatever you decide to do feels right for you to do it. There is really no rush to do the operation. Why, look at me; I've been contemplating a brain transplant for some time now, but haven't done it yet!"

"Why haven't you done it, Dik?" asked Sarah. "It would seem you could perform your doctoring in either state."

"Of course that's true," responded Dik, "but we were never sure about the resilience or longevity of the Project on Earth. I am the only living Gnorman left, and it was felt that since humans and I are quite compatible physiologically, I might be able to mate and at least have a chance at continuing the living line. Perhaps in time a colony of living beings like we had back on Mekan, as told to you in the Prime Mover's narrative, could have evolved. That was, and still is, a failsafe mechanism; although it is looking more and more like it won't be needed. Once we are sure, I most assuredly will opt for the longevity of the brain transplant and will accomplish it then."

"That is very noble of you, Dik," said Sarah, looking at him with her eyes shining. "Your words make me much more able now to handle whatever comes my way. In truth, I would like to stay as a living woman for at least a while if I return here to Mars." She squeezed his hand and they rose from their chairs with Dik holding Sarah's arm closely as he escorted her back into her hospital room.

"Try to get some rest, Detective Sarah," he said with a warm smile. "We'll see you in the morning." He impulsively bent over and kissed her on the cheek. "Good night, Sarah," he said softly, and left the room.

Sarah climbed into bed, noticing how strong she was in the low Martian gravity. Thoughts whirled about in her head. Her main deciding factor was that she still felt tied to her humanness and wanted to go back to her life on Earth. On the other side was an excitement for the obviously very noble Project of the Gnormen. There was the fact that she would be stronger, more sensitive, and live for many more years than she would on Earth. And there was the growing realization that Ellen might be right about Earth's people requiring a Gnor body to survive in the future; and she could be a part of that rescue! She began to understand Ellen's passion over the Project. The last thoughts that entered her mind before she drifted off to sleep were to admit that she was very much attracted to Dik Ran and that he might have some feelings for her as well.

Zeltor and Dr. Ran brought the scout vehicle with Ellen, Sarah and Molly on board close to the Earth in the evening and jammed the area electronically to avoid being detected from below. They began to instruct the three as to what would happen when the time warp mechanism was brought into play.

"Now listen carefully, ladies," said Dr. Ran. "When Zeltor activates the mechanism and sets the timeline back to just before the door opens on Carl's front porch you will materialize there and have no memory of anything after that time. We will materialize with our ship where we were in space at that time and also have no memory of what is to happen. I have located the hospital and the actual ambulance that we will have there to get Sarah and take her right to the hospital. I will send that message right before I activate the time warp mechanism and it will be strong enough that they will come very rapidly. Molly, you will be inside the house as before. If Sarah doesn't make it I'm almost sure that Ellen will want to have us reverse time and go back to Carl's porch and rescue her. We didn't have the time warp mechanism on the scout vehicle at that time so we will have to go back to Mars and get it. To save a lot of trouble and Sarah the pain of rescuing her again surgically, I am going to leave a note within the time warp mechanism saying that if you come back telling us Sarah is dead that I should activate the time warp mechanism to this current time and place when we get back to Mars to get it. This will bring us back to right where we are now and we can continue this timeline with Sarah knowing everything that has happened to her. It will leave the mystery of Carl's body on the porch, Sarah's parked cruiser and what happened to her, you, and Molly, but they will have to live with that as I don't want to put Sarah through that very painful surgery and recovery again if I don't have to!"

"Why, Dik," said Ellen, "I didn't know you cared for Sarah that much. Ha! I finally got you to blush!" And he was blushing, as was Sarah.

"All right, now ladies…there goes the message to the ambulance, and here we all go!" The ship and all its contents dematerialized.

As before Sarah approached Carl's front porch with her revolver drawn and called for him to come out. Again he pulled open the door and shot point blank into her chest, and as before she killed him instantly with two shots as she fell to the porch floor. Molly called out from within as before and Ellen rushed in to free her after she saw that Sarah was still alive on the porch. After the two of them returned quickly to the porch Ellen wondered what she would do to save Sarah as she didn't know where the local hospital was. She decided to call Zeltor as she did before, but before she dashed off to get her communicator an ambulance arrived on the scene and whisked all of them back to the hospital. Because of the message sent by Dr. Ran, the surgeons were waiting to treat Sarah and rushed her directly to the operating room. Ellen and Molly waited on a bench in the corridor of the hospital awaiting the outcome of Sarah's surgery. Even though she knew she should get in touch with Zeltor and Dik, she wanted to make sure Sarah was all right.

"In spite of her being a snoop," she whispered to Molly, "I'm quite fond of this woman, especially since she saved you! As soon as I'm sure she's OK we can leave and contact the scout vehicle."

About an hour and a half later a fatigued-looking surgeon walked slowly toward them in the corridor.

"I'm sorry, ma'am," he said, "we did everything we could, but there was too much damage to the heart and lungs and we lost her. She was a great policewoman and a credit to the force here. We all knew her and respected her a lot. When she lost her husband Jim last year we all thought that was a terrible tragedy, and now her as well; it's a lot to take. Are you related to Sarah?"

"No, doctor," said Ellen. "She actually gave her life to save my daughter from a child abuser. He's the one who shot her. She did manage to get off two shots that killed him instantly. You'll find his body on the porch of the house where the ambulance picked us up. Sarah's cruiser is parked there as well."

"Isn't that just like this gal!" returned the doctor, "always helping someone at a cost to herself! I can call the police and inform them of the body on the porch and Sarah's cruiser, and I'll call Jim's family since Sarah doesn't have any relatives. I'm sure the department will have a wonderful funeral for her; she was such a great gal, and wanted to be buried next to her husband, Jim, in the Woodlawn cemetery."

"I'm sure she was a wonderful person," said Ellen, who was already planning to convince everyone on Mars to send them back to rescue Sarah from Carl's porch, and then place her body back in the Woodlawn cemetery. Of course, she didn't realize that this timeline would be changed and would disappear forever if they were to save Sarah as they had already done.

Ellen and Molly left the hospital and contacted the scout vehicle to pick them up. When they were on the ship she told them that Sarah had died in surgery and that she hoped they could go back to Mars and get the time warp mechanism to return and rescue Sarah. Zeltor returned the scout vehicle to Mars where they picked up the time warp mechanism for their ship to return to Earth to rescue Sarah from Carl's porch.

"This is strange," said Dik, "there is a note inside our ship's time warp mechanism that was written from some time in the future and it tells me that if you return and say that Sarah died in the hospital, that I should set it to that future time and we can continue from that timeline. I have never seen a message like that before but I guess we should plan to honor it. I have a feeling that we may have rescued Sarah before and this is a way of avoiding a lot of trouble rescuing her again. It might change what you have determined will happen to Sarah's body, Ellen. If we rescued her before, and no ambulance arrived...say, that ambulance did come out of nowhere didn't it? Maybe we arranged for it to be there to give Sarah a chance to live here on Earth. If Ellen, who didn't know where the local hospital was, had decided to save Sarah, she would have had to have called us. If we took her back to Mars and Sarah survived, we would have had to take her back to Earth if she had decided to take a chance on living by the Earth hospital's treatment rather than undergoing a brain transplant on Mars!"

"Yes," said Ellen excitedly, "and we would have made sure there was an ambulance there right away to pick her up, since it was way out of town!"

"So just before we returned you to Carl's porch," resumed Dik, "this message was placed in the time warp mechanism to save Sarah from a repeated most likely very painful surgical rescue! That makes sense!"

"Well, Dik," said Ellen, "we'll see when we reset the mechanism."

Dik set the time warp mechanism to the coordinates mentioned in the note and the five of them reappeared on the scout vehicle just before they had returned to Carl's porch for the second time. Again, there was a note in the time warp mechanism explaining what had happened. Dik couldn't contain himself and embraced Sarah and kissed her full on the lips. Afterwards, he pulled back a little sheepishly and looked at the others.

"I can't believe that I'm so happy that someone died!" he exclaimed, and gave Sarah another squeeze. She smiled and reciprocated with a similar hug.

"Well, everyone, let's get back to Mars," said Ellen. "We've got a new member on our team now, one that Dik Ran is mighty happy to have there. Ha! I'm really catching up on causing blushing now!" And, indeed, both Sarah and Dik were quite red-faced at that!

Back on Mars the Prime Mover and the rest of the Gnormen and Gnor-humans were very happy that Sarah had decided to join them in their project; although the Gnor-humans felt a twinge of regret for her that she had succumbed in the attempt to save her in the Earth hospital. Sarah was introduced into several of the projects by way of assisting Dr. Ran in his dealings with the survivors. After a time she became a very good nurse and told Dik that she had actually taken a year of nurse's training before going into the police academy. She was also helpful to Ellen in her historical research since she had the intuition present in most good detectives. This enabled her to help determine which survivors were likely to be good or bad candidates for their Project according to the recorded activities in their past lives.

The Gnor-human pilots resumed their rescue of more naval personnel by first going after survivors of the sinking of the German battleship, Bismarck, which was sunk on May 27th, 1941 during WWII. The ship sank in fifteen thousand seven hundred feet of water three hundred twenty miles south of Cook, Ireland, and six hundred miles west of Brest, France. Several British swordfish torpedo bomber airplanes were lost in the campaign to find and sink the battleship, but finally contact was made and the ship was sunk. Ellen was able to get a list of the non-survivors of the sunken German ship, and of the British pilots lost. This kept all of the six rescuing scout vehicles quite busy finding and picking up the surviving pilots that went down in the ocean. There were five visits by different organizations by submarine to the sunken battleship Bismarck; so they had to be careful not to be discovered when they were returning the bodies to their watery graves. It had become a tradition for the Gnor-human pilots on the scout vehicles to play *The Navy Hymn* after return of the bodies to their sunken ship; and it was always emotional for them each time it was done. Even the Gnormen on the scout vehicles were affected by it as well, and it led to a closer relationship for both. During several encounters three other ships were involved in the fighting; and the British battleship, Hood, was sunk by the Bismarck with loss of one thousand four hundred ninety-eight seamen. Needless to say, the scout vehicles were very busy with their rescues during these sea battles. After the Bismarck and Hood sinkings were consummated the scout vehicles took on another navel disaster for their rescues. This was the sinking of the British steamship of the Cunard line, *Lusitania*, on May 15, 1915, by a German U-boat during WWI. It presumably was a passenger ship; but the Germans had intelligence reports that munitions were also on board as well. One thousand one hundred ninety-eight people lost their lives; and most of the bodies that were able to be recovered went to the port of Queensland, later called Cobh. This enabled Ellen to gather the history necessary to determine which people were not recovered and to give the scout vehicles the listing of who to rescue.

After the naval disasters the scout vehicle crews went to the

April 17th, 1906, San Francisco earthquake. It was a massive quake: 7.9 to 8.3 on the Richter scale. Seven hundred people died and Ellen had good historical research data that enabled the crews to get many more candidates for the Martian cities that had now risen to eight in number.

The next place considered for the Project was one where Ellen's historical expertise and intuition turned out to be very important to the Project's viability. They had decided to go after certain specific known famous intellects that had died of bubonic plague, during its scourge from 1347-1352. This so-called "Black Death" because of the black lumps or buboes that appeared all over the body, killed twenty-five million people or one-third of Europe's population during those five years. Many physicians who in fear failed to treat the patients affected often were killed for this refusal to care for them. Ellen thought that because of the great distance into the past and the consequent lack of technological evolution, there would be a great prevalence of superstition and fear of the unknown, even among the intelligent people of the time. She was convinced that even the most intellectual individuals would not be able to understand and accept the principles of the Gnormen's project. But because of the volume of people involved in the losses to the Black Death, it was decided to try one of the most advanced intellectuals of the time, Francesco Petrarch, to see if it might be feasible to use people from this era. The concept was obviously beyond Petrarch and he was unable to accept their Project and called them "demons of the damned" and "blasphemers of God." He was convinced that they had caused the Black Death to gather people's brains for their nefarious scheme. After this disastrous encounter, as was predicted by Ellen, it was decided by the Council that they would no longer go back into Earth's far past for candidates for their project.

The eight cities on Mars over the past five years had so increased in population from the project's many successful rescues that a more formal governing structure had to be created to enable them to function more efficiently. Each city elected a leader they called a mayor who presided over a city council. This was much like the Prime Mover who presided over the Council that governed the whole planet from their headquarters in the original city at the Candor Chasma in the Valles Marineris. The main Life Factory and Dr. Ran's oxygen quarter's complex remained in the original city. The other seven cities fanned out from the original city along the long canyon walls about five miles from each other. Much of their municipalities were partially underground, unlike the original city which was completely above ground; but each city had a protective force field over it to contain the heat and to protect it from space debris that might penetrate the thin Martian atmosphere. Each city was three to five miles in diameter. The inhabitants of the cities spent the majority of their time in preparing for or consummating various aspects of the Gnormen's Project. The rest of the time was spent on studying the Gnorman society and its technological, ethical, and moral characteristics. Gnor-humans that showed potential in different areas of Gnor learning and technology were shifted into those fields that they enjoyed working in and were competent in. The entire society functioned on a cooperative, not competitive basis, so there was practically no stress between any individuals, especially with the calming chemicals present in their brain's nutrient fluid. The mayor of the second city down was Lt. Joseph Kennedy and he had been allowed to name it "Hyannisport." The third city's mayor was Rol, and he named his city "Mekan II." The fourth city had John Scott as its mayor and he called his city "Harvard Square." The fifth city's mayor was Amelia Earhart, the only woman mayor, and she named her city "Electra," after her last airplane on Earth. The sixth city's mayor was Major Glenn Miller, and he named his city "Space Band." The seventh city had co-leaders, Dort and Zandor, continuing the close relationship they had had on Mekan. They named their city "Martian Seven" and a second Life Factory was situated here.

Ellen's school, the Martian Institute, was in Harvard Square and now had over 20 children of various ages enrolled. Jol had already produced several body changes for the children as they aged mentally. The children had been adopted eagerly by various Gnor-human couples, continuing to prove that human emotions were still a large part of the Gnor-human psyche. Dr. Ran still maintained the "oxygen quarters" complex in the original city, and for over seven years now Sarah had remained there as a living human and had not yet decided to undergo brain transplantation. The oxygen quarters remained necessary while the project still sought new brains for transplanting; and the two of them remained there as living, breathing beings. She and Dik had first become friends and colleagues, then lovers, and finally a couple living together. They had tried to conceive a child but so far had not been able to do so. Sarah had been pregnant three times, but the pregnancies always ended within a few weeks. She was not discouraged, however, because this had been common in her family history. In fact, Sarah had been the only pregnancy her mother had been able to carry through to term, and she was forty years old when that pregnancy occurred. Sarah's grandmother and great grandmother had each only had one female child later in life as well, so she felt her situation was not much different than that of the other women in her family.

Sarah was pregnant again for the fourth time, and this pregnancy was already in its seventh month so they had high hopes it would make it to term. Everyone, Gnor-human and Gnorman alike, was extremely excited about this apparently successful mating between a Gnorman and a human woman. The pregnancy proceeded without any further difficulties and Dik delivered Sarah's and his seven pound baby boy in the oxygen complex hospital two months later. He was very proud of his new healthy son, as was the infant's new mom. Everyone offered congratulations for the extraordinary mating, and Sarah was ecstatic to finally have been able to have a child by her Gnorman lover. They called the new little boy Ares, from the Greek name for Mars, the planet on which he had been born. There would obviously be some problems that she and Dik would have to face later on; since at some time they would have to close down the oxygen complex and consider brain transplantation. In honesty to herself she knew that now that she had had her child with Dik, she would definitely want to consider changing to a Gnor-human. She knew that Dik also had only been waiting for a successful pregnancy and for her to make up her mind to change, so she felt he would change as well when she did. This was definitely true since the Project had worked so well that there was no longer much need for Dik to remain in his living state. Also, Jol and his colleagues were close to completing development of the functioning synthetic higher brain center they had needed the Project for in the first place. Sarah knew that she and Dik would have to decide when would be the best and safest time to consider brain transplanting for their child. This was not as difficult a proposition for her as might be expected, as the Earth was continuing to show signs of advancing environmental pollution and disease. The greed of many companies and people had made charlatan complementary alternative medical care as popular as scientific medicine so that now many illnesses were not diagnosed or treated properly. Because of this discarding of science in medical care, pandemics had broken out in many areas of the Earth's population. Corporate greed continued to dominate the planet and cause hastening of the same downward spiral that the Gnormen had experienced on their planet. A strong Gnor body would ensure that Sarah's and Dik's child would have a much greater longevity on Mars; and also, if they went there, even on a decimated, polluted Earth where only such a body would be able to live. This situation had already been dictated on a similarly polluted Mekan that had necessitated the Gnor body's development in the first place.

One of the recent Projects completed had been the rescuing of some of the 3000 victims of the September 11, 2001 terrorist attack on the World Trade Center in New York City. There had been much soul-searching and discussion about this project as it had been directed against the economic elite of the U.S., the Wall Street financiers. There was concern about the self-motivated direction of the financial and business world's ethics, and possessing a Gnor body with its longevity and all it could do and survive in, certainly would be deemed extremely valuable. A company that could run a Life Factory and produce these bodies at an exorbitant price to the highest bidders would be worth a pretty sum indeed! There would be no doubt that armies of these Gnor-humans would be far superior to the present human ones. The ethics and morals of the Gnormen society absolutely forbid such uses of Gnor technology; and the way the corporate business world on Earth seemed to be heading, especially in some of the years that were viewed past the 9/11 time, it seemed it might be dangerous to allow these greedy businessmen the possibility of utilizing Gnor technology for their own profit. Since the twin towers of the World Trade Center was where some of the brightest stars of this financial and business world worked, the attack by the terrorists was an attempt to cripple the U.S. economy by destroying Wall Street's technological geniuses and the systems present there. The dilemma that was considered by the Gnor Project directors was whether it would be wise to transplant brains from humans that perhaps were highly intelligent but at the same time addicted to the greed and competition-oriented mentalities of many of the corporate business people of the current time. Of course there were some super intelligent people who died there that were probably above reproach, but it was obvious to Ellen, the Prime Mover, and the other directors that a very carefully planned choice of the individuals to be rescued would have to be done to avoid a possible disastrous situation occurring. As it turned out they were able to be sure about only a certain number of individuals as not much research was available describing all the victims of the attack. The ones they did rescue, however, were all excellent candidates and readily accepted brain transplant without any misgivings. They all fit smoothly into the Gnor society's functioning and none of them changed in their attitude towards the Project either as time went by on Mars.

It was the year 2050. The Gnorman base on the dark side of the moon (that never faced Earth) had been completed now for several years. There was now a functioning oxygenated Life Factory on the moon as well as two on Mars. The eight Martian cities now had a stable population with a smoothly running governing infrastructure. Earth, on the other hand, had continued on its slow downward spiral with many complex problems compounding the increasingly difficult time the people had for any kind of a comfortable life on their home planet. The economy had continued to sputter in a very volatile fashion, with the greed of corporate business funneling most of the Earth's wealth and power into fewer and fewer hands. These obscenely wealthy, powerful individuals no longer associated themselves with the people beneath them and isolated themselves in heavily guarded enclaves where they continued to consume far more of the Earth's goods than anyone else, while the rest of the world grew poorer and sicker. Most of the governments of the world found that their ability to continue funding basic projects was becoming impossible to accomplish. Still other powerful governments found their leadership infiltrated by ideologues that lied and cheated to insure that their cronies, their government, their beliefs, and they themselves would continue to receive more power and more of the world's goods. The global lack of funding caused a decrease in most cities' local police services which ultimately led to the consequent rise in the crime rate everywhere. All cities and towns became no longer safe to traverse at night and sometimes during the daytime. Lack of funding caused NASA and the European Space Agency to essentially shut down most of their space projects. This, of course, was a Boone to the Gnor base on the moon and their cities on Mars, as there were no NASA space vehicles launched that could discover their colonization. Martian launches done in 2003 and 2004 by NASA and the ESA did not place any craft anywhere near the Gnor cities, so they remained undiscovered. Because of the fear of this happening, Jol and his colleagues had incorporated cloaking devices into the force fields over the Martian cities and the moon base to conceal their presence at these sites. They felt now that with the shutdown of space missions on Earth they would not have to move to the concealment safety of the Olympus Mons volcano yet and reconstruct their cities there inside the fifteen-mile high mountain as they had been planning to do.

Disease had continued to ravage the Earth, with the AIDS epidemic now everywhere. Vaccines developed were only minimally effective, and mutant strains were poorly tolerated. This often led to outbreaks of rapid deaths in the overpopulated world that began to rival what had occurred with the Black Death in the 12th century. Many strains of common bacteria had mutated into organisms that no longer had an antibiotic that would destroy them. To add to this, SARS and other corona viruses had changed into forms that were much more easily spread among humans and lower animals, causing a tremendous loss of many of the pets and zoo animals around the globe. Increasing poverty in the world caused the death rates from common diseases such as tetanus, malaria, and tuberculosis to escalate to over six million people yearly with more dying every year. Mad Cow disease had made its way across the Earth by this time; and it was found that the etiology could be traced to certain companies that increased their profit margin by utilizing cheaper cattle food that was known to spread the problem. The increased greed of the corporate business world had caused widespread pollution of the air and land with skyrocketing cancer rates in adults and asthma in children. Decreasing fertility of the male sperm globally, added to reaction to the increasing surrounding environmental pollution by women's eggs, led to many birth defects in the increasingly fewer children born. Lung cancer had reached epidemic proportions as well, traced to aerosolized plutonium that occurred when five of the U.S.'s thirty low-orbiting missal defense space platforms powered by large nuclear reactors were shot down by terrorists causing the global plutonium pollution. Terrorists had also polluted much of the rapidly decreasing water supply of the world, which added to overall water loss secondary to the dramatically increasing desertification of many sites on the planet. Much of the oxygen-producing rain forests of the world continued to be decimated by greedy private and governmental developers, and the increasing global warming had begun to take much of the livable land away as the melting ice caps continued to cause the oceans to rise. The future did not look very good for the human race on the planet Earth!

The Prime Mover had requested that Ellen and the seven Martian city mayors meet to discuss what was happening to the Earth and for any suggestions they might have to try to help solve some of the problems there. They also had to consider what the policy would be if and when the Gnormen returned to their home planet, Mekan, since a synthetic higher brain center had now been successfully created and was performing very well in the first Gnorman implanted with one. If it continued to function flawlessly and the Gnorman implanted continued to learn and perform in a creative, intelligent fashion, the Gnormen would soon be ready to consider traveling back to their home planet. The Prime Mover had already begun construction of two new Spaceships; one to be left behind for the Gnor-humans to use as they saw fit, and one to carry additional Gnormen or Gnor-humans back to Mekan. All the scout vehicles would be left behind except for one each to be placed on the two leaving Starships. The Prime Mover opened the discussion.

"I have brought us all together to discuss what should be done as regards the ongoing policy towards the Earth. The planet seems to be declining very similarly to what happened to us on Mekan many, many years ago. This, of course, is why we eventually had to develop our synthetic bodies and the ethics and morals of cooperation, not competition. Such a philosophy required a fixed number of people to work well. This was fairly easily accomplished because we lost the drive to procreate that had been instrumental in producing overpopulation and the wars and pollution that decimated our people. Our current ethical and moral philosophy of cooperation, not competition, coupled with our ability to maintain a fixed population anywhere we settle, makes us able to fit into the Universe and survive almost anywhere we go. With the time warp mechanism coupled to Zandor's wave optics device we recently looked ahead in time to Mekan beyond the last surviving composite Gnorman there, and have found that the remaining synthetic Gnormen without a higher brain center have degenerated into violent behavior that has positioned them in a state not much different than the lower animals on the planet. We now have the weaponry and technology to take over the planet and reclaim these poor creatures back into functioning Gnormen once again. So you can see that our future looks bright indeed, once we are sure that the new synthetic brain center will continue to work correctly at the higher levels necessary. I must say, if the current design remains functional, we do have great confidence in designer Jol and his colleagues that they will continue to build better and better synthetic brains in the future. It should also be comforting to the Gnor-humans that Jol has been able to teach and train several Gnor-human surgeons and engineers in the design and construction of ongoing Gnor technology. But as I said earlier, there is more of a problem on Earth with philosophy than technology. Dag, as a knowledgeable financier, and as Ellen tells me, a true renaissance man, what are your thoughts on what is wrong with the Earth people and what might help correct the problems?"

"Well, Mr. Prime Mover," said the Secretary-General, "the biggest problem financially at this point in time seems to be a maldistribution of the wealth of the world. Some individuals and governments have much more of the world's goods than other individuals and governments. They may have earned their position legitimately (although that is less and less prevalent today) but certain basic needs and aspirations in the rest of the people are not being met with the current distribution. The wealth probably wouldn't even have to be evenly distributed either, but certain limitations on who holds what and how much must be accomplished before wars, terrorism, and violent behavior can be suppressed. You have accurately described another one of the biggest problems with humans, and that is the innate urge for sex and the increased procreation it engenders. That area is a prime example of why Earth's standard philosophy is competition, not cooperation. Indiscriminate procreation creates too many people and necessitates competition for the available goods, services, and land. The people who lose out in a world of competition must die or give up what they want or need, while the winners get all the spoils. The widespread philosophy now present throughout the world of putting yourself first and others second will have to be reversed to be able to start on the road to a cooperative society. In a planned population as has been achieved in the Gnor society there is a position for each person; so cooperation, not competition, is indeed possible. That is why the Gnor society fits into the structure of the Universe so well. When a new job is needed to be filled, a new Gnorman is built and trained to fill it. There is no competition; just cooperation. No fraud or subterfuge has to be done to protect a dwindling competitive advantage; something that has often led people and companies off in the opposite direction of progress. A competitive environment often leads to hasty actions and technology to beat out the competitor. This often causes disastrous results later on because things were not thought out far enough in advance to anticipate the problems that might occur; and when they occur people hide them for fear of losing their competitive advantage. In a cooperative environment, where there is time to think about future problems, it is much easier to fit seamlessly into the structure of the Universe. Cooperating individuals are oriented towards changing things right away when change is obviously indicated; there is no desire to hide facts that might create a competitive loss as is present in a competitive world. Cooperative philosophy is interested in doing the right thing for everyone and everything as far as can be seen at the time it is being done. As changes that should be done come into awareness in the future, there is no hesitancy to institute them and discontinue the old ones because no one is fired in this type of society; just furloughed, retrained, and reassigned. On Earth, that is perhaps already full of too many people to establish such a population-limited, cooperative society, it is obvious that something has to be done about reassigning the money of the world in new ways. I suspect, however, that even with the money distributed evenly there certainly would not be enough to let everyone have the lifestyle that most have in the developed world; probably not even enough for a much watered-down lifestyle. That means then that in practicality much of the population would have to be removed or accept a much more limited lifestyle to be able to accomplish a Gnor-like cooperative society. Of course, if the decimation of the population continues as it is now doing, a population size may be eventually reached that would be the right size to establish a cooperative rather than a competitive society. But, as you said, the reason you were able to keep that population stable was because you eliminated sex and the procreation that continually brought you back into overpopulation and the foibles of competition such as war, violence, and pollution that it inevitably created. Unfortunately, Mr. Prime Mover, I have great doubts that sex and procreation could ever be extracted from human beings."

"I'm not so sure about that, Mr. Secretary," broke in Ellen. "At least the procreation could be stopped just as we have done with the Gnor-humans in the Project. John and I are as attached and love our Molly just as well as Sarah and Dik love their Ares. I realize that making synthetic child bodies and advancing their form at the proper age is different than what has been done before in the Gnor society, but it has been very successful and has created no problems so far. And there is precedence with the age advancing of Gnormen every 100 years that is certainly a somewhat similar undertaking. When and if our services are needed in the future, there may be enough children present on Earth to continue for some time before a totally new synthetic child will need to be created. We will have to coordinate the children with what the society will need in the future, but that should be fairly easy to do. Thanks to our most able Jol, we have reconnected sex without disease to the Gnor body that everyone feels has been a very positive addition to the Gnor society. This sex is quite similar for all Gnor-humans so there is little need for worries about fidelity that might cause problems. Again, thanks to Jol, we have practically eliminated the need for procreation with his marvelous child creations. He tells me that the Gnor-humans he has trained are able to do his work almost as well as he does himself now. I'm sure that isn't totally true; no one could be like Jol! But we are confident that they are very skillful and can do the job necessary. Since it appears that it will soon be time for the return to Mekan for all of our Gnormen friends, we must decide on who will remain and what will be our policy for our activities on Earth from our Martian cities and base on the moon. My feeling is that we should continue our Project of rescuing

191

dying people in secret until and if we are needed on Earth to salvage our race as the Gnormen did theirs. We can approach the Earth openly at that time with offers of help to build a composite and/or totally synthetic race that can live in harmony with the Universe in a cooperative population-limited society. In the meantime, at some future point in time there may be a chance to help with projects in space in the way of radiation protection and propulsion technology without totally revealing our presence. We may be able to gradually introduce ourselves and assist in activities with the right people on Earth that would keep our secret. Again, I do feel strongly that we should continue as we have been doing for the present time. Our technicians will all want to get continuing training and practice when our Gnormen friends return to Mekan as they will be put to a great task if we have to restore the human race in the future."

"I will be remaining here with Sarah and my son, Ares," spoke up Dr. Ran. "There is little need for me on Mekan anymore, and great need for me here on Earth, Mars, and the moon base." Ellen acknowledged his offer with a broad smile.

"I knew you'd be one of us, Dik," she said. "We all owe you so much, and would hate to lose you!" Dort arose next to speak.

"Because of our original evolutionary experiments on the Earth's human ancestors, we both feel connected closely to humans," he said, "so Zandor and I will also remain behind. Besides, I would miss Glenn's orchestral concerts too much if I left!"

"I think I better stay around for awhile also," said Zeltor with a smile. "I want to iron out any bugs in the new Starship and someone has to watch those women drivers, Ellen and Amelia!" His remark elicited two wry smiles that blossomed into very warm ones from the two Gnor-human women.

"I also want to stay here for a little time yet," said Rol. "There is still some navigation I want to teach my pupils before I go back. And besides, my city, Mekan II is pretty much set up like the home planet so I won't be too homesick!"

"Obviously, most of us Gnor-humans will stay," said Lt. Kennedy, looking at Amelia and John. "We may have to save our human world as Ellen has said all along!"

"And what about you, friend Dag?" said the Prime Mover to the Secretary-General. "What will you do?"

"I have not decided completely," said the Secretary-General. "Since I would like to visit your world, I will go back with you to Mekan. By the time the Earth has declined into the position that it has to be saved by Professor James, I will return and help her establish a new philosophy of cooperation with a fixed population." He winked over at Ellen.

"Well then," said the Prime Mover. "It seems your Earth policies are all fairly well set and quite reasonable. We may be leaving soon for Mekan depending upon how Jol's new synthetic brain continues to perform. Please all come over to the Life Factory tomorrow and we'll introduce you to his creation; named appropriately, 'Atlas', for his dependent connection to Earth."

Atlas did remain stable; and Jol continued to improve his mental abilities until finally, by the year 2100, it was felt that they were ready to start back to Mekan to restart their Gnor society with totally synthetic Gnormen. But this time the synthetic men had excellent functioning higher brain centers that would enable the Gnor society to achieve the dream that the Prime Mover had had all along. There was no fear of danger from the lower-brain-capacity synthetic Gnormen they had left behind in their flight from the planet as most of these had long since died out or become similar to the lower animals there. By this time most of the composite Gnormen returning to Mekan had opted for the new totally synthetic brain and body and had assimilated most of the knowledge and training that had been present in their old composite brain. A few, like the Prime Mover, preferred to remain a composite and live out their shorter lives in that state, so that they could retain every single one of their memories. In transferring to the totally synthetic state some of those memories were often lost; and the Gnormen who remained composites did not want to lose any one of theirs. Of course, the new brain would start building up its own memories that could be much more easily stored and recalled than the composite brain had been able to do. It was decided that the original totally synthetic Gnorman, Atlas, would also remain behind to aid the surgeons and technicians in their continuing Earth Project. The three Life Factories would have the plans for his construction, but for now, no further total synthetics would be created.

The day of departure finally arrived and the two silver Starships

194

began to load the synthetic Gnormen, the remaining composite Gnormen, as well as a few Gnor-human composites that had preferred to stay that way, even though they were going to Mekan to live. Many emotional farewells were said and finally the Prime Mover ascended the entrance platform to the first Starship to give his last farewell address to those remaining behind.

"My friends, I shall never forget any of you," he said with obvious emotion. "Your diligence and participation has allowed us to realize my lifelong dream of a totally synthetic race descended from a living race. Thanks to you, Gnormen will have the chance to develop an essentially immortal, super intelligent, ethical and moral society with the required fixed population to accomplish it. I shall miss all you mayors and your Martian cities' inhabitants." He turned to the edge of the platform where two children and four adults were standing. "I shall miss you and all your dedication, Dr. Dik Ran, as well as your lovely wife, Sarah and your son, Ares." He moved toward the final three on the platform and embraced Ellen, who looked up at him with a sad expression on her face. "I will especially miss you three, Ellen, John, and Molly. You were our first Gnor-human family and we were very proud and fortunate to have you as our first." He turned toward the crowd below, "I suggest to you that Ellen be placed in charge of the Project in my place from now on. We are very grateful that serendipitous flaming plane crash rewarded us with her. Without her compassion, good sense, and passionate commitment to this Project it would never have faired as well as it has. Goodbye, my good friends; I wish you all possible success in the shepherding of your planet, Earth. I am in high hopes that we will all meet again. Please remember that if you ever need us in the future for anything at all we will always be available." With this the Prime Mover moved away from the six on the platform, raised his arm to the people below, and entered the first Starship. Shortly thereafter, the two Starships rose majestically over the rim of the Martian plateau and plunged off into the sky toward their home planet, Mekan..

"I shall miss them terribly," whispered Ellen to John, with her arms around his waist and Molly's shoulder.

"As will I," replied John. "I guess what he said is what we'll be for now, my love: shepherds of our Earth! Only the Universe knows what may be in store for us and our Earth in the future." John tightened his arm around Ellen as they all gazed skyward at the disappearing Starships.

Printed in the United States
17844LVS00001B/538-573